BROKEN CIRCLE

A GRAY GHOST NOVEL—BOOK ONE

AMY MCKINLEY

Broken Circle

(p) **ISBN-13**: 978-0-9994280-0-9

(e) **ISBN-13**: 978-0-9994280-1-6

Publisher: Arrowscope Press, LLC; www.arrowscopepress.com

Editing—Taylor Anhalt, Editor; Neila Y., Line Editor, Red Adept Editing

Proofreading—Kim H., Proofreader, Red Adept Editing

Cover Design—T.E. Black Designs; www.teblackdesigns.com

Interior Formatting—T.E. Black Designs; www.teblackdesigns.com

CHAPTER 1

*S*ecrets had the power to destroy, and Liv's could very well detonate her marriage. Still, she had to tell someone. Keeping the news from Alex wasn't her goal, and she would share it with him, just not yet. The elevator dinged, and Liv stepped inside, on her way to meet her best friend, Rachel, for lunch.

Her spirits lifted as she threaded her way through the crowded Manhattan sidewalk and drew nearer to the café. Weaving in and out to avoid a group of people to her left, she picked up her pace, ignoring the light bumps and jostles from the too-close pedestrians. A hard clip to her shoulder half spun her, and she stumble-stepped back.

The same man who'd bumped her shot his arm out to steady her. She blinked rapidly and dropped her gaze from his cold, tan features to where his hand tightly held her arm. *A butterfly tattoo?* Before she could study the mark further, he released her and strode away, the crowd swallowing him from her view.

With a shrug, Liv let the random incident slide from her

thoughts. The restaurant was only a few feet away. The click of her heels echoed along the pavement. She spotted Rachel and gave a breezy wave then flashed a smile at the host as she bypassed him.

Rachel leapt up and pulled Liv in for a hug before they took their seats. The pungent smell of Stargazer lilies, which sat on the center of their table, churned her temperamental stomach. Intermittent stirrings of nausea had plagued her the past week. She motioned to the waiter and had him take the flowers away before they placed their order for salads and drinks.

Across from her, Rachel grinned. "Did you survive 'the event of the season'?"

Last night, Liv and Alex had skipped a huge annual gala at the Radcliffs', a well-connected family her mother had continuously thrust on her. "Nope. I needed a break from socializing and the press."

"I don't blame you. But really, what do you expect? Your family's fortune—well, yours now…" Rachel reached for Liv's hand and squeezed it for a heartbeat longer than necessary. "Hun, let's face it. Even the Rockefellers would be jealous of you."

"Money doesn't buy happiness." She would trade it all if it would bring her parents back.

"Damn close, though, I bet." Rachel cocked her head.

Toying with the cup of coffee the waiter had delivered, Liv fished for information. "How's work?"

"It's going well." Rachel tucked a piece of honey-blond hair behind her ear. "Are you asking if I got the promotion?"

"Obviously." She grinned back. "I expect to be one of the first you tell. Alex has been very close-lipped regarding when or if you'll get it."

Rachel tapped Liv's hand. "I already heard. That's why I wanted to meet with you. You're looking at the youngest and newest forensic DNA analyst on the New York City Police Department."

Liv jumped to her feet, rushed around the table, and squeezed Rachel in a hug. "I'm so happy for you! But please don't use this as an opportunity to share your experiences on the job." She shuddered. "Some of the work you were doing kept me awake at night."

"Sure it did." Rachel's small body shook with laughter. "With that handsome, hot-blooded, Venezuelan husband of yours filling up your nights?"

Heat suffused Liv's cheeks. Rachel shook her head and stifled her amusement by taking a sip of coffee.

Liv picked at the corner of her napkin, her thoughts darkening. Rarely did they discuss Alex and the police force. As a detective who specialized in drug trafficking, Rachel refused to divulge information that would cause Liv worry. "Is…is there something going on at the office?"

"Always. What do you mean specifically?"

Taking a sip of her drink, Liv debated on how much to say. "It's just that Alex's attitude has been different the past couple of nights. There's this tension rolling off him. Then the other day…"

"What happened?"

"I overheard him on the phone late one night, just a small part of his conversation, really. It was the tone and hour that got to me." Growing up and watching her mother turn a blind eye to her husband's indiscretions hadn't left Liv unscathed. *Alex isn't like that.* Still, that little bit of doubt lodged its way into her mind. She hoped that confiding to Rachel would help dispel her mistrust. "There's something else. He used a different cell phone, because his was on the bedside table."

"Did he say who he was talking to?"

She shook her head, hoping that since Rachel worked with

him, she would have some insight. "No. It was the middle of the night. I fell asleep again by the time he came back to bed." A few words had made her think he was referring to their relationship. That had cast doubt over the call being about work.

For the first time since hearing about Alex, Rachel eased back in her chair. "I'm sure it was an informant, especially if he used a different phone and took the call that late. He wouldn't want anyone calling on a cell he'd answer unguarded. It's easier to compartmentalize that way. Hey, don't read into everything he does. He's not your father. I promise I'll tell you if there's anything weird going on that you should hear about. Benefits of working together."

Liv had to let go of her paranoia. "Okay, and I know you would. Thanks."

"The job has been really stressful, and Alex has single-handedly ousted an entire cartel and is on the way to dismantling another one. That's huge. They've halted their control in three states. It's crazy, the intuition he has. If we didn't know any better, I'd swear he had inside experience and firsthand knowledge about the inner workings of drug trafficking and cartels." She shook her head, her eyes taking on a faraway gleam. "So yeah, stress? He probably has it in spades."

"Okay, that's a relief. Well, you get what I mean."

Rachel laughed. "I do."

With that worry cleared up, Liv pressed her lips together, trying to contain the smile playing around the edges. "I have a surprise of my own." Rachel perked up, and Liv blurted out, "I'm pregnant."

"Oh my God, Liv! Have you told Alex?" Rachel rolled her eyes. "Well, of course you have."

Dread pooled in her stomach. "Actually, I haven't." *I need someone to be excited for me.* "He doesn't want kids, Rach."

Rachel's brows furrowed. "Never? Or just so soon after your first year of marriage and your parents…"

Grief stirred in her gut at the mention of her parents who had died five months ago in a freak accident. "We've never made it past discussing the 'I don't want kids' stage. I'm hoping he'll be happy, that his opinion will change once he gets used to the idea."

"Shit, Liv." Rachel shook her head. "He'll come around. Don't worry."

He'd been so adamant. Liv clasped her hands tight in her lap and plastered on a smile she didn't quite feel. "I'm sure you're right." The twisting in her stomach had nothing to do with morning sickness.

CHAPTER 2

*L*iv studied Alex as they dined in one of their favorite Italian restaurants. Deep shadows drooped beneath his eyes. Even though he was relaxed, fine lines were etched between his brows. For a few months, she had grieved hard, becoming an emotional zombie after learning of her parents' demise. Her anguish must have taken a toll on him.

While he cut up his chicken in sure strokes, she observed his mannerisms and his features with her artist's eye. His dark hair was disheveled as if he'd run his hands through it a time or two. She saw no slight narrowing of his left eye, which was his telltale sign that something was amiss. Aside from the circles and fine lines, he appeared content. So she relaxed as well—as much as she could with the looming pregnancy discussion.

She swirled a piece of chicken in the sauce before lifting it to her mouth. When she finished chewing, she broke the silence. "How's work going?"

The clatter of his fork against the china caused her eyebrows to rise. In the back of her mind, the phone call he'd had still festered.

He scrubbed his hands over his face. "It's going well. We're very close to bringing in the leader of a drug-trafficking outfit. I'm worried about this one though. This guy is slippery and very dangerous. It's taking more hours, manpower, and skill than I thought it would."

A chill skated across her skin. She dismissed the uncomfortable sensation. Alex's work was a world he mostly kept separate. This was due to his code of ethics, code of conduct, and desire to keep her safe.

The darker elements of his career were not something she cared for. Her only concern was that he was happy and doing what he loved, as she did. How he worked to disassemble drug rings, cartels, and gangs, she would never understand. Nor would she want to be thrust into that dangerous part of his life.

"Is that why you look so exhausted? Or is it because I've been a mess?"

"No, babe. It's not you, never could be. You give me energy. But this job, it's taking a toll. I want out."

She set her fork down and gave him her full attention, wishing she could smooth away the visible stress he wore with a simple touch of her hands. "You told me everything was on track to move into politics with backing from my father, Joe Radcliff, and Davidson, right?" She gnawed on her lip for a second. "I'm assuming my father set up a campaign fund and all the connections you'll need before he passed away?"

Alex's mouth pressed into a grim line. "He did, and I'm damn grateful for it. Although, I'd prefer if your parents were here and the senator position that opened was from your dad retiring instead."

She flinched, reached across the table, and squeezed his hand. "Me too. Even without them here, you've got this, right?"

Relief shone in his face as he grinned. "Yeah, I do. The governor called me. In a few months, I won't have the worry of my job and all the long hours at the NYPD. It's getting to be too much, and I'm ready for a change. Not much longer now."

Unease danced on the edge of her thoughts, and her smile faltered. "Well, it's a life with its own perils."

Alex shook his head, his eyes shining with excitement. "No, babe. It will be nothing like what you grew up with. We're a team. You're the best thing that's ever happened to me, and I'll never take you for granted."

Warmth filled her with his words. She knew it too. Not a day went by that he didn't do something to make her feel appreciated and loved. The only dark spot that nagged at her was her pregnancy secret, which could shatter their marriage, and the phone call she'd overheard. He'd sworn there were no secrets, and she needed to make peace with it and let it go. Still, her mind clouded over, and her lips pulled down in a frown.

Alex stood, came around the table, and drew her to her feet. "Let it go, Liv," he whispered before placing a heartbreakingly sweet kiss on her forehead.

Aware he didn't realize her thoughts had turned back to the call, she guessed he was talking about his worry over the case and the senate position he hoped to fill. He pulled his chair around the table, settled next to her, and drew her close. In quiet murmurs, they reminisced about everything from when they met and began dating to what they would like to have for lunch tomorrow. She laughed for the first time since her parents' death.

He did that to her—made her happy. She did the same for him. In his embrace, life was simple.

"How's your work going, babe?" Alex asked. "I didn't see any new gallery shows we're scheduled to attend. Everything okay?"

This time, she smiled for real. "We have a small break for the next several months. Giselle is introducing some new artists and wants to properly promote them before the next show. We'll go to that one." Alex went to the shows for her, not because he enjoyed looking at art. She gave his cheek a slow caress, and her smile dropped away. Fierce emotion kindled, blazed from her heart, and manifested into words. "I love you." Later, she could express her emotion with her body.

Alex paid their bill, and they exited the restaurant, hands interlaced, as they turned to walk back to their apartment. Goose bumps danced along Liv's skin the moment she sensed a change in their environment. Lifting her gaze, she gasped in surprise. The cagey-looking man who'd bumped her earlier headed straight for them. Shaggy brown hair fell in disarray across his forehead, and the jeans and black shirt he wore looked as though they hadn't been washed in a few days. Menace flashed across his face, and her veins felt as if they'd been injected with ice.

Alex tucked her behind him, obstructing her view. Lurching forward, Alex grabbed the man and shoved him against the wall. A dull crack from the man's head crashing against the brick made her cringe.

Liv stood helplessly as heated words volleyed quietly between the two men in Spanish. A few paces behind them, she strained to hear. Over Alex's shoulder, the man sneered at her. She tracked their every move. When the stranger lifted a hand to Alex's arm, her eyes narrowed on the blue ink between his thumb and index finger. She could make out the detail of the sharp-angled butterfly tattoo.

As fast as the altercation happened, it ended. Alex shoved the man away. Whatever he'd said made the stranger hurry down the street. Alex stood motionless, wearing a fierce frown, as he watched him leave.

Alex returned to Liv's side, and despite the miniscule narrowing of his left eye, he flashed a reassuring smile meant to put her at ease. "Informant. Being here, coming anywhere near you was a mistake on his part." He slid his arm around her waist and leaned in to brush a kiss on her cheek. "Ready?"

"If you're sure everything is okay." Her smile wobbled a little, but she firmed it up.

"Yes, of course. Forget about that. This is our night."

"I really don't get how you deal with that."

He tweaked her nose. "Walk in the park, Liv. What's important is you're by my side."

Even with Alex's reassurance that all was well, the man's last words played through her mind as he'd made a hasty departure. His English was heavily accented, and his message was odd. "He's waiting."

CHAPTER 3

Strong arms wrapped around her middle, and she leaned into Alex's embrace. She was a chicken. There'd been time to tell him at the restaurant, including the perfect moment when he'd sat beside her and kissed her on the forehead. She'd let it slip away.

Tilting her head back, she smiled. "Morning. Thank you for the flowers. They're beautiful."

He nuzzled her neck. "You're more so."

Desire stirred in her stomach. It would have to wait. Soon, Alex would head out the door for the day. "I wish we had a little more time this morning before your meeting." Reaching a hand back, she threaded her fingers through his thick hair.

"I'm not done, Liv." Turning her in his arms, he brushed his lips across hers, deepening the kiss when she parted for him. He backed her up and pinned her against the counter.

Molded to his body, she let all the tension from the previous night fall away and enjoyed how his mouth moved expertly over hers.

Too soon, he broke their kiss, a grin curving his lips, and he bent to whisper in her ear. "With how quickly everything happened last night, I didn't get a chance to give you a very delayed anniversary gift." His fingers traced the curve of her face, and banked passion blazed in his dark eyes.

A shiver raced down her spine. "Alex, you gave me two cases of my favorite wine from Savage Seas Winery for our one year. I told you that was the only thing I wanted." Their first anniversary had been six months ago, one month before the accident.

"It wasn't enough. Never is with you. I want to shower you in gifts." His shoulders tensed for the merest second. "You understand why we couldn't go on our honeymoon right away?"

Her smile softened, and she played with the ends of his hair at the back of his head. "Of course. Please stop worrying about that. There will be time for us to travel together. I get how important your work is to you. The timing wasn't right."

He grimaced. "I was so close to busting open the entire south-side cartel and mafia connection. It paid off, us waiting."

"It did. You're brilliant, and shutting the drug-trafficking factions down advanced your career by years. I couldn't be more proud of you. Just think how that'll impact the children who are exposed to that. You're saving lives for future generations. Even ours."

"Babe, we've talked about this. We can't have kids. I don't want them used against me. And they would be. It's just not a good idea." He softened his words by pressing a kiss to her pouting lips.

She frowned, her stomach a caldron of anxiety about telling him. Now was definitely not the time.

His grimace shifted to a grin. "At least with all the hours I put in, you had time to sculpt. You've grown. The finished pieces you sold at the gallery prove that. Although, I have my eye on the dancer you just glazed. Think we may have to keep that."

"You saw her? It's not in any shape for you to see yet. I need to fire it." She nibbled her lip, holding back her laughter, and very grateful for the change of subject. "Thanks for believing in me." Her parents had not when it came to sculpting, and the mantle of responsibility she'd worn weighed on her soul. When she had married Alex, he took a large portion of the burden off her.

"Be proud of what you are." He must have noticed where her train of thought had gone. "You're an artist, Liv. Your parents' goals don't define you." Before he could blink them away, dark shadows swirled in his eyes.

For the hundredth time, she wondered what secrets lived in his past. Someday he would confide in her. Refusing to let her insecurities be an influence, she rose up on her toes and kissed his cheek.

"Liv, I want to give you something before I leave for work." He drew a velvet box from his pocket and opened it. "It was my grandmother's."

Her hand fluttered to her mouth, and her gaze found his. An intricate silver design held a round stone of mercurial blues and purples. The antique setting looked very old.

Intense love collided with the swirling darkness that danced through his eyes. She recognized the strong emotion and the vulnerability that flashed in his brown depths on rare occasions. This piece of him, of his past with a grandmother he'd adored, meant a great deal, and the emotional weight of it caused her hands to shake. If only she'd had a chance to meet the woman before she'd died, or his mother, for that matter, who lived in Venezuela. For reasons Liv didn't fully understand, his mother had missed their wedding. "It's beautiful. I'm honored, Alex."

"I would have given it to you sooner, but after last night, I thought this was the perfect time to give you my grandmother's brooch."

Her brow furrowed. *After the confrontation when we left the restaurant?*

"My mother said this was my grandmother's favorite piece, one she kept with her always. Now, as my wife, it belongs to you"—he grinned—"even though I know you don't wear pins."

Laughter filled the air, and they said in unison, "Because they ruin clothes."

He tweaked her nose. "Our jeweler has the measurements and picture. This is temporary—the charm bracelet it's on. I think having it dangle like that could cause it to be hit too often and break. I'm going to have it mounted onto another design, one with a thin silver cuff."

"It's lovely, Alex." She ran her fingers over the smooth, fiery blue-green stone. *Paraiba tourmaline, perhaps?* A beat passed, and the air thickened as she looked from the gift to him. The strange seriousness of his expression caused her to pay closer attention to his next words.

"You hold both my past and future in your hands."

CHAPTER 4

lex. God, he was an inferno. Liv wanted nothing more than to wiggle against him and wake fully to the desire sizzling through her veins. Even with her heated body cuddled in Alex's arms on their bed, her mind buzzed.

Each new day held promise, and because of Alex, she was supported in her career, excelled at it even.

Careful not to disturb him, Liv eased away, moved his heavy arm from her waist, and dropped her legs over the side of the bed. Gentle rays of sunlight streamed through the gauzy curtains of their other home. The Upper East Side apartment she'd owned prior to marrying Alex was where they stayed during the week. If there was not a weekend function, they stayed in the Hamptons, which was her favorite.

Arms overhead, Liv stretched then stood. She slipped into her discarded top and panties and went to find where she'd dropped her purse, eager to find her pencils and sketchbook.

Her muse was Alex. Always. The images burned into her mind needed an outlet, and after sketching them, she wanted to immortalize them in clay. Her vision gave birth to a new series of sensual embraces. She longed to create lovers entwined in each other's arms and had already finished several of the pieces she'd imagined. Still, more called to her in various positions to design.

Even though she wanted to remain in bed with Alex, inspiration pulled her, and she smiled. He could use the rest while she worked, especially after last night, and he had paperwork to do later in the day. Her stomach fluttered, and she took note of how deliciously sore she was.

On bare feet, she padded over the stained concrete floor of her brightly lit studio. She plucked her sketchbook and pencils from where she'd dropped her oversized purse and went to the kitchen to make some coffee and do a little work. Clad in only ivory silk panties and matching camisole, she enjoyed the sensual connection to the form in her mind that cried out to be born.

She set her coffee on the table and hooked a toe onto the rung of her chair to drag it closer. She sat on the edge and flipped her sketchbook open. Pencil poised above the paper, she let the image she wanted to craft flow and take life as she began to sketch.

Mere seconds passed, and only a preliminary form had appeared when heat seared her backside once more. Strong, sure hands caressed the length of her arms and cupped the hand that sketched on the paper, bringing forth the emerging drawing. Alex caught her between his legs as he joined her on the chair, and her pulse kicked up. She dropped the pencil and shifted her fingers over the outline of the lovers that would soon be a sculpture. His followed.

She shuddered. Warm breath on her shoulder preceded the small pinch of his teeth as he gently nibbled her skin. The image in her head of her artwork faded, replaced by very real ones. He seduced her from her mind, bringing her fully to the present with him.

The tight clenching of her abdomen had her shifting to press back against his hard shaft. In agonizing slowness, his hand followed the curve of her shoulder, trailed over her back, and came around to brush the underside of her breast and flat stomach before pausing against the silk between her legs. Air whooshed out of her, and she sagged against him. The drawing sat forgotten on the table.

Alex released her other arm to grasp the back of her hair and tugged lightly on the strands at her nape. She tilted to the side so he could capture her lips. His tongue teased her, coaxing her to open for him. With a moan, she widened further as he invaded her mouth. Dizzying lust and need flamed higher as he hooked his feet on the insides of hers and spread her legs wide. Tormenting caresses over her silky underwear ceased, and she whimpered. Pressed against him, her skin heated, every spot he caressed hypersensitive.

His fingers skimmed the edges of her underwear, teasing. Arching, she urged him to touch her. He dipped inside her panties and slid his fingertips along her soaked seam. He spread the wetness over her clit in a slow circle, and she nipped at his bottom lip, desperate for more...for him.

Heat pooled at her center as his finger sank inside her. The world spun as another finger joined the first, stretching, accommodating her for when his shaft replaced his hands.

Uncaring of her charcoal-smeared hands, she threaded them into his thick, dark hair and pulled his mouth to her hammering pulse as she arched to the side, her legs still prisoner. He grazed his teeth against her sensitive flesh, and she cried out. Strong arms lifted her body, repositioning it so she sat astride him, face to face. Pressing against his hardness, she wrapped her arms around his neck. Her mouth crashed into Alex's, and her tongue tangled with his as he ground against her. With a growl, he maneuvered them enough to shove his boxers down and her panties aside. In one move, he sank fully into her wet sheath. She moaned, letting him hold her weight as he filled her, sending electric pulses through her entire body.

Finding a rhythm, he held her hips, taking over their pace. Head bent, he teased her nipples through the thin silk. Pleasure danced along her nerve endings. With every stroke, caress, and kiss, she climbed higher. Alex leaned her back more, and she braced herself on the edge of her table. With each thrust, he sank deeper and impossibly farther inside her. White sparks flashed behind her eyes, and her body tensed. Seating himself all the way, he filled her full and joined her in shouting his release.

The slide of his hands along her waist, ribs, and back only heightened her awareness of him. Several moments passed while their breathing regulated. He pulled her to his chest, and she nestled under his chin. The kiss at the top of her head made her smile. Her body molded to her husband's, sated.

In a sinuous move, he lifted her with him, and her legs automatically wrapped around his waist. Supporting her, Alex carried them from her studio, still imbedded within her. The twitch she felt deep inside stirred a small ounce of energy and a wicked grin. In a matter of minutes, she knew he would be hard once more. God, she loved him.

There were many different ways he made love to her. Sometimes he did so in a desperate frenzy, as if each moment, each time, would be their last. He already ruled her heart and her world, but the intensity of his actions made no sense to her. She was his. When he seduced her like he'd just done, those were her favorite moments.

Alex carried her into their bathroom, reached forward, and turned on the water so they could shower. Tensing, she prepared to slide down his body. His chuckle and strong hands holding her hips stopped her. She sank deeper, and he moaned, stiffening.

"Liv," his deep voice purred. "What could possibly pull you from our bed so early in the morning before I had you?" He chuckled. "Think I should punish you?"

She met his laughing gaze with a wicked one of her own. "Maybe you should."

He smacked her butt, stepped into the tepid water, and pressed her against the cool tiles. Time spun out as he thoroughly made love to her under their rainfall shower. Her husband was insatiable, and she loved him even more for it.

The bath mat beneath her feet bore Alex's wet footprints. Shifting, she sought a dryer portion as he wrapped a fluffy towel around her body, drawing her in for a hug. His warmth chased the chill away, and she leaned into him. Would she ever get enough of him?

He dropped a kiss on the top of her head. "What were you sketching?"

She squeezed him back, happy. "A new series I've begun to sculpt." She tilted her head, caught his gaze, and grinned. "You're my muse."

He laughed. "I am, huh?" In a slow up-and-down motion, he rubbed her arms. "Well, this muse needs breakfast. Have you eaten?"

"Of course not. Give me a few minutes, and I'll join you in the kitchen."

"I'll get the coffee started, and maybe some eggs too." He tweaked her nose then exited the bathroom so she could continue to dress.

In the distance, the doorbell rang. When she heard Alex answer the door, she thought she would have a few more minutes to get ready.

Running the brush through her hair, she studied her reflection in the foggy mirror. Flushed cheeks and bright eyes stared back. Alex did that to her—made her happy. So much had changed since he'd come into her life.

She suffocated under her parents' shadow in the role they'd cast her in. As an artist, she needed to create, not make political connections and have conversations over countless luncheons, dinner parties, and various events.

She slipped her legs into a new pair of panties and put on a matching bra before pulling slacks and a cream silk blouse from her closet. Liv couldn't help her mind from returning to the past and, not for the first time, she thanked fate for crossing her path with Alex's. Her life would have been very different if she had meekly caved to any of the senators' sons her parents had pushed on her.

Liv padded into the bedroom and saw that Alex had left the paper he'd been reading on his bedside table. She picked it up and froze at the smiling picture of her parents, one of many the aggressive photographers had taken of them when they were out. Their death had brought a flurry of reprinted pictures of their past. The paparazzi had always existed in their lives because of her father being a senator and her family's wealth that could be traced back more than a century.

With her finger, she followed the line of her mother's face in the photo. She was beautiful, no doubt. Her mother had maintained the same youthful mahogany hair she'd had in her younger years, an identical shade to Liv's natural color. Their only difference was that Liv wore her hair long rather than shoulder-length. With her Italian lineage, her mom's olive-toned skin had stayed flawless. Men had admired her full lips, high cheekbones, and her deep-brown, almond-shaped eyes, framed in long, spiky lashes. Liv looked like her mom, and they had often been mistaken for sisters. She smiled and dropped the article, pushing aside the melancholy that was trying to gain a foothold.

"Hey, Liv."

She knew that tone, the one dripping with teasing mystery that clung to her name. Alex had been even more attentive than usual after she'd heard him on the phone, determined to assure her there were no secrets and that everything was fine.

What did he have in store for her now? Her teeth sank into her bottom lip as she rounded the corner, anticipation crawling along her skin.

A grin stretched her lips wide, unable to hide her excitement. "I'm coming. What is it?"

Arms full with a sizable box, he walked from the closing elevator and bent to kiss her before walking toward her studio.

"Alex!" Laughter bubbled up as she followed him, quickening her pace to keep up. "What did you do?"

He set the box on her table, turned, and swept her into his arms. "A little present. Open it."

Liv peeled back the packing tape, ripped open the box, and sucked in a breath.

"Let me help you." Alex tore the sides and lifted two twenty-five-pound blocks of red clay. "Do you want this on the shelving over there, where the rest is?"

"Yes. Alex, it's so pretty. Is it from California?"

"Of course. I listen when you talk."

That was true, he did. He also confided in her when he needed someone to talk to. Their relationship was strong. She didn't keep secrets from him. Her pregnancy didn't count—she would tell him. And other than confidential aspects of his job, he didn't keep secrets, either.

"What are you going to make with it?"

She caught her lower lip between her teeth, sparks shooting through her body. "I've been thinking about it for a while." Up on her toes, she slid her arms around his neck and played with his thick hair. "I'm going to finish a series of us together and one other piece that's been hovering around in my mind." Laughing, she kissed the satisfied smirk that appeared on his face. "Since you listen so well, remember, we have that event tonight."

"I'm in good with the Radcliffs. I just had lunch with Joe, and I'm aware you weren't looking forward to going. He and your dad already locked me in as a candidate as your dad's successor. It's basically a done deal. Then after meeting Senator Davidson some time ago, thanks to you, I'm a shoo-in, no matter what."

Her smile fell, and she wondered at his conviction.

CHAPTER 5

*F*ive blissful days passed with no social obligations and plenty of time to work. It was the weekend, and Liv and Alex decided to stay at their home in the Hamptons again.

Alex had converted a back room adjacent to Liv's studio into a place to house her kiln. Shelves lined the wall and stored her works in progress. Glazes, washes, and her tools had their own space in a large armoire. A door separated the back room from her studio, which blazed with warmth and stunning views of the coast. Her workspace had big windows on two sides, allowing for maximum natural light. Situated off the back of their home, the studio was divided from the main house by a door.

If they ever moved, she would need another view to rival this one, with the inspiration of crashing waves as a backdrop.

The dancer statue that Alex admired, and must have peeked at a while ago, had been glazed and fired in her kiln. The finished piece was what she'd hoped for with its graceful posture and the life that radiated from the peaceful expression and bright colors of the woman's dress. It reminded Alex of his mother, which was why he wanted to keep it.

When he talked about his mom, her vibrancy filled the room. But there were times he refused to discuss his life growing up with a single mother, and that made her wonder. When he told the few stories he was willing to share, he painted a picture of her spirited and bubbly personality. Why occasional sadness permeated his words remained a mystery. Alex assured her they wanted for nothing, so the only answer in her mind was that he must have longed for a father figure.

Maybe she would keep the sculpture for him. There were others, completed ones she could put in one of the galleries that represented her work.

Her gaze skittered over the shelves, and she noticed the pieces that sat on them were dry. They would have to wait until the one she had just created was dry too. It would be at least three to four weeks before she would have to candle the kiln for her finished piece. Plan in place, she again focused on the table. Her tools were laid out, along with a spray bottle of fresh water to dampen the clay if and when she needed to.

Ideas came as her hands pressed into the unformed lump. The images were sluggish in materializing, but there. A tiny spark of excitement lit, and she moved her thumb in a sweep across the water-based clay. She knew what the malleable object would yield.

She began to form the head, which then determined the size and scope of the rest of the figure. As it always did, the clay became a connection to her thoughts, desires, dreams, and experiences. What was born wasn't always what she set out to create. That was the beauty, the gift. The finished product occasionally surprised her. Rachel would say that some pieces were an unconscious transference from Liv's mind to the clay, a premonition of sorts. It was a whimsical thing to say and held some merit, but those pieces were most likely a manifestation of her innermost feelings.

This one was no different.

Hours passed, and from the slant of the sun, Liv guessed she'd been in her studio the entire day. She stretched her hands over her head, elongating her stiff fingers and sore back muscles, as she observed the sculpture before her. The four figures represented her family: her parents, Alex, and herself. In exquisite detail, she'd duplicated her mother and father, their hands clasped. Liv's right hand seemed to slide partway into her father's large grasp, as if she was being pulled away. They formed a semicircle, facing one another, loosely mimicking *Circle of Friends* or Tom Friedman's *Circle Dance*. Her mother's hand was outstretched, reaching for Alex. Alex held Liv's left hand in a firm grip, stepping into their unit. *Or away?* His posture made it difficult to tell.

She would call this piece *Broken Circle*.

With a critical eye, she observed every nuance, ensuring it was complete before setting it on the shelf to dry. At least two to three weeks would pass before she could bisque fire the piece, along with the others waiting. When finished, she would use an under glaze to retain the intricate detail.

Even though she was exhausted, the need to work on the lovers' poses compelled her to continue, and she would...tomorrow. While Alex golfed, she would have plenty of time.

WITH THE NEW DAY, LIV'S ENERGY WAS RESTORED, AND SHE quickly began working in her studio once more. She molded the clay into Alex's form. As if she traced him, she imposed his characteristics in the manner he held his body—the cast of his head, angles of his face, and flow of his thick hair. The personality he exhibited to the world imprinted into the material and breathed life into the clay. His body language—the tilt of his shoulders and the way his body leaned both into and away from the blob she would soon craft into herself screamed of the conflicting push and pull of emotion.

Taut, sinewy cords in his arms popped. His slacks strained against the front thigh and slightly bent knee and pulled across his stabilizing back leg. It was near impossible to tell the outcome of his movements from his posture, even for her. Would he reach for her and clasp her hand in his, or was the separated contact a forced break?

The ache in her back and neck made her straighten from working on the facial features, and she observed the piece with a critical eye. A mask covered the top part of Alex's face, symbolizing the portion of his life she hadn't known about when they'd married.

She set her tool down then stood, stretched, and twisted her body to crack her back. One thing she had to remember was to get up every now and then and move around. When she was deep in her art, she found it difficult to pull herself away, or return to reality, as Alex would say.

A glance out the wall of windows showed her the sun had travelled a good distance across the sky. Despite the growl from her stomach, she couldn't bring herself to walk away from her work just yet. There was more she needed to do. The other half of her sculpture begged to be fashioned—the part that represented her.

A frown pulled her lips down as she studied the piece in its partially formed state. Would this be the last sculpture in her lovers' series?

Liv took her seat and, with tentative fingers, began on the next figure. The rough shape was almost the way she wanted, as if the inner workings of her subconscious had transferred to the clay. While Alex wore a shirt rolled up at the sleeves and soon-to-be black slacks, her body was covered in a breezy summer dress. Leaving the face for last, she molded the shape of the dress over her body to cling to her chest and abdomen.

As she worked the folds in the skirt that rippled away from her clay body, sadness swamped her, and tears rolled unchecked down her face. Absently, she swiped them away with a clean cloth. There was no doubt any longer about the outcome of the sculpture. Another thought formed—an idea that screamed premonition, one she refused to contemplate. The title for the piece sliced through her mind, leaving her bloody and bruised.

Fractured.

CHAPTER 6

*L*iv woke disoriented. With the weekend over, she and Alex were back in their apartment in the city. She wondered what had disturbed her as she peered through the dark at the red glowing numbers on her bedside clock. It was just past one in the morning. Another muffled sound reached her ears, and she threw off her covers and tiptoed down the hallway, halting when she heard the noise coming from Alex's office.

She was about to knock when his voice carried through the cracked door. Fury and frustration roared through his words. Instinctively, she froze. He sounded so…vicious. The scuff of his shoes against the hardwood brought him closer to the small opening of the cracked door.

"It's done. I've been setting things up." A beat passed. "I didn't tell you about her because it's none of *your* damn business. Keep your spies away from her, or I'll get rid of them myself." His words whipped out on a growl. "I realize what's expected."

Despite her resolve to leave him to his work, her curiosity and his cryptic speech held her prisoner. With small steps, she inched closer, worried for him, worried for herself. Through the sliver of an opening, she spied on his pacing form. Menace rearranged his features into a man she didn't know. The phone he pressed against his ear was black, not the silver one they'd purchased together.

His gaze met hers, and his palm smacked the door, slamming it shut and sending tendrils of alarm through her body. *What just happened?*

Shaking off her momentary paralysis, she continued to the kitchen for a glass of water. The phone call had to be in relation to the job, not anything to do with her or their life together. She must have misunderstood. His cases were intense, dangerous. With trembling hands, she took a long drink. It was just that Alex rarely brought his work home with him. There was a call here and there that he took in his office, but nothing like what she had just witnessed.

They'd been married just over a year. Did this mean his work world was converging with hers? Setting the glass on the counter, she continued to rationalize his behavior. She was acting foolish, wasn't she? He liked their lives to be disassociated from the details of his investigations. That was why everything —property and utilities—were in her maiden name. Safe. He always insisted they do whatever they could to keep her location and connection separate from him. Over and over again, she had experienced the depth of his feelings and compassion. She needed to do that again and extend her support and love in a time that was obviously tumultuous in his career.

Even so, worry licked up her spine, and she sank her teeth into her bottom lip. There was a reason she'd married him. He was not like her father or the majority of the men she'd grown up around, who were now lawyers, doctors, ran their daddies' companies, or in politics. At least he wasn't like that yet.

Soon, he would be entering that political arena, with her

father's and two other senators' full support. That dark gleam and dangerous aura that surrounded Alex when she'd first met him during her rebellious years lost some of its appeal. Was she being foolish?

A conversation she'd had with her mother surfaced. They had been having a heated discussion about what was expected of her. *Again.* She tasted blood as her teeth pierced her bottom lip. Her mother's taunt rippled through Liv's mind as clear as if Evelyn were still alive and in the room with her.

"Well, thankfully, Alex is driven and utilized the minimal effort you've made as his wife," her mother had said.

Liv flinched at the veiled disappointment in her mom's voice. "He has goals, Mother. I've done what you and Father asked and introduced him to the right people." She'd done what they had expected of her, but even so, she refrained from defining her and Alex's relationship. There was no talking to her mother when their social status was involved.

"You'll need to do more than that, dear, to ensure his foothold, and essentially yours."

"Stop, Mother. I don't want the same existence you have. It's brought nothing but heartache. Alex and I live a different life than you and Dad."

"Do you really think that, Olivia?" Her mother's voice dripped with cool disdain. "It's a small price to pay to put up with your father's minor indiscretions. In return, I have money, friends, social status, and the life I want. The only reason, and I do mean only, that you were allowed to marry Alex is because we didn't want you running off with some bohemian, starving artist who planned to strip you of your trust fund and your inheritance, and because his goals lined up with ours where you are concerned. Make no mistake, Olivia, your life is not that different than mine. Everybody uses each other for something. What do you think Alex needs from you?"

"Me! He wants me, Mother. There are no secrets between us." Even as she said it, the odd, pendulum-like moods her husband sometimes displayed weighed heavily on her mind.

"Don't be too sure, Olivia," her mother had said.

Shoving the memory from her thoughts, Liv pivoted to return to the bedroom so she could go back to sleep and came to a halt. Alex stood in the doorway, wearing an expression that was new to her. Was that fear? Regret?

Resting a hip against the counter, she ignored her racing heart and offered him a smile. "Did you want something to drink?"

Without a word, he opened the refrigerator, took a beer out, and downed half before he let it hang from his fingers by his side. A ragged whoosh of air left his lungs as he held her gaze, intensity oozing from his features. "That was work."

With a slight nod, she relented and gave in to her spiraling imagination, despite her determination to offer support only. "On a different phone?"

He tracked her every nuance as if assessing, reanalyzing, and finally coming to a conclusion. "Yes. That one's for informants and calls regarding specific cases…dangerous ones."

Her brows furrowed, unease still churning in her stomach at what she'd overheard. "I can't handle secrets, Alex. Living in a politician's household…"

He crossed the distance in a few steps and pulled her to his chest, one hand cradling her head. "I'm sorry, babe. I have no intention of hiding anything other than the job from you. There are no mistresses and never will be. You're it for me." He leaned back and tilted her chin up. "I need to keep you safe. That means the cases I work on have to remain separate from our lives, even if the call comes in the middle of the night like this one did. I'm a different person on those calls. Just bear with me. I don't want them bleeding into our private world, and I'm doing everything I can to ensure it stays that way."

She wasn't being fair. The job he did helped people, regardless of whether she had to endure a smidgen of doubt. Self-doubt and mistrust needed to stop. Relaxing in small degrees, she gazed into his eyes, worried by the repressed fury lingering there. She'd never seen him like this before. Needing to believe him, she rose up on her toes and pressed a kiss to his mouth.

She wasn't being entirely fair. The secret she held close needed to be shared.

A mass of jumbled nerves, she couldn't wait. "I know you are, and you're right. We shouldn't have any secrets between us. Alex, I have some news." Squeezing her hands behind her, she tilted her head back to look into his eyes. With his full attention on her, she forged ahead and ripped the Band-Aid off. "We're going to have a baby. I'm pregnant."

He stopped with the beer halfway to his lips. Silence reigned between them until violence exploded from his features in a menacing sneer and dilated eyes. "Fuck!" He hurled the beer, and it exploded across the backsplash diagonal from her.

Her heart hammered against her chest, and her breath sawed in and out.

Alex raked his hands through his hair, tilted his head back, and pushed out a breath. "How? How did this happen? You're on the pill!"

"My parents died, and I forgot how to live, and that included my birth control pills. I missed a few, or a lot. God, Alex, it wasn't planned." Sliding her foot sideways, she inched away, wanting nothing to do with him.

Raking his hands through his hair, he tugged on the strands then reached for her. His hands locked on her arms, and she froze. Several breaths wheezed through his nose, and his lips were tightly clenched. He drew out a blink, and his pupils returned to their rightful size. His reaction was more than unexpected. *Shock, sure, but violence?*

Caught in his remorseful gaze, she waited. The emotional blow from his outburst radiated pain along her insides.

"Liv, I'm so sorry." Enfolding her against his chest, he cradled her head, swaying from side to side. "I never meant... It was a huge shock."

Small tremors coursed through her stiff body. He'd never displayed his anger like that. In slow increments, her shock turned to outrage.

A small smile, which looked more like a grimace, flashed across his face. "A baby. So unexpected. It's just...we talked about this. I thought we agreed that, at the very least, we'd wait. Even then, bringing a kid into this world, especially with the dangers from my job... I don't want my past to touch our future. You hold my future."

"I'm aware of all that," she snapped. "Hearing you tell me, *after* we were married, that you didn't even think you wanted kids was upsetting. This wasn't planned, Alex. But it's happening, and you need to get on board with it."

A tremor shook his hand as he lifted it. "Sweetheart, you're right." His swallow was audible. "You're everything to me, and you don't even know it." With gentle fingers, he caressed her cheek. "I don't expect you to understand, or even forgive me."

"I get that you didn't want kids and that this is a shock to you too, Alex. You need to be happy, to accept this. Not throw a tantrum." She pushed his hands off her and paced the length of the kitchen floor. "The way you reacted, *throwing a beer*, doesn't make sense."

"It's the job, babe. The pressure is beyond intense, and my reaction was unwarranted. A baby with you is a good surprise, just not expected so soon. Dammit, I thought we'd have more time. I hoped we would." His teeth clenched, and he held still before he visibly relaxed once more. "I like having you all to myself." He pulled her into his embrace.

She tilted her head back, glared at him, and gave his chest a small push. Once he loosened his hold, she studied his face and the cocktail of emotions swimming across his features. Did fear swirl through the mix?

"Well, there's really no excuse for what I did." He dropped his arms from her and ran his hands through his hair, his mouth a grim line. "There are things going on right now. It's risky and dangerous, and I worry about it touching what we have." He flinched. "Then I go and do this instead. I promise I'll work harder to never let my stress touch you or what we have together."

She threw her hands up in the air, frustrated that he only partially understood her distress. "What happened here is proof. You're bottling too much up. You've got to let me in, even if it's just so I can understand what's going on. Because this, tonight, can't ever happen again. If it does, you'll lose me."

Needing to, she forgave him for his less-than-thrilled response to her news. Rachel had also told her that it was horribly intense at the station. Something was going down, and it must have been nearing a critical stage. Normally, he withheld everything from her about his job and his career. It worked for them. Upon the completion of a big case, or in the event of a promotion, he shared a few things...sparingly. She knew he needed time to decompress, and their dinners were usually just the thing to do the trick.

Alex opened the fridge for another beer then took a long drag before speaking. The mess he made went unaddressed. There was no way she was going to clean that. He would take care of it later, not Stephanie who cleaned for them, but him.

She stood there, unsure what would come next. Hopefully, he would show a smidgeon of acceptance and excitement at the very least. He would come to accept their baby, right? His fingers tightened on the neck of the bottle, and she worried further.

"Do you remember that honeymoon we never took?"

She frowned, her brows furrowing at the change of topic. This wasn't the first time he'd brought it up. "Of course. It was a pivotal point in your career, and we decided to put it off so that you could finish a big case. Since you were promoted right after, it was the right move."

"At the time, it was." A small smile came and left. "Let's get away for a few weeks. You deserve some pampering, and I could use the break from work."

She toyed with the bracelet dangling around her wrist, the one he'd fashioned with his grandmother's brooch. Maybe that was a good idea, an environment in which they could focus on each other and their expanding family. "Where did you have in mind?"

He threaded his fingers through hers and tugged her closer. After setting his beer down, he tucked a lock behind her ear then caressed the long strands of her thick hair in soothing motions. "I love you, Liv. More than you'll ever realize. And I'm so damn sorry."

The gentle squeeze on her hand brought her gaze to his, and she caught his guarded expression. "What is it?"

"Since we're expecting, we should go to Barbados, then to Venezuela."

"Oh, to visit your mom?" She smiled, excited at the opportunity to glimpse the world he grew up in, the one he remained a little secretive of, and to finally meet his mother.

He paused, looked away for a moment, and uttered yes. When he turned back, he was the Alex she knew with the mischievous, laughing eyes and sexy grin, not the closed-off one. What was going on?

Tired of the entire thing, she gave in and decided he was right. That was what they needed. In addition, she would go back to bed and leave him to clean the kitchen. The travel arrangements would be his to make too.

"We'll take that honeymoon we never had time for before we reach Venezuela." When he released her hand, he smiled, and she relaxed. The darkness swirling in his eyes dissipated. *Almost.* Something still lurked behind his dark orbs as he lifted her hand. He held her wrist and worked the lock of the charm bracelet he'd recently given her. "I'll get this taken care of before we leave."

CHAPTER 7

*T*he breeze ruffled Liv's hair, and she wrapped her hand around Alex's bicep. In between fluffy clouds, blinding sun shone down on them in golden shafts. The remnants of surprise still lingered from when Alex told her they would be flying to Barbados and spending time there before going to visit his mom.

Being in here was a dream come true and she enjoyed every moment of their vacation as they strolled hand in hand along the beach. With each step, their feet sank a little in the sand, leaving footprints, before gentle waves rolled over their trail and washed them away.

"How are we getting to your mom's?"

Alex's hand tightened for a fraction of a second, so briefly that she wondered if she had imagined it. "We'll take a boat to Caracas, Venezuela. From there, we'll drive to the airport and then fly to the small island I grew up on." The same island on which his mom still resided.

"Why don't we charter a plane for a direct flight from here to your mom's?"

"Let's not talk about leaving. Not yet, anyway. I want to spend as much time here with you as I can before my mom steals you away."

They changed direction and angled to where their beach chairs were. The sand grew hotter the farther they got from the water's edge. If she didn't know better, she would have thought he was stalling from the way he showered attention on her, almost as if he didn't want her to meet his mom or see where he grew up. She inhaled a breath and relaxed into the moment. They needed this trip, time to connect without all Alex's work stress before their baby arrived.

She dropped her wrap on the back of the lounge chair and lowered herself onto the royal-blue cushions. Even with the large umbrella overhead, she kept her sunglasses in place against the sun's reflection off the turquoise waters.

Listening to the breaking waves, she drifted, barely paying attention as Alex mentioned something about drinks. She heard him move around but was too comfortable to look.

"Hey, beautiful," Alex purred as he dropped a kiss on her cheek. He handed her a tall glass. "I brought you a drink."

"Iced tea?" She cleared her throat and accepted the glass, willing herself to stay awake.

"Yep, and I took the Long Island part and had them add it to mine. Yours is strictly virgin." He winked. "While I was up there, I ordered us lunch. It'll be delivered in about a half hour." He ran his hand over her still-flat abdomen. "I love this pink bikini on you."

She giggled. "It's coral."

"Well, this *coral* suit will look even better on the floor of our room." The scruff from his face tickled her neck as he brushed kisses along it. Holding his head in her hands, she sighed, wanting to take his caresses further. After a few heated minutes, he took a seat on his lounger, stretching his long legs out beside her. "You're trouble, Liv." His husky voice sent a thrill racing across her exposed skin.

She closed her eyes, enjoying the warm breeze. The beauty of Barbados was addicting. So far, they'd done nothing but take walks on the beach, swim, make love, and relax ocean-side. "Being here, with you, is like a drug. I'll never get enough."

"Hmm. Why don't we stay longer? I didn't tell my mom we were coming for sure. I'd rather keep you all to myself. If I need to, I can go see her for a day while you enjoy yourself here at the beach."

"What? No, Alex. I've never met her."

Silence fell between them as Alex drank half his beverage. The uncertainty of his quick glance brought an unpleasant realization crashing home. She came from old money, grew up immersed in time-honored traditions and expectations, led a privileged life. While Alex had plenty of money, it didn't touch the vast fortune of her family's, now hers alone.

Theirs.

The differences of their backgrounds, the circumstances surrounding their upbringing, could have been bothering him. Did he worry how his mother would react to her? Her family had tolerated him, at times barely, even correcting his speech from time to time. With their sights on the horizon of his aspiring political career, they'd relented.

"I think you've got something, babe. Let's make this our destination vacation place. I'm thinking we travel here at least twice a year."

She turned toward him and wrinkled her nose, choosing to let the comment about skipping the next leg of their trip go. He'd told her several times he wanted her all to himself. The relaxation of their vacation was needed, and she understood his perspective there. If his hesitation was due to the contrast of old and new money, she would prove to him how silly his fears were once she met Rita.

"If it's possible, let's stay longer next time." Even though she would never do anything to hold him back in his career, a small part of her didn't want him to advance any further. They would have to see if his job allowed the time. His plans to rise to the Senate were within reach, but first, he would have to win an election. The death of her parents didn't hinder his progress, as her father and all his buddies had made it known they were behind Alex's goals.

Her phone pinged, and she picked it up when she noticed Rachel's name flash across the screen.

Rachel had texted, *How's it going?*

Liv responded, *Amazing. Gorgeous here.*

Rachel: *So you're moving there and deserting me?*

Liv: *Haha. Nope. Although, Alex is being weird about me meeting his mom.*

Rachel: *Well, it's weird you haven't met her yet. Maybe she's a recluse?*

Liv: *Not sure. Worried he doesn't want me to meet her.*

Rachel: *You're high. That man adores you. It must be something with his mom.*

Liv: *Okay, fine. Chat with you later.*

Rachel: *Enjoy the sun!*

She set her phone down and leaned back. The combination of the heat and the hypnotic sound of the ocean lulled her once more into a blissful state of relaxation. Loud voices passing by their spot on the beach brought the people around them into sharp focus. She stifled a yawn. Had only a minute passed?

Alex laughed. "You've been zoning out for a half hour. Must be tired."

"Seriously? Time is moving way too quick." She lifted her

sunglasses and peered at the food that had just arrived. "I need coffee."

"What's the point, babe?" He flashed her a grin. "You can only have decaf with a baby growing inside you. I can kiss you awake."

"Yes." She sat up, intending to join him on his lounge chair, except the fresh pineapple and mango caught her eye. "Um, maybe after we eat?"

He chuckled. "Those hormones are really kicking in, babe."

She tossed her wide-brimmed hat at him.

Grinning, he caught it and plopped it back on her head. "You look like an avenging goddess."

"You're an evil man. I should swap out your coffee with decaf and see how you deal with the caffeine withdrawals."

His smile fell away, and he stabbed a mango. "Evil? Not with you. Never with you."

What? Her mouth parted to question his odd comment, but he slid a mango between her lips, and she closed her eyes at the sweet burst of flavors. Fruit was heaven. If the pregnancy hormones were amplifying her taste buds, she was in serious trouble. At least they also increased her sexual appetite, something Alex was not complaining about.

After eating fruit and a half sandwich, she leaned back, content to listen to the rolling water. Even under the umbrella, she wore her sunglasses to keep the glare of the water at bay. Alex was lost in his own world, and without him talking to her, she teetered on the edge of sleep, needing it in her first trimester.

She woke completely when her chair shifted. Alex hovered over her, fully focused on her mouth. A spark of desire ignited and sizzled through her.

"You're so beautiful." His hoarse words danced over her relaxed body.

The distance between them melted away, and his lips feasted on hers—gentle at first, then demanding. Her body hummed beneath his, craving skin-to-skin contact.

A gasp left her as he lifted her from the chair and carried her in the direction of their room. Being pressed against his lean body stirred her desire further. Each determined stride brought them closer. She couldn't wait. In his arms was exactly where she wanted to be.

The time it took to get to their room only heightened her need. When the door clicked shut behind them, he released her legs from the cradled position in which he held her. In a slow slide, her thighs brushed over his body until her feet touched the floor.

Liquid chocolate eyes stared into hers with an intensity that shot straight to her heart. His need, love, and intense passion blazed for her to see. Yet the silence he maintained told her something else bothered him, and she filed it away for later. He tumbled her to the bed then tugged at her hip and pulled her bikini bottom off.

Her coral suit lay on the rug a few feet from her as he bent his head to her abdomen. With a whimper, she begged for more.

Teeth scraped along her heated skin, intermingled with tantalizing kisses. He traveled higher, pressing his long body to hers. She arched her back and gave him full access to her aching breasts. When he took her nipple in his mouth, her breath left her lungs in a low moan. An underlying somberness skimmed around the edges of his gaze as he bent to brush agonizingly tender kisses on her mouth.

There were many ways Alex made love to her, and she loved them all. But this time, the quiet that blanketed them suffocated her with an uneasy cadence. With the passion he coaxed from her, she was unable to think and fully analyze his mood.

She gasped when he thrust into her. They fit perfectly. He

held still, seated all the way, gazing into her eyes. In slow movements, he built their desire, their need, as their breath collided in increasing bursts. With her arms wrapped around him, she clutched him as close as he did her. Dancing on the edge of her release, she moaned. When his hand slipped between their bodies and teased her sensitive nub, she shattered. He followed immediately after her, pulling her tighter to him.

She shifted and pressed her back against his chest, using his bicep as a pillow. His other arm draped over her hip and snuggled her close. To the quiet hum of the air conditioner, they fell asleep.

The next few days passed in bliss, and she almost relented to his comment about extending her stay. In the end, she didn't. Not visiting his mother after coming all this way would have been wrong.

Falling into a pattern on Barbados, she longed to remain in her bikini and fun crochet-and-fringe cover-up. Instead, she slipped on a sleeveless, gauzy knit dress with strappy heels. Alex said she overdressed, but it made her feel good, sexy. With the baby coming, she wanted to wear all her favorites before maternity clothes became the norm. Plus, this would be the first time she met his mom, and she wanted to make a good impression. She couldn't imagine Alex's mom would judge her appearance as her own mother had, but Liv didn't want to risk offending her. With her hair and makeup done, she left the dressing room and smiled at Alex's soft whistle. This was the right dress.

Jewelry was the only thing remaining. She slid the zipper to her suitcase open and rolled out the small pouch she'd brought. Running her fingers over a few necklaces, she contemplated which would look best. Here, her pearls were not needed.

"None of those." Alex's husky voice paused her search.

"No?" Smiling at him, she took note of the swirl of emotions in his mocha eyes.

From a box on top of the dresser, he pulled a delicate necklace. The pendant hung by shimmery strands of silver fashioned into a butterfly. An illusive memory tried to surface at the sight of the jewelry, but it was gone before she could fully grasp it. From the butterfly's almost angular wings, two rare blue diamonds dangled. Dainty and whimsical, the necklace complimented her dress.

"It's lovely." She lifted her hair so he could help her fasten it then turned to the mirror to admire the light bouncing off the gray-blue stones. Not her usual style, but beautiful all the same.

Picking up her wrist, he slid a silver cuff in place then secured its small latch. The inlay was his grandmother's brooch, the one he'd given her on a charm bracelet and took to have altered into another design before their trip. Stunned by the clever way he had it crafted, she smiled. He knew she would never have worn it as a pin. The design was a perfect compromise of both of their tastes.

"This is beautiful, Alex. When did you have time to do this?" She didn't miss the mix of emotions that flitted across his face. "Is everything okay?"

His gaze cleared, and he squeezed her hand. "Of course. I was just thinking about how I arranged our travel from Barbados. I should have chartered a private boat."

Why hadn't he? That was what they normally did.

He crushed her to his chest, and she laid her head against his crisp white shirt. Was he still concerned about her meeting his mother? It wouldn't matter what Rita Mudarra was like. Liv loved Alex with her whole heart and would face whatever lay ahead when they arrived. She slid her hand into the crook of his arm, and he pressed a tender kiss to her forehead. "Are you ready to go?"

The ride took no time at all, and soon they arrived at the boat that would ferry them to Venezuela before the plane and short trip to the island he grew up on. Neither did their time on the water. They strolled along the deck until they came upon tables with flickering tea lights. The romantic setting was not lost on them, and Liv leaned into Alex's side. He pulled out her chair and rested his hands on her bare shoulders for a brief moment before taking his seat.

He winked. "How are you holding up without your wine with dinner?"

She waited to answer as he placed their order for drinks with the server—nothing with alcohol for her. Still, the full-bodied cabernet she had at home would have been welcome, had she been able to drink it. "It's an adjustment, but not one I'm struggling with that badly. The morning nausea is what I could do without."

"Anything I can do to help, just tell me. This is a first for both of us, and I want to be there for you."

A smile spread across her lips. "Thanks." Toying with the napkin in her lap, she dove into the question she'd promised herself she wouldn't ask. "Are you worried about me meeting your mother? Is there anything I should be aware of?"

"No. My mom will love you."

"Then what is it?" She frowned at his guarded expression. "There are times you're so tense. Will anyone else be there we could run into who you'd rather not?" *An old girlfriend?*

His eyes shuttered, and she shivered from the loss of warmth. "It was not my intent for my past to collide with the life we've built together." He shook his head as she tried to speak. "I just didn't want to have to bring you here. It's not the safest place. There's nothing for you to worry about at my mom's. We'll spend some time with my mom and escape to some of the beaches and shopping if we want to be alone."

She knew about the dangers of Venezuela, Colombia, and Mexico and could understand some of his trepidation. But why that would affect her, she wasn't sure. It wasn't as though she would go anywhere that could be a hot spot for trouble. "All right." She reached across the table and squeezed his hand.

"Have I told you about the beaches there?" At her denial, he smiled. "They are some of the whitest sands, aside from Greece. Come to think of it, if we're able to cut this visit short, we should travel there too, take advantage of the vacation time I have. It's been too long since we've had any adventures. And there, the water is translucent. It's something to experience for sure."

Her heart soared at the thought of walking the historic streets with him. "I'd love to visit the Trevi fountain. Oh, wait. That's in Italy. Then the Parthenon sculptures. Well, any of the famous works of art would be amazing. If we could manage it, that would be lovely, Alex."

"A little research for your next piece?"

She laughed. "No. I'm content with my smaller sculptures."

Her anxiety over what they would soon face evaporated with the possibilities ahead. His unease must have been because he would rather not spend the entire vacation with his mom. Understandable. Who was she to judge? Her parents had loved her, and she them. It was the high expectations they'd set for her that she did not care for. Maybe he wanted to avoid a situation similar to what she'd grown up with.

THEY BUMPED ALONG IN A LITTLE RACER CAR ALEX HAD FLAGGED down to take them to the Caracas airport. From there, they would have a thirty-five-minute flight to Margarita Island, where his mom lived. They could have flown from Barbados, but Alex seemed to want to add any experience he could share with her before they arrived at their next destination.

Earlier, he'd called his mom to make sure she would be around this week, as they were going to surprise her. Why he had not paved the way for their stay, she wasn't sure. All it did was further unleash her nervous energy.

Liv intertwined her fingers with Alex's and gazed out the window at the passing countryside below. The blue water stretched as far as the eye could see.

Before she knew it, they had landed on the island, taken a short drive from the airport, and were pulling into a long drive-way. At the end sat a picturesque white colonial with a backdrop of the ocean. Liv's free hand fluttered to her chest. The scenic view was beautiful, and the artist in her longed to capture the feeling in clay.

"This is where you grew up?" her voice whispered through the car.

"Yes." No further information was given as Alex parked in front of the house and slipped his hand from hers.

"How did you ever leave?"

Rather than answer, he exited the car and went around to her side. He opened her door and helped her out. After he got their bags, she followed him up the winding path to the bold blue front door. Alex rapped his hand against the wood, and they waited.

A few moments passed before a petite woman who clearly resembled Alex opened the door. She had long dark-brown, almost black, hair and laughing mocha eyes that brought a smile to her face. When the woman squealed and launched herself at Alex, Liv was pleased she had listened to his wish to surprise her. His mother drew back, covered both cheeks with her hands, and kissed her son's face multiple times. A slew of foreign words rushed from the beautiful woman, and Liv almost groaned. *No English?* She'd taken only two years of Spanish, and that was in high school.

Alex pulled Liv close, and she blinked at one word she actually understood him say. "Esposa." *Wife*. A guarded look passed so quickly between Alex and Rita that Liv thought she had imagined it.

In flawless English, his mother welcomed her to their home. "I've heard so much about you, Liv. If I could have, I would have been at your wedding." Her thin arms wrapped around Liv, who relaxed at the genuine affection.

"Come. Come." She ushered them inside. "Alex will put your luggage in the other room."

A rushed exchange of dialogue in words she couldn't understand resulted in a frown from his mother before Alex turned to Liv with a wink and a promise to be right back.

Alone with his mother, Liv glanced around, getting caught once more by the glistening waters beyond the living room windows. "It's so beautiful here. I'm not sure why Alex left."

A breezy laugh filled the air before his mom linked arms with her and pulled her outside to the patio. "Sit. I want to hear all about you."

"I'm not sure what to say. I may be repeating what Alex told you."

"No, dear. Hearing it firsthand from you is an experience in itself. Please…" Her arm waved in a flourish, signaling that Liv should continue.

"The most important thing is your son makes me deliriously happy, Mrs. Mudarra."

"Ah, love. There is nothing better." She sighed. "Call me Rita."

"Of course, Rita."

"I'm very sorry to hear about your parents, dear. That must have been a terrible experience. Alex called me and said you needed to get away for a while, to cheer up after such a trying couple of months. I never dreamed he'd come here. I'm so pleased." She reached over and squeezed Liv's arm.

"Thank you. It's been difficult, but Alex is wonderful with all the attention he gives me. And he was right. We needed to get away, especially with the upcoming addition to our family and the stress he's under with his job. We can spend some time alone before our dynamic changes." Liv blinked, surprised at how Rita's face fell.

"Your family is expanding? You're with child?"

She didn't know? Alex said he'd told his mom about the baby before they had left for their vacation. "Yes. I'm sorry. I thought Alex told you." Her heart pounded, and her nails dug into her palms. Why had both Alex and his mother looked as if the world was about to end? Was having a baby somehow a bad memory for the two of them? What could have possibly been wrong?

"Please excuse me, Liv. I was surprised is all. This will change things, of course, but it's wonderful news. I'm thrilled for you both and expect to see that sweet little baby often."

Liv's smile wavered, and before she could reply, Alex walked onto the patio.

"Don't you have a call to make, Alex? Surely, you remember." His mother's eyes glanced at Liv's abdomen before they bore into his. Alex's jaw hardened. His tell that he was upset screamed at her—the subtle narrowing of his left eye. To anyone else, it wouldn't have been recognizable, but to her, it was a red flag. Alex wasn't happy.

"You're right. Liv, please excuse me for a few more minutes."

After the door shut, Liv pounced. "What's wrong, Rita? You can tell me."

Rita waved her concern away, her gaze shifting to where Alex had exited. "No. Nothing like that. We have a slight contention with his father. Alex needs to call him, tell him you've arrived, and the news of the baby."

"His father? I-I didn't realize Alex had any contact with him, or even knew who he was." Her brows furrowed. "When we were married, I saw his birth certificate, and there was no father listed."

Rita laughed. "That's merely a technicality, darling. His father is a powerful, amazing man." Her hand fluttered to her chest, and her eyes sparkled. "When I first encountered him, he swept me off my feet and spoiled me, promising me the world. After those first few weeks, my entire existence changed. You see, I was a Latin dance instructor when I met Juan Carlos. After that first night, he became adamant I would no longer work."

"I didn't realize you were married."

"Oh no. We weren't." She waved the issue away with a bubbly little laugh. "He has a wife. I am his consort. This house, everything in it, and Alex's education were provided by him."

Liv's throat constricted at the mention of his father's infidelity and Rita's easy acceptance of her part in coming between a married couple. Her unhappy childhood reared its head. Rita acted as though having an affair with a married man was an honorable thing, not something that tore families apart, undermined confidence, and sparked screaming fights. The way her father's infidelities had impacted her youth was earth shattering in her memories.

"They had contact while he was growing up?" Her mind whirled. Alex never talked about his father. Could this be why? Because he knew how Liv felt about cheating? She'd assumed he had never met or even been aware of who his father was.

"Yes, some when he was very young, and then more before Alex went away. Juan Carlos paid for me to fly to the United States and have the best doctors in my last trimester before Alex was born. I gave birth there, and…" she waved away the rest. "It's merely a piece of paper. Alex is aware of who is father is, how utterly powerful Juan Carlos is, and what that also does for him."

What exactly does his father do for him? Unease sat heavy in her stomach, and Liv leaned forward to pick up the tea Alex had brought when he popped out briefly. Her necklace dangled as she did so, and the happy squeal from his mom made her look up. Liv's gaze focused on the pendant Rita pinched in her fingers. It matched her own. Liv's hand went up to hover over her identical necklace.

CHAPTER 8

*V*ibrant sunlight reflected like tiny diamonds on the water as Alex, Rita, and Liv enjoyed tea, coffee, and croissants on the patio. Liv tore off a piece of the flaky bread and popped it in her mouth. It was so beautiful here. Her brows puzzled together with the sneaking suspicion that Alex's moving away had to do with his father, as he had never spoken about him.

They passed the morning telling Rita about their life in the States, and she, in turn, caught them up on friends of Alex's— who had married whom and who had moved away. There would be moments here and there in which Liv observed how fidgety he'd become, not at all his usual self. She'd even noticed him watching his mom, his left eye slightly narrowed.

When lunch rolled around, they again sat outside on the patio. There was something about eating fish and vegetable medleys that appealed to Liv in the Caribbean, or South America, rather.

"Mom, do you want to go sightseeing or to the beach with us? I thought I'd show Liv around some more."

Rita waved them off. "You're sweet to ask me, but no thank you, my dears. I wanted to go to town to meet a friend I was unable to get ahold of to cancel plans we had. You two run along and have fun."

That left Liv and Alex alone for the day, or several hours at least.

"What should we do?" Liv gazed longingly at the ocean spread out before them. Still in the first trimester of her pregnancy, she couldn't believe how much she craved sleep. An afternoon on the beach sounded like heaven. Hopefully, he would agree.

Alex chuckled. "You can't stand it much longer, can you? Get ready, and we'll go to the beach. Go." He waved her on. "I'll clean up here first."

With anticipation, she hurried to put on a bathing suit and wrap. She grabbed a wide-rimmed hat and sunscreen then tugged on her bracelet. Finally giving up on trying to get it off, she decided to wait for Alex to help her with the clasp and reached beneath her hair for the closure on her necklace.

Alex's hand halted hers as she worked the tricky clasp to the butterfly necklace. "Not that." The tick was back in his jaw. He nodded to her wrist and the handcrafted bracelet with the intricate fastening mechanism she had struggled to remove. "While we're here, you need to leave those on."

LIV EMERGED FROM THE BATHROOM AFTER SHOWERING THE NEXT morning. Her stomach growled loudly. God, she was always hungry lately. She made her way to the kitchen, bypassing the floor-to-ceiling windows at the back of the house, which showcased the sparkling lake beyond. She and Alex had spent precious hours yesterday afternoon walking along the beach, swimming, and relaxing in the sun.

If she had grown up here, she wouldn't have left. The small town inspired her, and she longed for her clay, even for just a few hours to create.

Rita joined them in the evening, a happy glow on her face. Alex's moods wavered from content to guarded. When they next had a moment by themselves, Liv would ask him about it.

Meanwhile, she soothed herself with the thought of traveling to Greece with her husband and having him all to herself once more. When they were alone, things were as they should be, and she was blissfully happy. With Alex's recent kaleidoscope of emotions, Liv guessed he would want to leave and spend time together, just them.

Well rested and showered, she followed hushed voices into the kitchen, only to draw up short at the dark expression on Alex's face and the serious one gracing his mother's. "I'm sorry, did you need a minute?"

Alex shoved his chair back, took a breath, and turned to her with a small smile. "Good morning, beautiful. Have a seat. I made a plate of fresh fruit and eggs."

Liv slid onto the chair Alex held for her and reached for the glass of water he'd poured. God, she wished she could have coffee. Decaf was pointless. *Only seven months left.*

He hovered in the kitchen and chatted for a moment while he finished his *caffeinated* coffee. *Traitor.* The heavenly aroma tormented her, and she swallowed another gulp of water that did not satisfy.

Alex leaned down, tilted her head up, and placed a kiss on her lips. "I'll be back shortly. Mom, no embarrassing *stories.*"

She narrowed her eyes, wondering about his stern expression and emphasis on "stories." A guarded look passed between Alex and his mom. What didn't he want her to hear?

He turned to leave, and Rita's satisfied demeanor spiked her suspicions. Getting to her feet, Liv caught a glimpse of Alex pulling his cell phone from his pocket. *Wait, that's the black one, the phone used for informants and case correspondence only!* Why would he need to use that one on their vacation?

In quick succession, he pressed a series of numbers as he let himself out of the house. Something wasn't adding up. His low voice carried, but only muffled noises drifted into the house, not enough for her to make anything out.

Following her instincts, she hurried and thanked his mom for breakfast before rinsing her plate. "If you don't mind, Rita, I'm exhausted from travel and, well, the pregnancy. Think I'll lie down for a bit."

"Of course, dear. I was beyond tired when I carried Alexander. I'll run a few errands while you rest." She patted Liv's shoulder and swept from the room.

In the bedroom, Liv paced. The sound of his mother leaving the house fueled her to take action. Moving the gauzy curtains to the side, Liv caught a glimpse of Alex disappearing down a trail within the tall palm trees. She slipped from her room, being careful to shut the door behind her so it appeared she was sleeping, and left through the back door. She hurried over to where she last saw Alex and entered the grove of palms. There was a narrow path, and she quickly walked along, thankful it didn't branch off…yet.

Swiping the perspiration from her forehead, she picked up her pace when she spied crystal blue water through the dancing leaves. The break in the foliage gave her a blinding view of the water…and Alex. He stood near the edge, peering out along the horizon at a boat that neared the little sandy cove. What was he doing?

Removing her sandals, Liv exited the tree line and

approached him. When she was a few feet away, she spoke over the lapping water. "What's going on?"

He whirled around, all color draining from his face. "Liv! Go back." He rushed her, gripped her arm tight enough to leave fingerprints, and hurried her toward the vacant path.

Yanking her arm free, she stepped away. "Alex, what's wrong?" The sound of a boat's horn caused her to lean around him, but her hair tangled in the breeze, partially obscuring her vision. The boat had moved closer, and she could make out two men on the deck—one with binoculars raised. And…were those machine guns strapped to their bodies?

She took a stuttered step back, and her gaze flew to his. "Alex, answer me. What's going on?"

A pained look flashed across his harsh features. "You weren't supposed to be here, Liv."

"Alejandro! So good you brought her along," one of the men yelled, now close enough that she could make out a few more details. He looked like an older version of Alex.

Alex cast a glance over his shoulder and swore with vehemence. "Fuck. It's too late."

The boat dropped anchor. The two men who had been on the deck approached in a dinghy. Only a few seconds remained until they would reach her and Alex. This would be the first time she witnessed his work. Her pulse raced. That was what this was, right? Work?

"Liv." His tortured voice breathed out, and his eyes pleaded for understanding, or forgiveness, as she nibbled on her lower lip. "I never wanted you involved in this. No matter what happens, I love you so much. More than you'll ever know. If nothing else, remember what you mean to me, how good we are together."

"Alex, you're scaring me." Her heart pounded, and fear clawed at her to turn and run. This was a mistake. She should have listened to him, stayed at his mother's house, and taken a nap. Now she couldn't change her rash decision, and it was too late. The men were upon them, and there was no running away.

Alex's hand clamped on her wrist, and he dragged her behind him as he turned. "Father." He nodded his head. "Mateo."

Father? Despite the heat, Liv shivered at the coldness emanating from her husband's tone. What sort of rift lay between them, and who was Mateo?

"Isn't this a surprise that Olivia came along?" A calculating gleam flashed in the older man's black-as-coal eyes.

"She isn't staying." Alex's voice rang with cold conviction.

"Step aside, Alejandro. I'd like to meet your wife, and I'm sure your brother would too."

Alex hesitated a moment then transferred the iron grip he had on her wrist to her waist, wrapping his arm around her as he stepped back and to the right so they were side by side.

Liv's heart pounded at the sight of the men up close. Doing her best to ignore the guns strapped to their chests and tucked into the waistbands of their pants, she offered a smile to the older man. Shorter than Alex's five feet eleven, the man eased his posture, and his lips twitched into a semismile. Despite the teasing quality to his features, she wanted to run far away. Even without the weapons, she detected an arctic cruelty within the depths of his dark eyes. Out of the corner of her eye, she caught the leer in his brother's expression as he perused her face and body, and she repressed a shiver.

"Olivia?" the older man asked. At her nod, he grinned. There would be no correcting him to use her nickname.

"I am Juan Carlos, Alejandro's father. I understand Rita's been keeping you all to herself. Imagine my surprise when she called about your arrival." He winked, his gaze locked on her, even when he no longer spoke directly to her. "Alex will have to explain his tardiness on informing me you were coming and the happy news." He rubbed his hands together. "Well then, Olivia, you'll have to come with Alex to my home."

"There is no need for her to join us, Father."

A hard glint flashed in Juan Carlos's narrowed eyes before he turned his attention to Alex. "I insist."

CHAPTER 9

*T*he boat ride from Margarita Island blurred by as Liv wrestled with her fear of the men onboard with guns. Rather than give in to a full-fledged panic, she focused on the passing scenery, as they stayed close to the shoreline. Questions buzzed in her head, but she pressed her lips together. She would wait and hope there would be an opportunity to talk to Alex without the others onboard overhearing. Except she did have a burning need to find out where they were headed. That, she would ask.

The moment she waited for came. No one was in earshot. She leaned closer to him and quietly asked, "Where are they taking us?"

Alex leaned to her ear and whispered their destination. "We're going to Northern Colombia."

Despite the warmth, she shivered. "Why do these men have guns?"

Alex's expression shuttered, and his brother, who stood just out of hearing distance—she hoped—flashed her a wolfish grin.

"What'll happen when we get there?" She'd dropped her

voice even lower, hoping he would at least answer that. He didn't. A tic pulsed angrily in his jaw.

Alex moved to speak to his father, and she turned away, uncomfortable with how his brother's cold, dead eyes followed her. The boat pulled alongside a lone dock and a shoreline thick with vegetation. Wringing her hands, she waited for Alex to return to her side.

An arm slipped around her waist, and she stiffened. Mateo gazed down at her. "Alex will be just a moment." He ushered her toward the boat's exit, where a dockhand waited to help her off.

She extended her hand to the stranger. The leer that spread across his face made her want to yank back. His grip tightened, and he pulled her forward. When her foot stretched across the edge of the boat, she gasped as the man's hand wandered up her leg and under her dress.

"Get the hell away from me!" she yelled, appalled at the brashness of his touch.

Teetering, she stumbled onto the dock, both his hands still on her. With a thump, Mateo landed next to her, grabbed her from the dockhand's grip, and pushed her to the side. A flash of silver arched toward the offensive man, and Liv yelped. Blood gurgled. He wobbled back. As life ebbed, he sank to his knees. With a thud, he fell flat on his face. A pool of blood seeped from beneath his body.

Chills erupted along her arms, despite the humid air, and she fought the bile that burned in the back of her throat. With her stomach churning, she clutched her shaking hands in front of her, afraid to move. A stream of angry Spanish words volleyed back and forth between Mateo and Juan Carlos before Mateo grunted and turned back to the prone body.

Frozen in place at the brutal violence, Liv followed Mateo's movements as he flipped the man over, withdrew something from his pocket, and splashed some liquid over the deckhand's face.

Mateo moved, and she caught a quick glimpse of the dead man's face melting into an unrecognizable mass of flesh, blood, and bone. He'd used acid. Jerking to the side of the dock, Liv lost what little she had in her stomach as she fell to her knees.

Oh God. Mateo killed him...for touching her? Her body shook, and when she was pulled to her feet, cold fear ran along her spine. Alex murmured something in her ear she couldn't recognize with the roaring panic in her head. His arm wrapped around her, and he guided her down the dock without another word.

What world had they entered?

Mateo stopped them, waiting until she looked at him. The words he uttered scraped her ears raw. *"It is our way."*

She flinched as he hooked the dainty silver necklace with his finger and pulled the butterfly pendant from beneath her clothes. In a fast staccato, he and Alex hurled foreign words at each other before her husband tucked her closer and led her away from the boat and the blood pooling behind them.

"The necklace needs to be visible, Liv." At her blank expression, he sighed. "To prevent situations like this."

Her gaze jerked to Alex's bare hands then to Mateo's then to the armed men who surrounded them. Everyone but her and Alex had a butterfly tattoo. Her vision swam at the realization she wore something that linked her to this awful experience, this group of people, and whatever it was they were involved in. Even so, she wasn't suicidal, and she would stop fighting him on wearing it in public.

A Jeep met them, and they traveled in silence over bumpy roads with low-hanging trees toward their destination. Dense foliage narrowly brushed the quick-moving vehicle. Off in the distance, she noticed a lean-to with men pouring and mixing over several barrels.

"Eyes forward, Liv." Alex's hushed whisper jerked her back to the dirt road before them.

Juan Carlos turned around, and his calculating gaze moved back and forth between them. "Interested in our business, Olivia?"

"She's not." Alex's clipped answer caused his father to smirk.

Shivering from Juan Carlos's maniacal laugh, she edged closer to Alex. They traveled a good fifteen minutes until they emerged in front of a sprawling Spanish-style home that boasted arches and hand-crafted tile work. Iron bars decorated the windows. Armed men peppered the roof and patrolled past windows and beneath arches. Humid, thick air pressed against her clammy skin. When the door to the house opened, she stepped inside to a chorus of noise.

Mind numb, Liv reacted on autopilot as Alex guided her sluggish body. They passed by a few children running through the main room, where several women sat and talked. One of them huffed, disgust clear when she caught sight of the two of them. Alex whispered to her after they walked by that she was Mateo's mother and Juan Carlos's wife.

Juan Carlos waved them off, and Alex propelled her down a long hallway, up a flight of stairs, pushed open a door, and ushered her inside a suite of rooms. With a quiet click, the door shut behind them. His hands lifted and shoved through his hair, disheveling it even more. "Why, Liv? Why did you follow me?" His gaze pleaded with her as he asked.

The anguish emanating from him shook her even more than their recent experience. "Your father, Alex? You lied to me."

"No, I did not. I just didn't tell you about him."

Anger fueled her, and she threw her hands up. "That's the same thing! It's lying by omission." She whirled on her heels and paced the length of the spacious room. "You could've mentioned something about them. I'm your wife. I deserve the truth about what's going on. What is he, what is this really, Alex? What does he do, and…oh my God, you came from *here*?"

"No, I didn't exactly come from here." The hollowness of his answer snared her attention. "I grew up in my mother's home, not here. You weren't supposed to meet him. It's not safe, and I wanted our life together separate. One thing—I wanted one thing for myself. And that was you."

She sucked in a breath at the naked pain on his face. "Then why were you meeting him? I don't understand."

He pushed away from the door and crowded her. One hand hauled her against his chest, and the other thrust into her hair, cupped the back of her head, and pulled her closer to rest his forehead against hers. "I didn't want you to come. I tried to send you back to my mother's." An anguished moan left his mouth. "I'll try to get you out as soon as I can."

She twisted in his arms, and his palms cradled her still-flat stomach. Helpless against his possessive hold and desperate for the closeness they shared, she leaned against him. Her hand reached up and around to cup the back of his neck, when the door opened.

Alex stiffened, his hands shifting higher as they both turned to take in who'd barged into the room. The dangerous gleam in Mateo's charcoal eyes as they dropped to her stomach shot panic through her body. In a flash of clarity, she remembered his reaction to Alex's father's mention of her pregnancy. *He knew.* For some reason, other than the obvious, she didn't want him to learn about the baby.

"A baby? How long had you planned to keep that from Father, Alexander?"

Something about his calculated tone sent raw fear to chase the earlier panic.

"He was told before we met on the beach. *That's* what the meeting was about, *Mat*. Pissed your spies didn't learn that back in Manhattan?"

Mateo's snicker cramped her stomach. Oh my God! That man—the one she'd seen when she'd gone to meet Rachel and after she and Alex had left dinner—was sent by Alex's brother. Why was Mateo having them watched?

"My wife and child don't concern you, which is why you were not included in our discussions. Where's Father?" Alex's controlled speech and subtle digs put her on high alert. The warmth of his body left her with an eerie sense of premonition. She never should have followed him.

Mateo laughed low and long. "Ahh, dear brother, that's where you're wrong."

"Wait here, Liv." His words were clipped, a command.

His odd behavior shocked her. When the door closed behind Alex and Mateo's retreating forms, she walked to the window, moved the drapes, and peered outside. Armed men came and went within her view. The closer she looked at them, the more she noticed every single one of them wore the same jagged butterfly tattoo.

How could Alex have come from this world? From all aspects, it seemed as though his father was a drug lord, the antithesis to Alex's career. With every fiber of her being, she hoped she was wrong.

Perhaps an hour passed, and in that time, Liv scoured her memories for any mention of his family other than his mother and grandmother. Nothing came to mind. Needing to talk to someone, she slipped her phone from her purse and shot off a text to Rachel.

Liv: *Rach. Freaking out here. Met Alex's FATHER and BROTHER.*

Not even a half a second later, Rachel replied.

Rachel: *WTF? He's never said anything about his father, right?*

Liv: *God, Rach. He's mafia or something. Drug trafficking. I'm not entirely sure yet. They have GUNS.*

Rachel: *Get out. You need to leave now! Did Alex know about him?*

Liv: *Yes. But I don't understand what's going on. He may be under-cover. Nothing else makes sense.*

Rachel: *If he is, you shouldn't be there.*

Liv: *Yeah. Seriously get that. I'll talk to him. But, Rach. Don't say anything to anyone, okay? Not yet.*

Rachel: *Um.*

Liv: *Swear. I don't want to jeopardize his career or anything, not if he's undercover.*

Rachel: *I know you love him but stop defending him. You shouldn't be there.*

Liv: *I'm not. Not really. I just have a bad feeling about word getting out before I know for sure. There's another issue, Rach. This is his FAMILY. I don't want to cause him to lose his job at the NYPD before I know what's going on.*

Rachel: *I don't agree. Not to you waiting or staying. He can take the risks but not with you.*

Liv: *I understand and fully agree. I should not be here. I wasn't supposed to, actually. I'll tell you all that later. I don't want to get caught on the phone.*

Rachel: *Please be careful. Text me as soon as you can.*

Liv: *Will. Love ya.*

She selected all the texts to Rachel and deleted them, just in case. A wave of exhaustion hit her, and her eyelids dropped to half mast. A yawn stretched her mouth wide. Reaching her hands behind her neck, she fiddled with the difficult little silver clasp. Unwilling to venture beyond the room without Alex, she sat on the bed, still toying with the clasp to the butterfly neck-lace. She understood the need to wear it in public, but it was so very uncomfortable to lie down with it around her neck. The rest of her jewelry didn't bother her, but the pendant felt as if it was strangling her. Her distraction with removing the jewelry caused her to miss the sound of the door opening and the approaching footsteps.

"Leave that on." Alex growled as his hands locked around hers, lowering them from the clasp. "I told you not to remove that while we're here."

"I was going to lie down."

Alex clenched his jaw. "Not even then."

The grim line of his mouth gave her pause. This wasn't the same man she'd come to know, to love. The minor behaviors she'd witnessed while he was on the black cell phone at home were in full-blown appearance, and she was worried. The man before her no longer resembled her husband.

"I came back to check on you. I need your brooch cuff for a little while. I'll give it back in an hour or so." He clamped her wrist between his side and arm, his back to her.

She felt the release of the bracelet but wished she could have watched him take it off her. That clasp wasn't something she'd ever wrestled with before. *So weird.*

"Rest. I'll be back as soon as I can."

"Wait! Where are you going?" The fear she worked to keep at bay shot its way to the forefront. If Alex did not want her there in the first place, what did that mean would happen to her, to them? "Are you leaving me here? Please don't lie. I-I can't take the thought of being in this place without you."

A mild softening in his gaze reminded her he was still in there, somewhere. "No. I'm not going anywhere without you. I have a meeting with my father, this time without Mateo present, which I'd hoped for before my plans went to hell." He pressed a kiss to her forehead. "Promise I'll be back."

～

LIV WOKE TO A DARK, EMPTY ROOM AND DOWNWARD PRESSURE IN her abdomen. Pulling her knees up, she pushed out a calming breath. *It must be stress.*

She felt another unusual tightening and moaned. Slowing her breathing, she waited it out as her mind whirled. Could something be wrong with her baby? Shoving the unwanted thought away, she peered at the bedside clock. Several hours had passed. Stretching her hand to the side Alex should be on, she frowned. The sheets were cold and the pillow still fluffed, no indent from his head. Worry for their child and for her and Alex plagued her, and she wished he had returned.

With her discomfort egging her on, she rose, crept out of the room, and hoped she wouldn't run into anyone other than Alex. Maybe tea would help. With that thought, the kitchen was her destination.

The stress of her situation must have been the root of what affected her physically—a position, she recognized, her husband had tried to shield her from. Again, the same question haunted her about the secret he'd kept. Because it was a secret. Buried underneath her fear, she was more than disappointed about his lies.

The reason for his planned visit to see his father and what exactly he was doing there ran through her mind on a treacherous roller coaster. Could it be he was working to expose his father's organization? If so, why hadn't he said anything to her? Or were there listening devices in the rooms that she wasn't aware of?

Retracing the direction they had come together would be easier, but she remembered glimpsing another set of stairs closer to their room. That probably led to the kitchen since she didn't remember seeing it on their way up the other staircase. She moved quietly, with muffled steps, on the red floral carpet runner that ran the length of the long hall and approached the steep flight of stairs. Soft light illuminated the landing. She put her hand on the wall and slowed. Dull aches radiated through her stomach, and she took measured breaths. Just a little ways and she would arrive at the landing. Hand outstretched, she stopped when deep voices snared her attention.

Nervous and wanting the reassurance of her husband, she leaned against the wall, and her focus snagged on the light seeping through a cracked doorway just ahead. She nibbled on her lip. Would she make it past there without the door opening and someone catching her outside her room? As the discomfort subsided, she became even more aware of a semiquiet conversation.

Step by step, she inched closer. Clipped voices shattered the quiet, and she paused. *Alex?* Unable to stop herself, she leaned forward, her body tense.

The bark of Juan Carlos's voice strung her body tight, and she debated about the wisdom of her actions. She should leave, quietly. As she crept carefully away, her ears strained to catch their words. What she heard made her blood run cold.

"She stays. You'll have to figure out how to keep her in line," Juan Carlos ordered.

"She wasn't supposed to be involved in anything here," Alex argued.

"But *you* need to be. It's high time you do more than your pampered job in the States." He paused for a beat. "You'll have your political career. I've already seen to it. You understand what you need to make it look legit." Another pause, and Liv heard Alex grunt. "If you ever want to prove your importance alongside your brother, you'll increase your efforts with our family business."

"I've done more in my short career over there than my brother has to advance—"

"Enough! Now let's look at the shipping routes and make

sure we have the right people paid off. This is very important, Alejandro. We are filling four tons in barrels. Mistakes will not be tolerated."

They discussed Alex's involvement with the family business —*cartel* business. Her hand flew to her mouth, stifling a gasp, as she quickly backed away. She'd heard "coca fields" and put two and two together. *Cocaine.* That was what they'd been doing in that field.

Tears flooded her eyes, making it difficult to see as she rushed down the hall to the opposite set of stairs. She needed a plan, a way to get out. With each frantic beat of her heart, the rest of what she'd heard filtered through her thoughts. Did his father mean to *fix* the election for Alex? A muffled noise made her pause as her foot dangled over the first step.

A hard thump to her back caused the air to whoosh from her lungs. In a free fall, time suspended. Her surroundings blurred as she tumbled down. The ground waited. So did pain. On impact, time fast-forwarded, and her awareness rushed back. Her bones moved in a way they shouldn't.

Sound rushed back, and splintered distress slammed her entire body. Shallow breaths moved her battered lungs. Warmth trickled down her face—blood. She lay in a crumpled heap, and agony spread like a spider's web on each breath. Alive—that was what the needles of pain screamed. Moaning, she cracked her eyes open and blinked away black floaty spots.

In the distance, a door slammed, and footsteps pounded to the beat of her throbbing head. She didn't move. Before they arrived and crested her line of sight, she fixated on the top of the stairs. It was empty. The dark void above held its secret close. *Who pushed me?*

Pain separated into dull aches and sharp stabs, differentiating their location on the bruised map of her body. The throb of her ankle, the rhythmic pulse of her head, and the ache in her back did nothing to distract from the warmth spreading between her legs. *God, no.*

Tears welled, only to spill in a continuous cascade down her face. Her mind raced, replaying her flight down the stairs, and she tried to determine if she'd imagined being pushed. *I'm not safe here.* Again, she flicked her gaze to the top of the steps. Inky darkness met her strained vision.

What seemed like hours must have been mere seconds, or maybe minutes. The footsteps she heard racing materialized.

"Liv!" Alex halted at the upstairs landing, Juan Carlos not far from him. Horror pulled Alex's features tight as he flew down the steep flight. She cast her gaze between the two, afraid to move. A thunderous cloud hovered over Juan Carlos's face before he shuttered his expression to hide the raging emotions.

In a slow blink, she lost sight of Alex until he kneeled by her side. Feather-light touches trailed along her arms, legs, neck, and face. She pleaded with her eyes for him to tell her everything would be all right. *The baby. Please don't let anything have happened.*

She shut her eyes, blocking the sight of the terror she'd glimpsed briefly on his face before he yelled for someone to pull a car around.

THE STERILE ANTISEPTIC SMELL PERMEATED LIV'S FOGGY awareness, and she cracked open her swollen eyelids. Big mistake. Bright light forced them closed and she waited for the sensation of glass shards to subside before she tried again. The sounds and scents told her she lay in a hospital bed. In fuzzy bits and pieces, the events from the night filtered through her brain, and she sucked in a shaky breath.

They'd arrived at the hospital after her fall down the stairs where they'd ushered her in, past rows of beds filled with patients in the hallway. Hospitals in South America were very different than in the States. By some miracle, or the frightening presence of Alex's family, she'd been given a private room. For the room alone, she was grateful.

Alex's tight grip on her hand linked them, if only physically. She inhaled his spicy cologne, momentarily comforted by his presence. But she couldn't sense the one she desperately needed. It should have been too early to tell, but she could. She knew, just as she'd sensed it was a girl. It never stood a chance. "Our baby's gone, isn't she?"

"Shh, babe. I'm here." With one hand, Alex scrubbed his face, his eyes wild. "Shit. I never wanted..." Audibly, he swallowed, and his hoarse voice sought her. "I tried to keep you away, to protect you. But with the baby's pending arrival, I had no choice."

His gentle touch made the tears roll faster down her face, and she melted into his careful embrace. The caress of his lips on her forehead and the slide of his fingers through her hair nearly undid her. Underneath her heartache festered a deep anger for whoever had pushed her. She wouldn't share that detail with him. He'd blown her trust. He'd kept this part of his life secret.

Processing his regret-filled words didn't matter right now. What did was the moment of grief they shared. This was the man she'd fallen for, the man she needed, and the man who held her heart.

The other one was a virtual stranger. Sheltered, she hadn't seen that side of his life—his work persona. That had to be what it was. Content to live only in the world they'd created, she let him have his other identity. Or maybe it was him that defined the separate lives.

For now, she sank into the comfort he offered. The rest of

their problems could wait. They needed to leave this terrible place.

She craved their life back home, where she could heal and recover. This…this was a nightmare.

Sleep pulled her back under, welcome arms where she sought their baby in the in-between. She floated in a gray mist until a nurse shook her from slumber with a gentle prodding as she checked her vitals. Liv's gaze lurched to Alex's, fear and despair barely held back. Her free hand fluttered to him, and he gripped her with reassuring strength. In silence, she waited for the nurse to go, for the all-too-ugly reality to go fuzzy again. When the door shut with a soft click, she shifted closer to Alex, needing his warmth and shared grief over their loss. It didn't matter that he hadn't confirmed the loss. The emptiness in her soul was answer enough for her.

Nothing was broken. She should have been grateful. She wasn't. "How much longer?"

"Shh, Liv. Don't worry. I've got you." He motioned for her to move over, and he joined her in the hospital bed. Lying on his side, he pulled her close, and she burrowed in. They stayed like that for some time. Hours may have passed. Time didn't mean much. As long as he was with her, the caring man she'd married, there would be some way she could crawl out from the dark hole she found herself in.

When he shifted, Liv's eyes popped open. "Don't leave me here, Alex."

"Relax." His hand rubbed her back, and he pressed a kiss to her head. Pulling back, he cupped her cheek. "How are you feeling?"

Her lower lip quivered. "Physically, I'm sore but fine. The lights hurt, and I'm a little dizzy. I—I miss her, Alex. Even in that short time span, I loved her the moment I learned of her existence."

Air brushed along her cheek as he sighed. "One day, we'll try again. When we're both ready."

I was ready.

Shifting, she pulled back so she could scrutinize his face. "Did you truly not want our baby? Even after you said all those things to me, the time alone, the beach, and cruise."

"Liv, every part of you is a gift. It does not matter if I wasn't ready to begin a family, I'd welcome a baby into our lives because she or he would come from you. You're the best thing in my life. Always."

The truth swirled in the dark depths of his eyes, but she let it go, mentally exhausted. Over their few years together, she'd loved what they had. Not now.

Whatever she'd wanted, he provided. And he had seemed to instinctively understand she wanted a soul mate, a partner, someone to lean on. Even if, for her, their relationship had begun as a rebellious and impulsive act, it had morphed into a dream, nothing like the empty, businesslike one her parents lived. All her life, she witnessed her parents' effort in climbing the political ladder, instead of focusing on their lackluster commitment to their marriage and friendship. She even questioned their love for one another. With Alex, that was the one thing she never second-guessed.

But this place… "Alex, I want to go home. Now. Let's leave straight from here."

His features shuttered, and she shivered from the sudden chill.

"At the very least, let's go back to your mom's."

"Liv, it's too late." The seriousness of his tone twisted her body into a mass of anxiety and, beneath that, simmering anger. "Why were you out of our room? I told you to stay there, to wait until I came back. What made you leave?"

Whatever they were planning or involved in, her being

detained sent heightened jolts of alarm through her. "I was worried and not feeling very well." Her gaze searched his. The man she knew receded, and the mask of the stranger, the one she'd only caught glimpses of this past month, returned. "I want to get out of here, Alex. Let's go home, forget about this place, whatever it is. Please, just take me home."

Silence met her plea, and the slight narrowing of his left eye told her he wasn't happy about something, or that he was lying. ·

With slow, deliberate movements, Alex raised the sheet higher on her chest, tucking her in. "Did something happen that caused your fall? Did you hear anything while you were out in the hallway?"

"No. Nothing. Should I have?" Her eyes narrowed as every nerve in her body screamed to keep what had happened, and what she'd learned, a secret. It would only stir the pot even more and cause her trouble if he knew.

"Why can't we leave, Alex?" she demanded. Though from his closed expression, she sensed she wouldn't get an answer. The silence told her enough—he planned to stay. She did not.

Feeling sick from what had happened and the bone-deep loss she'd suffered, she stayed vigilant while staring into the cold gaze of her husband, a man she now understood she truly did not know. But she did realize one thing—if she wanted to survive, she had to leave.

𝒶 lex leaned over and tucked her hair behind her ear. "Are you comfortable, Liv?"

"I'm fine." She'd barely moved from the hospital bed. It'd been two days so far, and she really wanted to leave.

"I'm going to talk to the doctor again, look into your release for tomorrow, and check in with my dad's men." At her nod, he left, closing the door with a soft click behind him.

She moved the bracelet up and down on her wrist, her fingers smoothing across the stone. Alex had put the bracelet back on her, making it clear once more that she was not to remove it. She wasn't sure why he was so adamant about his grandmother's brooch staying on. Maybe having her wear the jewelry gave him a connection to something good in his past. Perhaps it was the only thing that helped him through seeing his father and brother.

Shifting, she pulled her purse onto the bed and rifled around inside the big bag, pushing her sketchbook, pencils, and wallet aside until she found her phone. She needed to text Rachel, see if she'd heard anything yet.

Liv: *Hey, Rach. Did you find out anything at the precinct?*

Rachel: *No. No one has information about Alex being undercover.*

Liv: *Rach! Did you tell them? What if he is and we just blew his cover?*

Rachel: *Liv, I love you, but get your head out of your ass! Something isn't right. Please tell me you left.*

Liv's fingers tightened on the phone, contemplating her words before she sent them.

Liv: *I love him, Rach.*

Rachel: *Sweetie, I get it. I do. But you have to leave. What you've told me sounds really bad. Please get out of there, or I'll have to tell the chief.*

She'd begun to doubt Alex too the more they were around his dad, brother, and the entourage of machine gun–toting men. That killed her, but love didn't just go away. They'd been there for each other; he was her everything. Even if Alex were guilty, how could she just abandon him?

Rachel: *Liv, you still there?*

Her friend was right. There wasn't any point in denying she had to get away. Still, the thought of Alex being a part of his father's organization didn't sit well with her, and she clung to the idea of him working undercover. Rachel had to be wrong. Even so, Liv wasn't crazy.

Liv: *Yeah, I'm here. I'll leave tonight. Please don't worry, I'll be okay and will text you when I'm safe.*

Rachel: *Be careful! Please text me as soon as you can. If I don't hear from you, I'm calling the chief and the FBI.*

Liv: *Love ya. Will text when I'm alright.*

Rachel signed off with a kissy face, and again, Liv deleted all messages. She shoved her phone into the zippered pocket so she could find it more easily next time, set her purse on the bedside table, and rested against her pillow.

Alex's involvement with Juan Carlos blew her mind. She just

couldn't wrap herself around that reality. Since Juan Carlos was his father, maybe that was why Alex had originally gone into law enforcement—to stop what he knew was happening, what he'd most likely seen firsthand growing up. Liv had no idea how much exposure he'd had as a kid.

But abandoning Alex? She chewed on her lower lip. In her heart, she couldn't. If she stayed there, who knew what else would happen. She'd paid a terrible price.

The whoosh from the door opening accelerated her heart rate, until she saw who it was. "Alex."

"Just me," he reassured. "I spoke with your doctor, and you're all set for release tomorrow."

"Where will we go?" If it was anywhere other than his mom's or home, she needed to step up and follow through with her decision, with or without Alex.

His lips pressed together in a stubborn line. "I've told you— we need to return to my father's house. A few more days, at least. Then we'll go home."

She tucked her clammy hands under her sheet, the bracelet catching on the edge. There was no way she was going back. "I don't need all these things hooked up to me anymore, do I? It's uncomfortable."

"No. I don't see why you would. I'll talk to the nurse about removing them in a little while." A beat passed as he pulled a chair up to her bedside and took one of her hands from beneath the sheet to hold. "Don't worry, babe. Everything will be okay. Just make sure you stay where I tell you. This will be over soon."

In small increments, her heart broke. No, it was just beginning. Her gaze traveled over Alex's handsome features, losing herself for a few moments in his warm brown eyes. She dropped her gaze to the firm lips she'd kissed a hundred times. The visceral memory of him was deeply imprinted on her psyche, and she clung to the hope that he was truly on her side. She would give him that, even though she couldn't do as he asked and return to his dad's. She would stay vigilant and make her escape.

CHAPTER 11

A loud clang from the hallway disturbed the relative quiet and dragged Liv from sleep. Awake, she blinked in the inky darkness, waiting for the tiny room to take shape. Soft light leaked under her door.

Hospitals were difficult to get a good night's rest in with staff moving in the hallways and coming in at all hours to check vitals. Not that she'd slept well since her introduction to Alex's father and the family business. Why had he brought her around them? If this was a job to him, if he was working to break their organization wide open, she shouldn't have been there, and he should have told her. Whatever he planned to do, she would no longer be a part of it. The cost of their baby's life had proved to be too high.

Disgust at her blind naivety where Alex was concerned churned in a nauseating mix in her stomach. While there was a chance he did work undercover and had to maintain the façade even to her, the likelihood of it was small. At that point, she was not one to risk her safety. Too much had been sacrificed in the small amount of time since she'd been introduced to his other world.

She was running out of time; her stay in the hospital was drawing to an end too fast. In the morning, the doctor would discharge her. On the outside, she would heal well enough, in time. With her womb cleaned, the bleeding had stopped. So they'd pronounced her well, despite her bruised body and soul.

The minor sprain to her ankle, not to mention the concussion and a myriad of bruises, would fade, and she no longer needed to be under observation. Even so, they watched her. Armed men stood outside her door—for her protection, Alex had said.

Who would protect her from them?

Now she understood Alex's need to keep his work and family separate from their lives, but the secrets surely would've found them at some point, like now.

The frightening part of his job did not belong in bed with them. He told her that over and over. One mistake, and she stepped in the serpent's lair, inviting them into their bed.

Air wheezed from her strangled soul as her plan formed.

If he weren't willing to leave with her, then she would go on her own. When he settled whatever *business* he needed to, maybe she would welcome him home…*if he was innocent.* Her doubt had amplified since overhearing him and his father talking.

Now she would run.

Alex sat softly snoring in the chair next to her bed, a fraction of the loving and caring man she'd married. Tomorrow, he would take her back to her prison, his father's house. Tomorrow, she would slowly die. Tomorrow could never materialize in that manner.

Tonight, she would escape.

With careful movements, she took inventory of her surroundings. Her purse, thankfully, was next to Alex on the small table. He kept it close. There was money in there. Not a lot, but some. And she had her jewelry on. *Thank God!*

Clothes were her next order of business. Before she had closed her eyes for the night, the nurse had taken her off the pulse and heart rate monitor, which would have alerted them if she'd removed it. Only an IV remained. In gradual movements, she sat up. She pushed the covers back and slid her legs from the bed. No one stirred. Alex's snoring continued, so she stepped with care over to the unit. Her pulse raced as she pressed the power button so there would not be any alarms. Clamping her lips tight, she peeled the tape back. With shaking fingers, she pulled the IV from her arm then quickly grabbed Kleenex and pressed it against the small wound.

Dropping the IV, she sucked in air to chase the dizziness and nausea away. Alex stirred. Frozen, she kept him in her sights, afraid to move a muscle lest she fully wake him. Sadness clung to every beat of her frantic heart.

The sound of light snoring roused her from immobility, and on silent feet, she made her way to the wardrobe across the room. A dull throbbing ache from her ankle worried her that she wouldn't be able to run if she needed to. It was a chance she would have to take. The cabinet gave a soft click when she opened it, and she glanced over her shoulder, relieved when she saw her husband still slept.

The usual noise of the busy hospital filtered through the walls, but the door remained closed, unbroken light spilling beneath. Could it be her guards weren't right outside her door?

She didn't have a clue when the next shift would be in to take her vitals and couldn't make out the foreign words on the whiteboard. As fast as she could manage, she dressed in her clothes that, thankfully, were folded on a shelf in the cabinet. She would have to exchange them as soon as possible for something else, especially since blood stained the once pristine fabric.

With shoes in hand and purse slung over her body cross-ways, she tiptoed to the door and peeked into the hallway. The relatively clear, free of her guards, hallway.

With care, she slipped her shoes on her feet in case she had to run while keeping a watch beyond her room.

A nurse walked down the hall, checking on sleeping patients that lined the corridor. The nurse's back was to her, and Liv breathed a sigh of relief that the armed guards had abandoned their post and were standing down the hallway, chatting with a pretty nurse at what looked like the main desk for her floor. The men with guns bore the same butterfly tattoo she'd come to associate with Alex's father's organization. Why were they there, or rather, what made her so important to Alex's family that she warranted guards?

By the hub, the woman checking on patients stopped when one of the men smiled at her, and she leaned a hip against the counter. This was Liv's chance. While the men and the nurses were engaged in conversation, she slipped through her door and headed in the opposite direction.

With slow steps, she crept to the nearest hospital bed, where a man with an IV drip slept. Crouching down between two cots, she peered around to see if anyone had noticed her. Their backs were still to her, so she maneuvered around the beds, grateful for the noise of the patients and staff.

With her head down, she bypassed the elevator and made her way to the stairwell door and opened it just enough to slip inside. With a slow push, she shoved open the door, closed it carefully behind her, then rushed as fast as she could down the flight of stairs until the number over the door indicated ground level. Once in the hall, she tucked her chin, taking care to avoid any people or staff whose paths she crossed.

She snuck out of the hospital with her face averted from any passing people. Aside from her floor, the halls were surprisingly empty. No alarms had rung, but several armed men had rushed to secure the doors. With luck on her side, thankfully, she'd managed to sneak out of one of them to the street before the guard turned down that hallway. Once outside, she didn't waste time. She hailed a cab, thankful the driver spoke English, and had him drop her off at the marina.

In the early hours, the dock bustled with activity to begin the day. Most of the ships had left port. The few that remained were busy, with crews shooting leering looks her way. Maybe there was another way off Colombian shores, or possibly one with fewer crew onboard.

She needed something to help her blend in. Wearing the expensive sundress screamed money.

Liv strolled past a pub and gift shop before spotting a clothing store. She decided to duck inside as a dark-haired woman unlocked the door for the day. Several of the woman's long, wavy strands brushed against Liv's arm as she scooted out of the storeowner's way. Yanking her necklace out from beneath her clothes, she turned to sort through a cluster of skirts, when the woman gasped.

"Porque estás aquí?" she demanded. "Why are you here?"

Liv froze at the frantic tone. Would the woman turn her in? With trembling hands, she plucked the first long, flowing skirt from the rack. "I saw your store and thought the clothes looked beautiful, that I'd try some on."

The woman grabbed her elbow and turned Liv around. Face to face with her, Liv winced. The storeowner stared directly at her butterfly necklace.

"No. A member of the Ramirez family"—she angrily gestured to the pendant hanging from Liv's neck—"would not shop here." Her fingers bit into Liv's arm. "Are you wondering what I look like? You've heard of me, of Marita, and"—her lips pressed into a furious line—"you can have him. I *never* wanted him."

"Please." Liv cleared her throat to get rid of the shakiness from her voice. "I don't know who you are, and I want nothing to do with them. I'm only here to purchase clothes. And"—she took a chance due to the venom in the woman's voice—"to get away."

Sultry eyes framed in thick black lashes regarded her. Finally, Marita nodded and released Liv. "Hurry."

Not wanting to risk being found, Liv grabbed the skirt and a shirt that looked as though it would match. She rushed into a dressing room as fast as her throbbing ankle would allow, removed her clothes, and replaced them with the new ones. Bundling up her sundress, she pushed the curtain aside and almost ran into the woman who stood in front of the dressing room, barring her from going any further.

"Here." With deft fingers, Marita twisted Liv's hair, knotted it, then slipped the silk scarf over her head, covering the shade of her hair. Pushing a pair of sunglasses into Liv's hands, she took the bundled clothes from her. "Go out the back and do not come here again."

Liv opened her purse, but Marita waved her away, her gaze trained on the store window. Not wanting to risk the storeowner's goodwill further, Liv did as the woman asked and exited through the door beyond the storeroom.

Putting on the sunglasses, she shielded her eyes from view. She only had a handful of bills. Not good. She would need more. The one thing she wanted to get rid of was the blue-diamond butterfly necklace. It represented a world she wanted no part of. But she wouldn't yet, not until she left the country. For some crazy reason, it was meant to brand her, to keep her safe, at least while there. It was an illusion she despised.

She hurried down an alley, scanning the shops, until she

caught sight of a pawnshop. What choice did she have? With escalating wariness, she pressed her palm against the door and pushed. The bell above announced her arrival, and she moved toward the back of the dark and dusty interior.

A heavyset man sat behind a glass counter with his head bent over a ring. When she neared, he lowered his eyepiece and flashed her an eager smile.

Hoping he spoke English, she addressed him first. "Hello. I would like to sell a piece of jewelry for cash."

He motioned her closer and, in stilted English, asked to see what she wished to part with. She approached the counter, and his gaze dropped to her necklace. His eyes rounded, and he raised his hands then took a step back. His ruddy face was pinched in fear. "No. I cannot help you. What could you possibly need that *they* wouldn't provide?"

Frustrated, she lurched forward and gripped the metal frame of the counter. The desperation in her actions conveyed her urgency. His wide-eyed gaze fell once more to her necklace.

"Not this." She wasn't that stupid. The hated thing seemed to ward off people, marking her as protected by Alex's family. "Something else." She tucked her hair behind her ears and showed off the diamond studs she wore.

The man stared at her earrings, deep lines of worry etched between his brows. Liv took off her one-and-a-half-carat diamonds and laid them on the counter with a determined clink.

Seconds passed as the proprietor picked each one up and inspected it, his thick mustache twitching as he ran his finger over it. When he looked up with greedy eagerness in his gaze, he offered the equivalent in pesos for five hundred American dollars, severely undercutting what the earrings were worth. After he counted the money out, Liv snatched it up.

The man jumped up and came around the counter. Heart

thudding, she backed away, but he bypassed her and ran to the door. *Dammit! They're here.* She saw at least three men with guns. Her mouth fell open as the owner frantically motioned one of the many members of the Ramirez cartel over.

Shit! She flew to the back room in the tiny store, hoping to find an exit. In her haste, she stumbled over a box and fell into an old TV, only to have it crash to the floor beside her.

With a quick look behind her, Liv picked herself up and rushed to the small light she'd spied while on the ground. *A door.* She burst through it and slammed it closed behind her, effectively silencing the frantic flurry of Spanish the store owner spewed to one, or many, of the men she ran from.

Sweating and probably pale, she shoved the large sunglasses back onto her face. As she neared the dock, she noticed the increase of people, mainly men.

Soon, they would all be onto her, thanks to the pawnshop traitor. Eyes darting, she ducked her head and hurried to the docks, keeping out of sight as much as possible. There had to be a way out of this port. With her head down, she caught several glimpses of tattooed hands, each with the small outline of a jagged butterfly. The men carried guns out in the open; the law would have very little influence over them. Her breath came faster, and she fought dizziness as she risked looking at the boats. A few remained tethered. She would have to risk boarding one. One of the men closest to her turned, and she hid behind a group of people, narrowly escaping the trafficker's view.

Half a dozen men or so weaved around people on the dock as she hovered behind a few crates that were bundled and waiting on wooden planks for one of the ships. She chanced a peek around her hiding spot and noted the armed men had stopped and were questioning people. *And shop owners.* How many of those shop owners were employed by Juan Carlos?

Now that she knew what to look for, she saw the blue

butterfly everywhere—hanging from a window, in the corner of a doorway, on a necklace of a local woman. The woman's necklace wasn't as elaborate as hers, but it was unmistakable, delicate, and deadly, just the same. Butterflies meant life, but they no longer represented that to her. By the looks of the machine gun–wielding rough men searching for her, she doubted it did to them, either.

Who would help her?

She scanned the few remaining boats along the port, looking for an immediate means of escape. A shout sounded in the distance, followed by a frenzy of movement. She'd run out of time. There had to be a way out.

A ferry! People poured off the boat in droves. With a careful eye, she studied the flurry of individuals, realizing they must have traveled from one of the islands for work. Where would the boat go next?

It didn't matter. If she didn't go now, the armed men would capture her. She should never have tried to sell jewelry there. The risk was clearly too great.

Taking care not to rush, she walked the few paces necessary to board the boat. By some small miracle, none of the Ramirez men took note of her. It appeared as though they were now questioning the shop owners a ways down. Liv slipped closer when no one was looking then rushed up the ramp. She thrust a handful of bills into the attendant's hands and went to the farthest part of the deck, where she would be out of sight.

Weak, aching, and with a pounding heart, she quietly asked a nearby woman where they were headed. The lady's brows furrowed before she answered. "*Caracas.*"

Relief washed over Liv. They were going to Venezuela, where there was a larger airport. With nerves strung tight, she waited for the ferry to depart. When it did, she exhaled the first unencumbered breath since she had escaped the hospital. With the money in her purse, she stood a small chance of successfully escaping.

The worry that the Ramirez men knew where she'd been still sat heavy in her stomach. There would be no stopping for her until she was much farther away. She'd learned a potentially deadly lesson from her tumble down the stairs.

With a few minutes of peace and possible safety, her mind wandered. A warm breeze blew in from the ocean, drying the sudden trail of tears, and she thought back to the hospital and her escape as she locked herself inside a bathroom on the ferry.

Her fingers pressed against the necklace underneath her T-shirt. Inside, she quietly cried—for her baby, her sham of a marriage, her naivety, and now the threat to her life. She would do as Alex said and keep the necklace on until she was out of South America, possibly even until she was somewhere safe. There was not much choice in the matter. She thought about all the tattoos she'd noticed on the men, and a familiar memory sparked. She realized their reach spanned the distance to New York. That night she and Alex had gone out to dinner before their trip, one of Alex's father's men approached him—she was sure of it. Home wasn't an option, not yet.

Her home would not be a sanctuary, not until she figured out what was really going on. There would be time to rest when she was safe…or as safe as she could be from a drug cartel, her husband, and his family.

With her sunglasses shoved on top of her head, Liv rinsed off her face. The flash of her diamond rings caught the light. *Too dangerous.* She turned them so only the platinum portion of the bands were visible. Curling her hand into a fist, she hid them further so they wouldn't draw attention. A wave of dizziness swept over her, and she leaned against the mirror, resting her head on the cool glass.

If she pawned all of her jewelry at once in Caracas, they

would find her easily. Wouldn't they? Money was necessary. She'd checked her oversized purse and noted only a few hundred dollars within, and she knew enough not to use her credit cards. The sale of her earrings to the pawnshop had gotten her more but not nearly enough. The rest of her jewelry could easily be traced back to her.

With the skittishness of the shop owners, she decided not to push her luck and risk selling her jewels so close to Alex's family's home. No, she would wait until she was farther away. It didn't matter where she went, so long as it was away from Colombia. That was, if she could find a way out before they found her.

CHAPTER 12

The hustle and bustle of Caracas's airport buzzed around Liv and the lone booking agent, but she paid no attention, intent on securing a flight out of South America. Clutching her purse to keep her hands from shaking, she pleaded with the woman. "There has to be a seat left."

The young attendant's eyebrows drew together as she shook her head. "There is nothing open until tomorrow." Her focus returned to the screen, and her fingers flew across the keyboard in a light staccato.

No one stood behind Liv, but she knew that wouldn't last. Neither would she if she waited much longer. Cartel lackeys, identifiable by their tattooed hands, were crawling all over the surrounding area like ants in an anthill. Soon, they would find her there.

Checking the woman's name tag, she tried again. "I'll pay anything, Gabriella. I have to get away *today*. The sooner, the better." Liv readjusted her purse to get her wallet, but it slipped from her grasp.

When she bent to retrieve it, Gabriella's focus dropped to

the necklace that had come loose from beneath Liv's fuchsia shirt, and her mouth pressed into a thin line. The bruising that inked Liv's face became another focal point for the booking agent. She nibbled on a fingernail while looking up and down the terminal. Facing Liv, she continued to scan the area as she leaned forward, keeping her voice low. "Will you be traveling alone?"

"Yes." Liv rushed her reply, desperation clinging to her affirmation.

At Liv's adamant response, Gabriella dropped her voice. "Are you involved...what I mean is, do you plan to come back here?"

"Never." Tucking the damning butterfly once more beneath her shirt, she mimicked Gabriella's body language, sensing something, commiseration maybe? Could it be this woman knew why she fled and would aid her? She understood why Gabriella would not want to see her again. It could mean the woman's death. For Liv, there was little choice but to accept whatever offer of help was given, even if it led her into the waiting hands of Alex's dad's organization. She had no other option.

"I may have a way for you to leave. He's helped others."

Liv dug into her purse once more, intent on pulling out money.

"No." With a subtle glance, Gabriella indicated the door a flight attendant had just gone through. "When the next person goes through that door, wait until it's almost closed then slip past it." She leaned across the counter, closer to Liv, and dropped her voice lower. "Go to the hangar, all the way to the end, where the smaller planes are housed. Find Trev."

Hope bubbled inside Liv's chest. "Thank you."

As she turned to leave, Gabriella snagged her shirt. Liv looked over her shoulder and caught her whispered words.

"Tell no one how you found out or that I helped you."

"I won't."

Liv did as she'd been told and waited for the next person in uniform to go through the heavy gray door. As quickly as she could, she shoved her hand between the door and frame to stop it from closing, locking, and throwing away her chance to escape. She opened it only as far as needed and slipped through. With hurried steps and a tight grip on the railing, she made her way down the stairs and pushed open the exit door on the ground level. Immediately, a wall of heat blasted her, and she shoved her sunglasses back on against the glaring sun.

As Gabriella had instructed, she hurried to the last hangar, blocking out the aches in her bruised body. Head bent, Liv ignored the men refueling and driving the baggage carts to various planes. The adrenaline that pumped through her body was fading, and she pushed herself to move faster, even with her throbbing ankle. When the rush finally depleted, she feared she would crash hard.

Almost running into the open hangar, she searched for a man who looked as though he could be Trev. Maybe that was short for Trevor? Only one man walked from a small plane, toolbox in hand. When she took another step, he turned toward her, and she froze. Her gaze immediately scanned his hands for markings and his body for guns, but there weren't any that she could see.

He stood about six feet tall with tousled, dirty-blond hair and day-old scruff on his square jaw. Aviators hid his eyes from her, but she could tell he was finely tuned to her presence in the predatory stillness. A beat ticked by, then in a few strides, he was in front of her. She tilted her head back, refusing to show fear.

Gentle, albeit grease-streaked, fingers gripped her chin and turned her face to the side. He scrutinized the bruise marring a good portion of her temple and cheek. He hooked a finger under the silver chain peeking from under her shirt, and she took an immediate step back, but not before the damn necklace pulled free so it was in full view.

He grunted. "You're on the run?"

Shoot, was he the right guy? "Are you Trev?"

A quick nod of his head confirmed he was.

What the hell, if honesty would aid her in her plight…she didn't have anything else to lose. *Other than my life.* "Yes, I'm running away from a very bad situation."

A moment passed before he answered. "I can take you to Rhode Island. There is a buddy of mine that'll help from there."

The fast and instant relief made her dizzy, and she swayed. His hand clamped on her arm, and he directed her to rollaway stairs he pushed to the opening of the plane he was working on.

"Thank you."

Again, he only grunted. "Go on in and buckle up. We leave in ten minutes."

"I can pay."

His abrupt head shake stopped her from saying anything further. "I'm going there, anyway. Doesn't cost me anything to take you along."

She thanked him before hurrying up the stairs to fall into a seat. With a click, she secured the belt. Liv clutched her purse in her lap and laid her head back. With a few minutes to herself, free from the constant worry of how to get away, sadness over all she'd lost flooded her system. Refusing to cry, she pushed out a breath and willed her tired mind and body to heal, hoping she had put her trust in the right man this time.

SHE STOOD WITH TREVOR IN RHODE ISLAND, OVERLOOKING

boats tethered to the pier.

"My buddy's is that one over there."

A sporty, luxury boat bobbed at the end of the pier where he'd pointed and a tiny amount of tension eased in between Liv's shoulders.

Trev flashed her a grin and motioned her over to it. He jumped aboard, helped her on, and yelled for Liam as he went down a flight of stairs to the cabin below. She stayed where she was. When his head popped back up above deck, he grinned. "Well, this should be interesting."

Alarm slammed into her, and her body trembled. "What?"

"He's not here."

"Oh, maybe I can find somewhere to stay, then." She looked behind her at the dock, worried that Juan Carlos's reach extended there too. Keeping out of sight until she heard from Alex would be the best course of action. But she'd ditched her phone. In its place sat a burner cell she'd picked up when she and Trev had stopped for a bite to eat after landing. Alex didn't have that number.

"Nah. He'll be back. I couldn't get ahold of him to tell him about you, but I texted him." He winked. "Just make yourself at home and be sure to tell him Trev brought you."

"Okay." She looked around at the boat, at a loss for where she should sit that would be out of the way while waiting for this Liam person to arrive.

Trev chuckled. "You can wait in the cabin. Liam won't mind once you mention me."

The smile of relief she flashed him made him shake his head, and he gave her shoulder a light squeeze. "Take care of yourself and stay out of sight until he gets back."

After hearing Trevor's parting words, she did exactly as he told her and went below deck to wait for what fate brought her next.

CHAPTER 13

*T*he powerful inboard cabin cruiser worried Liv, especially since one of the ways the Ramirez cartel smuggled their cocaine was over water. That wasn't her only concern; her other was who the owner of the boat might be. But that wasn't a big enough reason for her to leave. Desperate to sit down, she sank onto a cushioned seat below deck, out of sight. The flight and constant anxiety had exhausted her, and the gentle rocking on the water helped soothe her frayed nerves. An hour passed, and the threat of discovery hung heavy. Her hand splayed over the seats on either side of her. While comfortable, she longed for the softness of a bed and the safety of her world before she and Alex had left.

With nothing but time, Liv pulled her phone from her over-sized purse. She opened her browser and typed "Ramirez cartel" into Google. She scrolled through the titles, hovering over the YouTube videos, but instead clicked on a link about territory wars. The article loaded, and her gaze shied away from graphic pictures. With her stomach churning, she read on.

Widespread panic ensued in the tiny village as two rival factions fought to establish claim to the small town's water access. A sea of black-masked men collided. The Ramirez cartel rose to the challenge the Los Elegido cartel had thrown down. They would not relent their position or their territory to the spreading Mexican cartel.

The sound of gunshots, bodies hitting the ground, and the screams of the dying rang through the surrounding forest.

The cartel members were not the only ones slain on this day. Caught in the crossfire, the dirt roads were littered with mutilated residents. Blood ran freely, and dry dirt turned to a reddish-brown mud. Those that could hide did. Others were not so lucky.

After the gruesome attack, members of the Ramirez cartel drove the rivals back, piling up body parts in a gory wall, warning others not to pass.

Bile inched up Liv's throat as she skimmed over pictures of maimed and bleeding people. Unable to stomach any more, she powered off her phone, again taking the battery out.

How could Alex have come from those people? With a shaking hand, she pushed her hair back, grateful she'd escaped but horrified for all those who had not. As each minute passed, she focused on regaining control of her emotions. *I'm safe. They can't find me here.* Soon, Liam would get there, and they would hopefully leave, lessening her chances of being found even more.

The boat gently dipped from the weight of someone stepping on board. Footsteps sounded on the deck, and her abused stomach muscles tensed. Fear made her dizzy. When the footsteps hit the stairs, Liv's fingernails dug into the cushion. A man's legs came into view in that second, and her body went into fight-or-flight mode. Adrenaline surged, but she locked her muscles down and remained sitting.

Nothing had prepared her for him. He looked about thirty or thirty-one, very close to her twenty-eight years, and…*holy hell.* Narrowed, bright-green eyes met hers, assessing. Tall, broad-shouldered, and with a strong chiseled jaw, the man filled the doorway. The hollows of his cheeks only added to his allure. His mouth pressed into a tight line and made her sit up taller. With her smaller size, Liv became anxious at his very large presence. She shivered. Tension rolled off him like waves on an ocean after a storm. No other emotion graced his shuttered features.

Liv's fingers curled on the cushioned seat, her words momentarily held hostage by her stunned mind. She had been foolish to wait below. The large man filled the doorway, making it impossible for her to pass.

His tight collared shirt stretched over rippling muscles, and his biceps flexed when he gripped the top of the frame, leaning in as if he had all the time in the world. If only she did too.

She narrowed her eyes right back at him, refusing to show the worry clawing inside her. In the silence, she continued to assess him for a potential threat. Her muscles slowly relaxed as his brows drew together in what looked like concern. He could be an asset.

Capable. That was what his broad shoulders broadcasted. A portion of the duct-taped vigilance she had maintained to hold herself together eased.

She nibbled her lower lip as a new thought popped into her head. What if he denied her help? Her emotions bounced like a yo-yo as she waited for him to speak, silently coming to a variety of conclusions about him and about the current position she found herself in.

A frightening thought screamed through her mind, waking her to the precarious situation she was in. He looked like military with his short haircut—a bit long for active duty—and his controlled stance. Did he have connections with the police?

Seeming to come to a decision, he leaned back against the bulkhead, his arms crossed over his impressive chest. "Why are you on my boat?"

A single question, and her fate hung in the balance of her

answer. Steel laced his slightly accented words and infused her, aiding her determination to successfully escape. Anywhere, even Rhode Island, existed too close to the threat she fled from. She ran through her options and decided the least information might gain the best results. "Trev flew me here. He said you'd be able to take me farther away."

"Away from what?" His gaze scrutinized her bruised face, and his jaw clenched. "Or whom?"

Colombia. My husband. His family. "Just away." Would fear darken his eyes and refusal color his words if he knew who she fled from? Letting him incorrectly assume that she was running from a battered marriage seemed the safer bet to elicit his aid.

He stood straight and spared a quick glance at his phone— no doubt the text from Trevor he'd failed to read. "So, you're Liv, huh?"

That was what she needed, confirmation he'd read Trev's text. This was Liam for sure. It had to be. "Olivia, I mean Liv. I go by the shortened version." Oh my God! What was her problem? She should have given a fake name. First the clothing store owner, then Trevor, now Liam? *I'm not cut out for life on the run.*

"Liam." He smirked, in a good way. "I'm headed to Maine. Is that far enough?"

The rapid percussion of her pulse skipped at the news. *Nowhere would be safe.*

The crinkles in the corners of his eyes eased her anxiety further. "Yes, Maine is perfect. I-I have money. I can pay you."

Liam's gaze roved over her, from head to toe. "Keep it. I'm going there, anyway."

She breathed out her relief. The small wad of bills sat heavy in her purse but would be necessary for her survival later. No way could she attempt to touch her bank accounts, use a credit card, or present identification that could lead them to her. Unfortunately, she was an open book with her name. She longed to call Rachel, but dragging her into this mess might not have been the best idea.

"Thank you." Tears misted her eyes at the chance for safety, and she dug her nails into her palms to gain control. The soft burr of Liam's Irish accent helped to ease some of her anxiety.

He opened his mouth, about to say something, when a noise sounded above. All trace of emotion erased from his face. The immediate sharpening of his focus eased her worry. This was the right move. He appeared as though he could handle himself, maybe not against a mob of Juan Carlos's men, but definitely if a few boarded.

Without uttering a sound, he went topside. Holding still so no noises carried, she strained to hear. Liam exchanged a few words with whoever had come aboard, but she couldn't make them out. Steps receded, and the boat swayed as the person left. When Liam came down with grocery bags and set them on the kitchen counter, she tentatively followed him back up to help.

He moved aside, grinned, and gave her a light bag while he took armfuls. "Why don't you head below? I'm about ready to push off." A crooked grin pulled his lips up but did not meet his eyes. "That bright outfit doesn't help you blend in."

Her hand flew to the scarf Marita had wrapped around her hair, hoping to change her appearance enough to throw off immediate pursuit. Liam had a point, and she refrained from correcting his assumption of her disguise. The cabin offered shelter from prying eyes, and with a nod, she rose and ducked beneath the hull to follow the stairs below.

Light filtered in through the small portals as she made her way through a galley kitchen, past a built-in table, and to the front of the boat. A bed loomed ahead, and she was powerless against its pull. Exhausted, she nudged off her flats with her toes before crawling into the bed. Her head hit the pillow, eyelids fluttered shut, and welcoming darkness caught her in its arms.

Blind trust became her only option.

~

THE NUDGE AT LIV'S BACK PULLED HER FROM WARMTH. SHE rocked in a slow side-to-side motion and withstood the pull to wake. Safe in Alex's arms, the tears for their loss fell in wild abandon. The heat from his hand on her shoulder made her burrow deeper into his embrace. All she wanted was the man she loved to shield her from the world, at least for a little while longer.

A sob racked her body and rattled her from the safety of her dream. With a slow blink, the cause of the disturbance, the heated palm on her shoulder that gently shook her, came into focus. *Him. Liam.*

She sucked in a breath and wet her dry lips. Oh God, did he want more than she could give him? The fact that she was on his bed didn't escape her notice. She shifted away. "What's wrong?"

A frown marred his face. He stood back rather than looming over her and tucked his hands into the pockets of his jeans, probably to appear less intimidating. It didn't work.

"You've been asleep for sixteen hours."

Sixteen? "I thought Maine was only a few hours away."

"It is. I had another sales stop, and it added time. Not to mention, we dropped anchor to sleep."

With a quick look, she noticed the lack of indent on the pillow beside her, and she relaxed. "Oh, I'm so sorry." Her much smaller frame would have done fine on the couch, where there was no way he could fit.

"We'll be in port in an hour to refuel. Is there anything you need?"

"No." She dropped her hands into her lap to still their shaking. Out at sea, they couldn't find her. But on land…that was an entirely different story.

His teal gaze captured hers. "We aren't there yet. Why don't you join me on the deck? A little sunshine will help."

Nothing would help, not really—except, perhaps, enough distance. When Alex returned home, she would too. Maybe, if it was possible, they could resume some semblance of normalcy. Internally, she winced. She was dreaming in regard to anything being normal again.

Icy fingers crawled up her spine, and she faced the truth. Their lives would never be the same again. She'd met the other side of Alex and feared it. Since learning about his family, her doubts about his true identity swirled like an angry hornet's nest. Her former life, her marriage—it was over. It was time to let him go.

She had to run. Staying there had killed her baby. If she'd stayed, she would have died there as well. She sensed that deep in her bones. At random times, she would remember their baby girl. Then she would play a game of what if. What if she'd agreed to remain behind in Barbados? What if she'd remained in Rita's house when Alex had left to meet his father? What if she'd never stepped foot outside the room she and Alex were to stay in at his father's house?

Liam's voice startled her, and the pillow she held fell from her arms. "I'm sorry, what did you say?"

"I asked if you were coming." At her blank stare, he repeated what he'd said. "Up top to get some sun and fresh air."

That, she needed. "Yes."

Wind whipped her freed hair, and she sucked in a deep breath of sea air. Despite the darkness that clung to her soul, she smiled. He was right. She needed this.

Liam steered the boat, his attention on the direction they headed.

Sinking into the captain's chair next to him, Liv grinned. "It's beautiful."

He flashed a smile, and she volleyed back with a wobbly one, tilting her head as she scrutinized him further. With the backdrop of the sea, he resembled a mythological god, one she needed in her situation. He looked powerful, with chiseled features, a strong jaw, and a body to rival any man she had met before, so different than Alex's lean build.

Leashed danger surrounded both of them, but for some reason, Liam's didn't cause her wariness. No doubt he could intimidate anyone he chose to. That, she could use. Regardless, a small voice inside her head warned she had made a mistake in her judgment with Alex.

Even when they had first met, Alex's mysterious aura stirred her self-protective instincts. But with her parents' constant meddling and imposed restrictions, the time had been ripe for her to rebel. Her risk had turned into a dream, one her parents had oddly come on board with. Not once had Alex caused her to worry…until recently.

Tired of her useless train of thought, she cast her gaze once more to the vast blue of the sea before them. Where had Liam gone that required him to take them so far off course? Puzzling over the possibilities, she startled when he chuckled. He must have been watching her as her mind spun and her expression turned curious.

"I had a few restaurants to visit, and they were spread a good distance apart. The last was a referral, and I took a chance to sell to them as well. We won't be much longer."

"What are you selling?"

"Mainly wine this time. Normally, this is all handled on the phone, but first contact, I like to do that myself."

"That's wise to establish a relationship."

"Exactly. Then they have a face to put with the vendor."

The wind worked against their words in an attempt to whip them away. They lapsed into silence, and for a while, Liv felt better. With the sun beating down on them, her dry, scratchy throat became too uncomfortable, and she made an excuse to go below again.

She ran the water until it was cold then dipped a glass under the faucet and took a few sips. At the taste, she pursed her lips. It was definitely not the bottled water she preferred. She set the cup in the sink then hobbled over to the small couch. After her punishing dash and anxiety over being found, she hadn't spared a thought to her still aching ankle.

The worry in Liam's gaze as she'd made her excuses hadn't gone unnoticed. She would be fine. But even as she told herself that, nausea rolled. Liv lay back down and shifted to her side. It would take some time for the cuts and bruises to fade, her ankle to fully heal, and her heart to mend.

Sweat beaded along her hairline and above her upper lip. With a shaky hand, she swiped it away. If only the boat would stop rocking.

If she'd stayed in the hospital, she would have received another day's worth of strong antibiotics, not to mention the pills the doctor had told Alex she needed to continue for a week. Those pills were supposed to ease her aches and pains. Part of her worried she still needed the meds, that her injuries and the stress had turned into a minor infection, one that was gaining a foothold rather than subsiding. Although the clamminess and weakness could have just been a result of overtaxing and her battered body's attempt to heal.

While topside, Liam had asked if she was unwell, to which she'd replied no. She'd lied. With a gentle prod, he asked her again whom she ran from. She shook her head while he studied her. His calloused hand pressed against her forehead before she knew his intentions. Mouth tightening, he said he was stopping to get her medicine. Panic had bubbled, and she'd made him swear not to involve the police or hospitals.

Their words swirled around in her head as she slipped in and out of a restless sleep. Frustrated and hot, she sat up and drew her knees to her chest.

"I made some soup. Come have some with me topside."

She startled at his voice. How he managed to enter and exit without her ever hearing confused her skittish mind. Even so, soup sounded like something she could stomach. *When was the last time I ate?*

Pushing to a sitting position, she slid to the edge of the bed then rose. With a gentle grip, Liam helped her navigate the small cabin to the stairs, and she fought herself from pulling away. He only aided her so she wouldn't fall on her face; there was no reason for her to be rude. Once her hands gripped the rail, she climbed to the top and welcomed the fresh air. It was exactly what she needed.

Seated on a captain's chair, she curled her legs beneath her and accepted the hot mug from Liam with a grateful smile. Even with his imposing build and watchful eyes, his Irish lilt put her at ease, and she relaxed back into the cushion.

"Have you ever been to Maine?" Corded muscles rippled as he lifted the cup to his lips, and she was helpless against following his motions. He exuded strength, and for now, she would borrow from him to get her far from Colombia.

Soon, she would have to fight.

"No. Not a lot of traveling over the past two years. Maine would've been nice. We've been to Paris for an extended week-end." Her heart fluttered at the memory of their time away in the quaint cafes, decadent mornings in her husband's arms, and the romantic evenings out.

"We?"

Softly uttered, his question almost made it past her shields.

His quiet attention to detail made her curse herself for the slip. Trusting him with what had happened during their vacation to Colombia needed to remain off the table. Maybe she could tell him in the future if it became necessary. For now, the less he learned, the safer he would be.

The mistake had occurred because her mind continued to stray to the happy times she and Alex had shared. The boat ride and the days on end on a beach in Barbados had been the last of them before stepping foot onto his homeland soil. The blue of the water all around her pulled her back, over and over again, to those recent memories. If only they'd changed their plans when, in a fleeting moment, Alex had mentioned it. Not meant to be, they had stayed on course. Should she have remained by his side amidst his frightening family?

Her hand fluttered over her flat stomach that would have swelled with their child. No, the cost had been too high. Her choice and her survival had dictated that she leave.

"Just a trip with friends." Another sip of the soothing hot soup preempted a new discussion. "This is delicious. It's not from a can, is it?"

He chuckled. "Yes and no. It was canned for me to take with, or jarred rather, but it's homemade."

"Really? It's very good. Is this part of what you do?"

"No. I'm friends with a couple of restaurant owners along the coast and managed to snag a few batches of lobster bisque before I left last week."

A handful of moments passed, and she looked out to the horizon. Nothing but blue water, the perfect place for her right now—away from civilization, from people. At some point, she would have to go home. The thought of leaving Alex still hurt, but it was necessary. He wouldn't leave Colombia and had refused to help her. Only a tiny part of her assumed he worked undercover. Her suspicions were high that he was on the take from his family. It made sense now. His career had come too easy, and he had too much money for his position to generate. The phone call she'd overheard, the conversation that night between him and his father, and the necklace around her neck that branded her as one of theirs—it all added up.

If—and that was a big if—he worked undercover, would he be the same loving husband when he returned to her? Would he return? Would she believe him?

"Trev called while I stopped, but he didn't say where you wanted to go once we reach the port in Maine. Do you have somewhere to stay?"

"Um, no. I don't." Great, that sounded innocent. Her heart pounded. Where did she want to go? To her husband's side, but that would not happen. At least not while he remained in the fold of his family. Her mind spun in tormenting loops. What plan did Alex have? His erratic, unusual behaviors over the past month had led her to believe he was plotting something, although he'd never before mixed their personal lives with work. The puzzle of it clanked around in her head, making her sick with confusion.

Her fatal mistake had occurred when she'd followed him. Perhaps he'd never meant for her to be involved. *Too late.* Now, only one option made sense.

With escape as her primary goal, the next logical hurdle terrified her. Going home at this point might not be the best decision. There would be paparazzi and questions to deal with. She would lie low.

Liam took another gulp from his mug, his gaze locked on the empty horizon. "I live on a farm with plenty of space. You're welcome to stay until you have a plan."

Could she? With no other options, she turned to face him. Chiseled features met her view. Nothing about him looked soft, but despite his imposing presence, she did not question her safety. With that thought, her answer became crystal clear. "Thank you, Liam. I'd like that. At least until I make other arrangements."

"You're welcome."

He never pushed for information, making it easy for her to slide into a compatible silence with him as she enjoyed the fresh air and sunshine.

With each passing league, her future looked possible once again.

With a crook of his finger, Liam motioned for her to rise and come to him. Should she? He laughed, and she smiled from the deep cadence of it.

"Come here and take the wheel. I'm going to rinse our mugs."

"Oh. No, I'll wash them." She went to snatch his cup, but he pulled it away, instead taking hers.

"Stay here and hold the wheel steady. It won't take me long."

With a tight grip, she kept them on course. Or at least, she hoped she did. It didn't take her long to relax and enjoy having control of the boat. That was probably why Liam had her take charge. She fought a smile, pleased to learn another aspect of his personality—one in which he empowered her and gave her some control back.

"I brought your scarf up."

"Oh, right." She lifted a hand to her hair that flew around in the wind. Her large sunglasses helped to both shield her eyes from the glare glinting off the water and keep her hair from whipping into them. "Thanks."

"We have about thirty minutes before we stop at the next port. I'll need to refuel for the last leg of our journey. Did you want to walk around when we're there? It will probably take an hour."

"No." Her abrupt answer didn't draw his notice, and she breathed easy. No matter what she did, he seemed to take it in stride. For that, she was grateful. "Well, maybe." Her finger tapped against her leg. They were far enough away from Colombia; surely the port would be safe.

CHAPTER 14

So far, all Liv had learned from Liam was his name and that he owned a farm. Not much else about their destination was discussed, nor did she care. Escape still occupied most of her thoughts. After Liam's comment about how light she traveled, she had agreed to go into port and purchase a few things. It wasn't as though she could live in the same outfit day after day until she was able to go home.

With no other option but to wear the same clothes again, she slipped the sunglasses back on and climbed to the deck. After double-checking her appearance, some of the anxiety at stepping foot on solid ground eased.

She should have kept her sundress, but it was the last thing she'd worn, and anyone associated with Alex's father's organization could have a description of it. Even though it wasn't her style, the outfit she wore instead worked well enough as a disguise. The sunglasses helped to hide her eyes.

The boat slowed, and the rocking increased. She longed to be above in the fresh air but remained below, safe, until Liam poked his head down.

"We've docked. I'm going to refuel. You can walk around the port until I'm done or wait, and we can grab something to eat in a pub."

Her fingers threaded behind her back to hide the tremors that shook them. "I'll wait here until you're finished. Thanks." She smiled in an attempt to distract him from her nervous behavior. When he disappeared once more, she went to the bathroom to recheck how she looked with a critical eye. Her goal was to downplay her appearance in any way she could. The glint of the gold chain winked at her, and her hand pressed over the blue-diamond butterfly. The necklace was safely tucked beneath her shirt, and she refused to remove it. Why, she wasn't quite so sure. Here, it would not be needed. She hoped. Alex's behavior had given her the impression it would help to keep her safe, untouchable to those working under Juan Carlos. For that reason alone, it stayed on.

Minutes ticked by until Liam called to her. With a deep breath, she climbed the steps that would expose her to view. Her sandal-clad feet touched the deck, and her gaze darted along the dock and port. People went about their business. No one took notice as she and Liam exited the boat. Liam's strong grip ensured she did not fall. As soon as she stepped onto the wood planks, she moved away from him.

She walked alongside him as he no doubt slowed his longer strides for her. When they came to a small boutique, he offered to help her, but she declined. After picking out a few outfits, she left the store with the bag in hand. They cleared a few more stores until the scent of food wafted their way. His hand settled on the small of her back to guide her into a bustling pub along the port. The tantalizing smells filled the air. Not fine dining, but it smelled delicious just the same.

Liam pulled out a chair for her, and she accepted the plastic menu from a harried server. Aside from the loud chatter in the restaurant, silence settled between her and Liam as they looked over their menus.

A gum-smacking waitress walked up to their table, tapping her pencil against a pad of paper. "Are you ready to order?"

Liv grinned at Liam, enjoying the experience. They placed their orders and settled back to wait. She wrapped her fingers around the cold beer that had been dropped off in a rush and lifted it for a taste. A jolt hit her when she thought about being able to drink again, but she pushed it to the pit of her stomach, where she couldn't feel it.

Normally, she would enjoy a glass of wine, but it was probably better to do the opposite of her usual habits, at least while she was there. She could try to get one thing right while being on the run.

After their food arrived, she and Liam chatted, and her tension dissipated. No one paid them much attention, aside from a few steamy glances from women at Liam. She ignored the pang in her heart. That had happened with Alex all the time.

"How much farther until Maine?"

Liam settled back in his chair, stretching long legs out and effectively caging her in. Instead of feeling claustrophobic, she relaxed. He exuded protection, something she sorely needed. *For now.*

"Two hours." He flagged down the waitress and gave her cash for their check before she flew off again. He rose and helped Liv do so as well. Beside him, her five-foot-seven height felt petite. He had to be an inch or two over six feet.

They moved toward the exit, when a familiar face flashed across someone's phone, catching her attention. Inches from the person watching a video, she stood frozen, staring at the picture on the phone. The image tugged at her memory. *The pawnshop owner!* Barely registering the fact that she'd inched closer, she found herself at the table, glued to the tiny video playing across the screen as the sights and sounds took her back to the store, the man, and his betrayal.

A scene unfolded of men from the Ramirez cartel surrounding the man she'd sold her earrings to. A few broke off, searched the shop, then returned. Forceful words volleyed back and forth until one of the armed men whipped out a knife and slit the man's throat. He fell at their feet, blood painting the ground crimson.

The room spun.

Liam's firm grip settled on her arm, and his soft murmur that they should go kick-started her reaction. Sucking in a breath, she met his gaze. Her fingers found her sunglasses on the top of her head, and she pulled them over her eyes as she exited the restaurant with him. They made it to the boat in no time. With his help, she climbed aboard and pivoted to look at him.

A fisherman jumped off the deck of his boat, pole in hand, and waved Liam down. Liam sought her gaze, and with a slight nod, Liv conveyed she was okay.

"Harold." Liam greeted the older man as he walked several feet down the dock to shake his hand.

While he engaged in a conversation, she removed the prepaid burner phone from her purse. Dialing her lawyer, she left a brief message on his private number's voice mail, telling him she was okay but hiding after crossing paths with a cartel. Doing so would circumvent any legal repercussions due to her allegedly running away. Hanging up, she pressed the sequence for Alex's cell.

When he answered on the third ring, she pushed past the pain and spoke. "It's Liv. Please tell me you're not involved with your father's cartel and the death of that man on the news."

"Where are you?" he ground out.

"Safe." She swallowed. "Alex, I need you to tell me the truth.

Are you tangled up in any of this?" Tears filled her eyes, several flowing over to trail down her cheeks. *Please say no.* There was no way he would engage in the things his father did or others executed on his behalf. She prayed Alex was undercover. That was the only explanation. And she clung to the slight possibility of it with an iron grip.

"Liv. How do you think it looks that you left, that I don't have control of my wife? You have to come back here. Immediately."

Control? The blood drained from her face, and her body shook at his shocking, harsh words. What happened to him? *Do I even know him?* "I-I can't come back. What's going on there… the way you're acting—" She choked back a sob and covered her mouth with her hand. With the phone pressed to her ear, she waited for his response, hoping against everything in her that he would whisper it was only a cover, that he loved her with all his heart, and she should go home, where their lives would continue as normal.

None of that happened. There was no more denying his involvement.

"Now, Liv." His voice sounded resigned. "You won't like the consequences." Shuffling met her ears before another voice broke into their conversation.

"Your place is by your husband's side, Olivia." The heavily accented voice of his brother, Mateo, filled the line. "Now, do as you're told. Tell us where you are."

The phone fumbled, but she managed to disconnect the call, slip the battery out of the phone, and throw both into her bag. Her gaze scanned the dock as Liam ended his conversation and turned. Her entire body shook.

With his brother standing so close, Alex's actions may have been involuntary. But she doubted it. They had demanded the same thing—her return. Even if there was an explanation, it was too late. Too many opportunities to confess to her had slipped by.

She gave up the last thread of hope that Alex was undercover.

She let go of her old life.

She gave him up.

As Liam neared the boat, she started to turn away so he wouldn't see her tears or what a mess she was. Before she turned, she stopped and stared at a tall man with his hand shielding his face from the sun. Not too far away, she mimicked his behavior, and her eyes narrowed. *Oh my God!* Her heart jumped. The man—on his hand, there was a tattoo.

CHAPTER 15

"I just marked your death," Liv whispered as Liam joined her on the boat.

"You'll need to be a little more specific."

Liv jerked, realizing too late she spoke aloud. Her unwavering stare remained on the lanky man as he lifted a cell phone to his ear, observing them. With a few steps, she moved enough to obscure herself from direct view of anyone in the harbor. With no other choice, she met Liam's intense gaze. No other option existed except to tell him. Three deaths already stained her soul. His life was now at risk. She should leave.

"I'm so sorry, Liam." She swallowed the terror back. "I shouldn't have involved you. Dangerous people are after me. They'll stop at nothing to bring me back. I-I don't want your death on my conscience. I need to go." Clutching the strap of her purse like a lifeline, she maneuvered around him.

His arm snaked out, stopping her from moving past him and off the boat. "You'll be safe with me. Go below, and I'll get us out of here."

"No. They saw me and are aware I'm onboard. They'll

follow me. I need to go, to throw them off my trail, and hope-fully off yours." Her mind raced. "Hide the boat. Maybe that'll stall them." The tremors she had tried to hold back erupted with a vengeance, and her teeth rattled.

Before her, Liam changed. The easygoing man looked at her with a clenched jaw and hard eyes. Within their depths, compassion lurked. Deep down, she sensed the protector in him, eliminating her raw fear.

"It'll take them a while to puzzle through how this boat is registered. There isn't anything to worry about. Go below and rest. I'll get us out of here. We'll talk when we're a good distance away." He ushered her beneath the deck while pressing a small bag into her hands from the store they had gone to before eating.

With her stomach rolling, she nodded and made her way down the steps. What choice did she have? She could continue with the plan of getting as far away as she could with Liam or endure untold misery as soon as she stepped off the boat, because the man who had recognized her waited.

Guilt stabbed her. *Liam doesn't get the danger, the risks, not really.*

Hovering in the small stairwell so the top of the boat was in view, she tracked Liam's movements as he untied them from the dock. She knew she would not be able to remain out of sight for much longer. Needing something to do, she opened the bag he'd handed her. Several different pain medications were inside. He must have purchased them while she was distracted in one of the stores or while she was in the boutique. With her nausea and low-grade fever, she suspected her body was worn down and in need of additional rest. She took the recommended dose of one of the pain pills with a sip of water.

The boat rocked as they left the harbor. When their speed noticeably increased, she walked back up the couple of steps, unable to sit in the small kitchenette and worry. Soon, Liam would demand the entire story. He had a right. Even so, her mind swirled with how much to share.

She fell onto the bench seat toward the back of the deck. The velocity they were traveling at caused them to slam into waves. The wind tore through her hair, and she regretted leaving her silk scarf below.

"Hold on." Liam looked at her over his shoulder and frowned. "It's going to be okay."

His confident words didn't quite shake her trepidation. Images of Mateo slicing through a man's neck ransacked any calm she could possibly attain. She had pushed past the first shocking induction to the violence of their world when she exited Juan Carlos's boat, but the televised murder brought it back with a vengeance.

Mateo had sliced a man's throat for helping her down off the boat with a small, inappropriate caress. The only thing that had occurred between her and the now-deceased man was her accepting his offered hand for aid. He had taken that as permission to lean in and whisper suggestively to her while touching her. Whatever he'd said was wasted, as she didn't speak Spanish. How that warranted his death failed her even now.

And Alex. Oh God. He'd taken what his brother did in stride. There'd been no change in his expression as blood spurted and arced through the air. How had she not noticed that then? The gurgle of death… She'd clung to her husband, but the look he had given her chilled her to the bone. No remorse, only annoyance, and cutting disappointment—in her.

"Liv." Liam's sharp tone broke through the loop of misery she'd been lost in. "We have company. You need to go below."

Her fingers gripped the seat as they crashed against waves, jarring her with their force. The roar of an engine fast approaching prevented her from moving. Even though logic told her it was not Alex, she looked back, shoving her tangled hair out of her face, and scanned the water to see who chased them. A sleek racing boat closed the distance. Two passengers. She could barely make them out, although the driver's carriage and build looked similar to the man on the harbor.

Liam's firm voice urged her to get out of sight, but she couldn't do it, not when he risked his life to help her. She would stay and fight, even the odds. Besides, those men wanted her, and she wasn't about to hide when they pursued her and Liam.

The boat gained on them. Liam's flew over the water but couldn't compete with the power of the lighter speedboat. In no time, they drew alongside.

Liam yelled at her again, but she had to try to reason with the men at the very least. She didn't think they were supposed to kill her. Plus, Liam's life depended on it.

"Hold on!" Liam yelled.

She gripped the seat tighter as Liam swerved at the smaller vessel, causing them to adjust their course to avoid being hit. The speedboat slowed, readjusted, then sped up in their wake. The man that wasn't driving climbed to the very front of the boat. Clinging to the bow, he ordered his partner to get him closer. Again, Liam yelled at her, but she didn't register his words. Instead, she looked around for anything heavy to throw at the man on the speedboat or swing at his head if he got close enough.

In a crouch, the man waited. In a burst of motion, the speedboat shot to the side of them and forward enough for the man to jump over the side of their boat. He launched himself into the air, straight for her. She ducked, and he tumbled over her onto the floor, but not before a sharp sting struck her bicep. Blood dripped down her arm.

Furious, she rushed to him before he could get up and kicked him in the stomach as hard as she could. Liam gripped her wrist and pulled her away from the man's grappling hands. She teetered a moment before regaining her footing.

The boat jerked. No one manned the wheel. With Liam busy, that left her. She hurried to take his place. Keeping the boat straight, she looked behind her at the two fighting men.

Her attacker got to his feet, and Liam's fist cracked into his jaw. As his head jerked back, Liam buried his fist in the assailant's gut. The man thrust his balled hand up. Before it made contact, Liam grabbed his wrist, used the momentum, and twisted. A scream sliced through the air as the man's now-useless arm dropped to his side.

Liam shoved the attacker to the floor then jammed his knee into the man's back. As Liv watched, Liam wrapped an arm around the attacker's neck and locked his head tightly. With his other hand, Liam wrenched, and the man's body went limp.

Before the dead man could fully drop to the ground, Liam picked him up and tossed him overboard. The body slammed into the side of the pursuing boat. The driver did nothing to help. Greedy ocean waves grasped the dead man and pulled his prone body beneath the surface.

"Go below," Liam growled as he whipped off his shirt and wrapped it around Liv's seeping wound.

With a shake of her head, she pulled herself back onto the seat, her grip firm on the wheel. Breaking eye contact with Liam, she sought the threat chasing them. Her gaze locked with the cold one of the driver. With a sneer, the man turned the boat away. *He's giving up?* Her breath came easier, and she moved on unsteady limbs to make way for Liam to take the wheel.

The driver made one last attempt, and the loud pop of gunshots caused Liam to push her to the deck then return fire. Even on the floor, she studied the look in his eyes and the lock of his jaw.

Liam increased their momentum and got them back on

course as he steered the boat. "They'll send someone else or ambush us when we get to port."

Those men couldn't have acted on Alex's order. The attacker had come at her with a knife, his intent to harm or maybe even kill her. So if Alex hadn't sent him—and she still had trouble believing her husband would go to such extremes—then who?

She rose and gripped the chair next to his. The gun he'd held moments ago was once again stowed in a small compartment under and to the right of the steering wheel. "I'm so sorry. I brought this mess down on us. Please, you have to drop me at the nearest harbor. I'll make sure I'm seen so they don't follow you."

A moment passed while Liam studied her, reading something in her expression. "You're safer with me. I need information about who's after you and why. No more withholding, Liv."

She owed him. She lifted her good arm to shove her hair from her face. The tangled strands whipped behind her, helpless against the unforgiving wind. "It seems my husband is involved in a drug-trafficking organization." From beneath her shirt, she drew out the butterfly necklace and held it up for his view. "The Ramirez cartel. I left, and now they're after me."

He nodded. "Why are they after you?"

"I'm not sure. The only thing I can say is they're thorough in their pursuit, in the way they gain knowledge. I sold my earrings before I left the port. Remember that video I stopped to see in the restaurant? It was him. They killed him for...well, I don't exactly understand why. Whether he ratted me out or not doesn't matter. He paid with his life."

Her gaze tangled with Liam's green eyes, and sadness nearly choked her. *I hope you aren't next.*

Sun glinted off the water, blinding Liv to the view around her, to life. It moved and flowed, but her awareness became a muted version. The stinging burn on her arm tethered her to reality, to the existence she'd traded on a whim when she ignored her husband's wishes.

Would things have been different if she'd listened, remained at his mom's? Would Alex have returned to her, a replica of the man she'd married?

Over and over, the events played in her head as she and Liam rode the water to Maine's harbor. She'd witnessed the first brutal death, learned of the senseless one. Then there were the potential ones of all who'd helped her and the pending ones when they docked. The beauty of her surroundings contrasted with the ugliness of her train of thought. The image of the recent fight swarmed and competed with the escalating battle she waged with her husband and his men. The confrontation looped in her head—the difference in the way she thought Alex would have wanted her handled and the effortless way Liam dealt with the attack.

Death entered her world on a recurring basis, and the crack of their attacker's arm, his neck, and the final splash as he met a watery grave only amplified it. That was not the end.

Liam had fought before. He was a warrior—one she was glad to have on her side. After the incident on the water, she knew. Her best chance for survival would be with Liam.

CHAPTER 16

ALEX

*D*ry heat slapped Alex in the face as he exited his father's home. Mateo leaned against the stucco wall, wearing a smirk, mocking him. Alex fought the urge to clench his fists and keep his emotions in check, something he'd learned to do at a young age with his *brother*. Mateo wanted to prove Alex's inability to lead. It would be another way to taunt him, an example to their father of Alex's worthlessness. His brother would not get the upper hand.

The ground scuffed beneath Mateo's shoes. Dressed in ill-fitting slacks and a partially buttoned-up shirt, his brother looked like a cheap pimp, unworthy of the assumed, higher position in their family business.

With Alex paving the way Stateside, respect and power within his father's organization were his for the taking. He had labored long and hard to climb all proverbial ladders, and nothing would take sweet victory from his grasp.

The power play with Mateo wasn't why he'd come outside. He wanted information from the men who'd returned from searching for his wife.

Five men stood waiting, talking among themselves while their eyes shifted from Mateo to Alex. There had been news. He needed to deal with this situation before all he'd worked so long and hard for imploded.

Crossing his arms over his chest, he widened his stance and glared at the men in silence…waiting. It didn't take long.

The biggest one in the group, Rodrigo, spoke. "We heard from Pedro. Diego died before they could grab her." His eyes narrowed, reeking of disrespect. "Your wife travels with another man, one with skills."

Rage exploded. She could have been hurt. "These men were under your control. Explicit instructions about the mission were given. No incidents were to happen. If you can't keep them in line, you will be disciplined."

Rodrigo dropped his gaze to the ground, and the others shifted a hair away. "I understand."

"Explain what happened." Alex caught a very brief amused glance between the two men standing next to Rodrigo. They thought him beneath the power of his brother, unimportant to truly follow. Alex lunged and grabbed the closest insubordinate and, with three punishing punches, dropped him to the ground. He demanded obedience, and they would comply. Too much was at stake.

Mateo chuckled, turned, and went inside. Alex's anger soared to new heights. His brother would not undermine his authority. Dismissing that problem—for now—he focused his attention back on Rodrigo and the others.

Seconds ticked by, and a low growl rumbled in Alex's chest at the man's audacity of making him wait. His impatience spurred Rodrigo to talk. His brother would have killed one of the men already, but that wasn't his way.

"Pedro was forced to turn back to the harbor after Diego jumped onboard your wife's boat. When he leapt across, his blade nicked her arm. The man helping her, he killed Diego."

Fury painted Alex's vision red. "She was injured?" In two steps, Alex stood nose to nose with Rodrigo, knife in hand. "If you heard from Pedro anything other than he's returning with her, then he failed to do his job."

Rodrigo quickly raised his hands. "Pedro has his name. We traced the name of the boat and have the location where she'll go. The man who owns the boat is Liam Savage, and he lives in Maine."

I've heard that name before. Nothing came to mind immediately. Another matter took priority.

"Bring her to me. *Unharmed.* No one stands in our way." Alex wiped his hands of the dirt and blood that covered them from pummeling one of the idiots who preferred to follow his brother. Disgusted, he turned for the house, dismissing the bunch of worthless thugs.

If he had gone after Liv himself, none of this would have happened. But to leave his brother alone with his father would have been a bad move. Mateo had his father's ear, and Alex needed to undo the damage his spiteful sibling sowed.

The cool, dark interior did much for his temperament. Liv. God, what a mistake bringing her turned into. He'd never meant for her to come to his father's. He had only wanted her to meet his mother. Somehow, he'd thought he could keep her from this world.

Calm settled over him, and he took in everything around him—the machine guns, the wealth, and the rightful prestige of his birth. He should not have to prove himself, as he too came from the same father. With a frown, he took his phone from his pocket and punched in the number of a trusted member in their organization. In clipped words, he outlined what he wanted from David. If he could've guaranteed the loyalty of the men his brother had undoubtedly sent to hunt down Liv, he wouldn't have been in this predicament.

The next steps would happen fast. He understood his father's thinking, and a group would be set up. The familiar slam of the door behind him stiffened his shoulders. The disappointment and anger he'd experienced would be nothing compared to his father's. Now things would move quickly.

Soon, he would meet with Mateo's group that was ordered to swarm Liam's home. But first, he had to deal with the regiment that had returned to their fold and delivered news of his wife. Plans formulated in his mind on the disciplinary measures he needed to take.

Finally, the time to assume his role had presented itself. Liv had made her choice. Now he must make his. Decision made, he met the cold gaze of his father.

THE JEEPS BOUNCED OVER ROUGH ROADS OF DIRT AND ROCK, deep in the Colombian jungle. Alex rode in the front with Mateo. Each vehicle carried members of their cartel, all heavily armed. On the floor, between two of their members, sat a chainsaw his crazy brother had brought. Sick dread churned his stomach at what he knew would follow.

Cresting the last of the trees that bore low-hanging leaves, they burst into a clearing. If only Alex's mother hadn't told Juan Carlos about him from the outset. Years of exposure to his father's world, to his brother's, had changed him, molded his life in ways he wished he'd never experienced and didn't have to participate in. Now he had to jump in and do what he must, or

Liv's life would be in even greater danger. His father could change his mind about Liv, and Alex knew he wouldn't like the outcome.

Alex sat in the passenger seat, shedding layers of skin to reveal the monster crouched inside, as they entered the small village by the river. They came to a screeching halt, and Alex jumped out, hitting the ground before Mateo did. With his teeth clenched tight, Alex felt the pressure in his jaw increase to the point of pain. They'd received word that a rival gang had infiltrated their territory. The gang had to be dealt with. Alex had made the decision to make his presence known in the Ramirez cartel. He had to do this. If he didn't, he would lose ground with his father. Then where would Liv be? What would happen to her?

Mateo smirked. "You're out of your element, City Boy."

Clicking the safety off his gun, Alex refused to rise to his half brother's bait. Knife in one hand, gun in the other, he fell in line with Mateo as they moved through the village strategically located next to one of their exit points for shipping up the river.

Behind them, some twenty-odd members of their cartel followed.

"Find them," Mateo shouted to their crew. "Let's make an example."

Men, women, and children scurried inside huts, some crying and some begging. A few stood their ground. They weren't who the Ramirezes were there for, and those who stayed within sight were well-known supporters of the Ramirez cartel.

The villagers around the bend saw another opportunity—a detrimental one.

The acrid scent of betrayal and fear permeated the air. Dusk kicked up around the villagers' hurried feet. Gunshots rained all around them. Alex grabbed two people from a hut and dragged them to the center of the road, where a younger member of his organization, probably about eighteen, stood with his gun pointed at the villagers who opposed them.

Tears fell, foul words were silenced, and the pile of disloyal villagers grew. Mateo broke apart from the others, meandering over to the group as Alex herded another supporter of their closest rival to the group. Why they'd turned didn't concern him. Standing alongside his brother and securing his presence and position in the eyes of their people mattered.

Mateo flipped a switch, and the metallic whirl of the chainsaw rose over begging and sobs. The rival supporters were already dead; their deaths marked the moment they had made a deal with adversaries of the Ramirezes. Alex and his men would execute the deathblow—some quicker than others.

Alex motioned for Rodrigo to retrieve the garbage bags from the jeep. Alex walked to the quivering group in the street, opposite where his brother stood. He would deliver mercy as quickly as he could, before the excruciating pain of the chainsaw cut like butter, elongating the people's suffering.

Moving fast, Alex swung, severing the flesh of a man's neck. Blood spurted and poured over the front of his dusty clothes.

The grind of the chainsaw motor stopped. "Alex! What the fuck are you doing?"

Widening his stance, Alex faced Mateo with blood dripping off his knife. "The point is to send a message. Torture won't make a difference."

"You're a rookie. No wonder no one follows you." Mateo spit on the ground and slapped a hand against his chest. "They follow me."

"Fuckin' crazy is what you are." White-hot rage pulsed in his veins. Rather than give in to the urge to cut Mateo, he bent to his task, doing it his way. Following Mateo's example of senseless torture wasn't what his father had done all those years ago. Brutal and agonizing disfigurement was not his father's, nor his, way. Soon, his father would see that Alex was the way of the future, not his crazy-ass fool brother and his adrenaline-junkie shitheads.

With quick and powerful movements, Alex took care of ending the lives of those he could before Mateo could reach them. He didn't ease all of their suffering.

Screams filled the air, echoing through the village. Anguished cries festered in horror from those who lived, including himself. Arms and legs were sliced through with the chainsaw. The streets ran with blood. Rodrigo picked up the severed limbs and shoved them into one of the garbage bags.

"Take some of the bags and dump the body parts along the east boarder," Alex ordered Rodrigo and the others helping him. "Do a drive-by to our rival's closest village and drop the rest of the bags there."

The coppery scent of blood filled the air. So did Mateo's laughter.

Sick fuck.

Alex pulled the small, hard plastic container from his pocket and poured acid over as many of the dead people's faces as he could. Mateo finished up the rest. That horrific practice would change when he led. Blood splattered Alex's clothes, but Mateo was soaked in it, his skin red from the amount spilled.

It didn't take long to finish their job.

CHAPTER 17

*S*eagulls circled overhead as the motion of the boat slowed. Some semblance of sense slid into her mind as to why Alex didn't want children. Even though they were married, that didn't necessarily mean she had to become involved with his family. But a baby tied them all together with grandparents and uncles. At some point, she and Alex wouldn't have been able to stop their child from being exposed to that world.

Liv sat quietly, reflecting and rejecting parts of who she used to be. There would be times when sadness would overthrow her resolve, but no matter what, she was prepared to fight—for her life, for those who helped her, and for her freedom.

The quaint beauty of Maine's Down East Port wasn't lost on Liv, and the artist in her stirred. It had been too long since she had created, and her soul screamed for release. The dark world she presently resided in sucked too much from her, and her fingers curled at the thought of sketching and manipulating clay. She longed for some normalcy.

Liam lined up the boat with one of the docking ports. With

her artist's instincts taking over, she studied him. His powerful shoulders moved with ease, the tense bunching now relaxed. The muscles in his back rippled beneath the thin gray cotton of his T-shirt. Her focus whipped to his face as he glanced at her over his shoulder, and his mouth pulled into a sexy lopsided grin that made her laugh.

Feeling lighter, she tore her gaze away and took in the small harbor. Docks stretched far into the blue water, and a pretty inlet looked to have access out as well. At least she was feeling better and hadn't taken any more of the pain pills. Things looked brighter, at least for the moment.

Liam maneuvered the boat alongside the dock, and her heart skipped a beat. The thought of exposure worried her. Cartels were not exactly a part of her life, and since Alex had refrained from bringing his work home with him, her knowledge was sadly lacking. She should have taken a greater interest in what he was working on, what he did. If the day came that she entered into another relationship, she would not make the same mistake of staying in the dark.

The fact that she and Liam had encountered someone connected to the Ramirez cartel in the last port shocked her. How far did Juan Carlos's operation reach?

Liv removed the silk scarf from her head and shoved it in her purse. Too many people from Alex's dad's cartel had seen her in it. Instead, she gathered her hair into a high ponytail, something she rarely wore, and twisted a band around it to hold her long strands in place. As Liam jumped off the boat onto the deck to tie it, she went below and slipped on one of the outfits she'd purchased when they stopped to eat. The tan shorts and breezy shirt looked sweet and gave her the illusion of being carefree.

After changing, she shoved her meager belongings into the shopping bag and went up to the deck. Liam stood a few feet away and spoke with some of the fishermen. Their quiet voices were impossible for her to hear, despite how much she strained to do so.

Liam noticed her right away, broke apart from the other men, and moved to assist her down.

"Oh, wait." The twinge in her abdomen as she twisted bothered her mentally rather than physically. "I forgot my purse and sunglasses." More than anything, she wanted to be able to take the time to mourn the loss of her baby, the betrayal of her husband, and the confusion and hurt those things had caused. Despite all that had happened, a part of her would always love Alex and the sense of freedom he'd given her. If only she could shut her emotions off.

The small thread of hope that Alex was working undercover had snapped with their last communication. She had to let him go, no matter how difficult it was. That decision had taken root the moment she snuck out of her hospital room.

She had time to think now that her head was clear, no longer weighed down by pain and fear while traveling alone. One thing still nagged. Who had been on that landing with her at Juan Carlos's estate? Through the whirlwind of the past few days, the worry of who had pushed her down the stairs and murdered her baby kept resurfacing. Because someone had.

With her belongings in hand, she went back to where Liam waited. He reached up, and she grasped his extended hand to disembark. Shaky from the sway of the boat, her foot caught on the low rail. Liam's arm wrapped around her waist and steadied her. Unnerved from the fright of falling and the memory it gave strength to, she gripped Liam tighter. But this was not that moment. Feeling safe, she put her hand flat against his chest and gently pushed. He released her instantly.

All her life, people had wanted her to be someone else. When Alex had given her wings, she'd fallen even harder for him. Now she needed to use them to stay safe, to remain just out of range of her husband and what he was a part of. Because she had very little faith after the recent events that he was innocent.

To regain her mental footing, she turned to observe the coastline. In quaint beauty, shops and restaurants lined the busy harbor. Even with the large number of people coming and going, the small town appealed to her. She took a step, but Liam's large hand on her arm stopped her with a gentle tug.

"I need to unload a few things from the boat. My truck isn't far." At her nod, he continued, his hand still touching her arm. "Do you want to wait in the coffee shop before we head out? I won't be too long."

She shook her head. "No."

"All right, I'll show you where my truck is."

She loved to listen to his Irish lilt. "Have you always lived here?"

"No." He waved to an older woman coming out of a store. "I was in the military, and that took me all over the place. I'm not exactly active duty right now, and it's nice being back home."

"Can't say I blame you. It's beautiful here." Liv pushed the large sunglasses farther up the bridge of her nose. One hand gripped her purse, and the other found its way into Liam's reassuring grip. He made her feel safe. She wanted to wrap herself in that safety and hibernate for a while.

A short distance from the dock, he pointed out a black F-150 truck. With a beep of his key fob, he unlocked the cab. She climbed inside and took the keys from his offered hand.

"I'll be about fifteen minutes. You all right?"

She nodded, not quite trusting her voice. In reality, she wasn't, far from it. She needed answers to too many questions. The one burning a hole in her mind—why did the cartel want her so badly?

Liv clasped her hands in her lap. A loud bang rocked the truck and made her jump. She turned while aftershocks shook the vehicle and caught Liam's wink.

"Sorry, should have warned you." Muscles bulging, he lowered the other crate that rested atop his shoulder with less impact to where she sat.

A group of women walking along the sidewalk drew her attention, and she laughed. They didn't spare her a glance; their attention focused solely on an awe-inspiring Liam.

He held up his index finger. "Give me another minute."

"Sure." Instead of going in the direction of his boat, he headed toward the rows of shops. Liv tracked his movements until she lost him around the corner. Ten minutes ticked by, and her stomach rolled and knotted. Her gaze fixated on where she'd seen him disappear. When he finally rounded the building, two very full grocery bags hung from his hands. She sagged against the seat, irrationally worried for his safety, which was foolish, as she'd seen him in action.

He opened the driver's-side door and set the bags between them. "We wouldn't have had any milk or eggs. I picked up a few other things too, not sure about what you like. Are you sure there isn't anything you want while we're here?"

"Coffee and creamer?"

"That's part of the survival supplies I grabbed."

"Thank God we think alike. That's about all I need right now." *Supplies to sculpt.* She would have to wait until she returned home for that, if she ever did. The only other thing she thought of was her freedom. Even though she longed to stroll through the shops and sit by the coast with a coffee, she did not dare. The more people that got a look at her, the greater the danger all of them were in.

Liam drove along a winding road. As the miles passed by,

her curiosity got the better of her. "Where exactly are we going? You mentioned something about a farm?"

He chuckled. "I was wondering when you would ask. We grow wild blueberries and hybrid grapes. The land and business have been in my family for longer than I can remember."

More people. Her heart dropped. "Will there be anyone else there?"

His attention stayed on the narrow road. "Not in the house, at least not until Friday. Lucy comes once a week to clean. I have a crew that works the land and another to help with manufacturing and shipping, but it's relatively quiet."

"With your accent, I assumed your family came from Ireland."

A wide smile curved his face. "That would be my mom. My dad's side has owned this land for generations. When my mom met him, she was fresh off the boat."

"Why the accent then if you were raised here?"

"Eh, I think it's mainly from being around her and all the times her family would visit. We'd go there too when we could."

She smiled at how happy he sounded. "It must have been nice."

He laughed. "We're a loud bunch when we're together. There was always someone getting in trouble or a party going on. Now it's pretty quiet. I do miss having more people around."

"But you have all those people who work for you."

"Different, though."

"Yeah, I suppose it would be." With so many people there working, the appeal of staying on his farm diminished. At least the house would be empty. "You mentioned a cabin?"

"Yes. It's small and not too far from the main house, in the wooded area. It used to be for the crew leader. I use it for guests now. You're welcome to it if you like." His focus left the road for a moment and landed on her. "I don't think it's a good idea with what happened on the water. I'd prefer you were closer, and I can protect you better if you're under the same roof."

There would be no arguing. She feared what could happen if, or when, the cartel found her. Worry for his life weighed on her conscience. "I don't want to bring trouble to your door." *Even though I already have.*

His expression remained the same, as did his response. "That doesn't concern me, and I don't want you worrying about your safety. There are lots of empty rooms, and you'll have enough space to give you the illusion of a private residence."

What could she say to that? While she planned to fight with all she had, she lacked the necessary skills. Those, she would need to learn. Until then... "Okay. Thank you."

The truck bumped over a rough road and around another curve. Rows and rows of wild blueberry bushes sprang into view as far as she could see. They rounded the next bend and drove beneath a large sign that looked to be the entrance to a farm. What had it said? She twisted in her seat and looked out the back. Seas Farms? No, it couldn't be. A memory of Alex's gift to her flashed in her mind—a case of her favorite cabernet from Savage Seas Winery.

CHAPTER 18

*L*iv opened her mouth to ask Liam about the name of his farm, but her words faded away as his home came into view. A sprawling, white two-story Victorian soared with a wraparound porch and the backdrop of the ocean. *Magnificent.* In every direction, she glimpsed rolling hills, lines of crops, and a grove of trees to the left. Behind all of that stretched miles of water. How she longed to sit outside and sketch.

When they stopped, she pushed open her door, climbed down from the truck's cabin, and fell into step with Liam. The grocery bags were looped over each of his hands, and he lifted one to point out where the blueberries and grapes were grown. Liv walked beside him to the front door, her attention drawn more than once to the sight of the shimmering blue water.

The click of the lock and rush of air as Liam opened the door pulled her focus back to the house. She stepped over the threshold and again sucked in a breath at the beauty around her. Hardwood floors gleamed, and sunlight streamed through large windows.

Liam shut the door behind them and headed inside and to the left. "Go ahead and look around while I put these away." He lifted the groceries higher. "I need to unload my truck too, so take your time."

"Oh, okay. Thanks, but do you want me to wait until you get back in?"

"Nope. Have at it."

Unwilling to set her purse down, she went from room to room with it over her shoulder. She moved from the entryway, with its antique chandelier, to a family room that urged her to sink into a welcoming and stylish sectional or relax on a stationary armchair with ottoman—her favorite. An enticing fireplace in the corner offered the promise of cozy evenings on chilly nights. This room drew her like none other. Windows soared and depicted a view of the bluff and miles of ocean.

With difficulty, she tore herself from the family room to stroll into the dining room. Her breath caught at the oversized natural-wood table. Trailing her fingers over the polished surface, her gaze darted to oil paintings of scenes around Europe.

Room after room offered comfort and beauty. Her mother would have both loved and hated it. Liv adored every nook and cranny she came across. The atmosphere of the home, the landscape, and Liam's protective presence worked to ease the sadness festering inside her.

After going through the main rooms, she walked to a set of French doors that led to a patio out back. She turned the lock, pushed them open, and stepped outside onto gorgeous slate. A wrought iron table and chairs with fluffy pillows took up one corner. Two outdoor lounge chairs set near the rear of the patio, facing the bluff, drew her in. She passed by a built-in grill on the left before lowering herself to one of the loungers and dropping her purse on the ground between them. In front of her, a gas fire pit waited for use.

Any time of day or night, this back area would have been heaven. Her head rested on the raised back of the lounge chair, the waves lulled her, and she let her eyes drift shut for a few moments.

A whoosh cut through the silence and startled her awake with an involuntary gasp. Flames climbed the air from the now-lit fire pit before her.

Liam lowered himself onto the seat next to her, two beers in his hands. He set them on the small table in between them, a good enough distance from the warm fire. "I didn't mean to wake you. As the sun goes down, it gets a little chilly."

She stretched her legs out and crossed them at the ankles. Then she pulled herself into more of a sitting position, too relaxed to even think of getting up. The fire he'd lit offered the perfect amount of heat and light in the approaching evening.

"I started the grill up a few minutes ago. I hope you like burgers."

She smiled. He was too sweet. "Of course. What can I do to help?"

"Nothing. They'll be ready soon." He popped open the beers and handed her one. "This okay?"

"It's great. Thanks." She would have preferred wine, but there was no need to be rude. Instead, she took a swig from the bottle and noticed a plate of fresh veggies when she went to put it down. She took a few cucumbers and nibbled on them, racking her brain for something to talk about. "Are you the only one in your family that runs the farm?"

Liam settled back with a handful of carrots and a cup of dip. "Yes. It's pretty much mine now. My parents spent a lifetime here, raising me and my sister and taking care of the day-to-day operations. Now they get to travel the world when the whim hits."

"So they still live here?"

At her raised brow, he elaborated. "My sister is married and lives in Ireland. She and her husband have two little rug rats, and my parents find it difficult to be far from them. So they plan a few trips a year and purchased a townhome nearby."

"Don't you miss them?"

"I do. We get together as often as we can, definitely for Christmas."

"Do you enjoy running the farm?"

"Yes. While it's a lot of work, or it was before I hired the right managers, there's enough freedom to keep me happy." He grew quiet for a moment, gazing at the water before he spoke again. "Are you ready to tell me about why a drug cartel is after you?"

CHAPTER 19

S ettled on the bench on the back of Liam's property, Liv opened her sketchbook and set it beside her. The soothing, repetitive crash of the waves as a backdrop helped her to do what she knew she needed to. Before coming outside, she'd slipped her burner phone and battery in her pocket. Escaping into the sketches that begged completion would have to wait until she did a little research on Juan Carlos's organization.

She reattached the battery, powered on the phone, and ignored the missed calls, not ready to talk to Alex, the only person who had this number.

To try to figure out what she and Liam would be facing, she would gather as much information as possible. She pulled up an Internet browser and plugged in the words "Ramirez cartel" just to see what popped up. Her stomach knotted at the amount of sites and videos that filled her small screen. Ignoring all but the most recent ones, she tapped on a video stream.

The terrain in the footage began in a small town. What froze her in place were the dead strewn around a street filled with a mixture of what appeared to be police and cartel members.

Bloodied bodies, pools of red, and death littered the area like forgotten garbage. Neither side paid the least bit of attention to the lifeless people or the few who grieved at a distance.

Her stomach clenched and rolled at the inhuman, compassionless demeanor of the two factions that looked to be in charge. Gripping the phone with two hands, Liv listened as the voice documenting the carnage spoke of long-standing rivals. The Los Elegido cartel fought for territory over what had previously been established by the Ramirez cartel. The location was a key point of business, of exporting their product for distribution to Mexico and various states in the US.

The ones who paid the price for the devastating loss of lives were the townspeople, or sympathizers to the Ramirez cartel. From that point, Liv paid closer attention to which gun-toting hands bore tattoos while mingling with those who should have been in authority. It was clear to her there were no rules, no boundaries, and no borders.

What did that mean in terms of Alex retrieving her? Lives would be lost, and innocents would pay the price there in Maine too. She would have to tell Liam; there was no other way. Even though he was military, he couldn't possibly keep her safe against a group of lawless cartel members.

What she failed to understand was why her return was necessary and whether the Ramirezes meant to take her back with little abuse, or dead. There had to be a reason Alex and his family wanted her back. She just needed to figure it out and see if she could use it as a bargaining chip for freedom—for herself and for those she'd interacted with.

The clip droned on, showing more death, and she pressed the back arrow, looking for anything that showed Ramirez movement or what they had planned. There were more video clips, but she didn't need to watch them, as their dates were older than the one she'd just viewed.

Frustrated and deeply worried, she powered off her burner phone and popped the battery back out before slipping both into her pocket. She didn't have any options right now other than to share everything with Liam. Maybe he would be able to learn something she couldn't with his government connections.

Taking several deep breaths, she worked to calm her nerves. Twirling a graphite pencil between her fingers, she pushed all thoughts of violence out of her head. Needing a complete break from the brutal images, she picked up her sketchpad and tried to take her mind off what she'd seen. Then she could talk to Liam.

After a good twenty minutes, she was back in control, enough to distract herself with the scenery around her. Not only did she need the distraction from the graphic videos and pictures she'd just seen, she also needed something to take her mind off Alex and what he might be involved in. The sense of failure circled around in her mind and was too much. When she added that to what she might have to share with Liam, she needed a moment, a small moment of peace to try to come to terms with her drastically different new world.

The sight and sounds of the water inspired her creativity, and she let the location wash over her as her pencil flew over the sketchpad. She became so immersed in what she drew she didn't notice Liam's approach until he spoke over her shoulder.

"That's beautiful."

Liv glanced at him and caught his laid-back smile. She appreciated his easy manner around her. A few pieces of her shattered heart fluttered, and her brows furrowed in response. He confused her. After all, she was a virtual stranger. Yet he offered her sanctuary when he most likely thought her husband caused her bruises and was the reason she'd run. After the boat incident, did Liam suspect something else?

Offering him a small smile of thanks, she turned back to the landscape. Thankfully, the picture she'd sketched first lay behind the book, a page away. That, she was not ready to share.

Ghosts of the past.

There would be time to finish her sketch and immortalize it in clay. Creating would expel the ghosts. Nothing was without sacrifice, and it would take so much emotion and effort to achieve exactly what she wanted. If she were lucky, healing would result.

Guilt rocked her, once again, at the realization of how she was holed up in Liam's home, risking his livelihood and his life. "Is there anything you need me to do? I-I really shouldn't impose on your hospitality." Even though it was too late. Alex and his men would know she was here, probably sooner than she expected. She owed Liam the truth.

Liam frowned and crossed his arms over his chest, creating an even more imposing force. "There's nothing you need to do, except explain in detail why you're running and what they want from you." At her anguished silence, he scanned the area before speaking. "It would help to understand what we'll be up against, Liv."

Guarded, she nodded, still unable to speak past the horrible images in her mind and the fear of what was coming. *He'll be in even greater danger.* Her lips pressed together. She would tell him. Each moment she didn't put him in more danger. It was a vicious circle, and she needed to figure out how to explain it. How did she admit out loud the detrimental mistake she'd made by marrying into that world?

She owed Liam so much. One part of it would be easy to tell. "I told you before a drug cartel from Columbia is after me. What I don't understand is why. What benefit my return will give them." Her lips clamped together, and she blinked her eyes in a fast pinch. She could do it, tell him everything, including all the mistakes she'd unknowingly made.

A deep frown marred his face. "I figured as much from who chased us."

Her silence was the only answer.

"When you're ready to tell me the rest, I'm here, Liv. Just make sure it's soon." The lines around his eyes eased. "I made some sandwiches if you're hungry."

The thought of food turned her stomach, and she shook her head. Her stay of execution from sharing everything, reliving it in the telling, would be short lived. But she was grateful nonetheless. She wanted to stay outside, at least for a little longer. Something withheld her from confessing everything. But she couldn't figure out what that was—nerves, fear of voicing out loud that she had made an enormous mistake in her marriage, or possibly something else. She would tell him, just after she let her mind ponder a little bit more what held her back.

"I want to tell you. Everything. Just give me a few minutes, please? I'm struggling with admitting it, but I have to tell you it's bad, and we aren't safe." A very tiny part of her worried about her obvious lack of judgment where Alex was concerned, and she wondered if putting her trust in Liam was warranted.

Gripping the wrought iron back of the bench, Liam leaned forward, his gaze once again skimming the area. "I have a few phone calls to make. When you're ready, come find me. All the workers are busy, finishing up a harvest. No one will disturb you back here." The frown returned. "If you notice anything, hurry inside and get me."

Fear skidded along her skin. Time worked against them. She had to make a choice sooner rather than later. Could she really trust him?

After he retreated to his office, she flipped back to the sketch that consumed a portion of her thoughts. The first one she did depicted two lovers reaching for each other. The man wore a partial mask, while a layer of hair semi-shielded the woman. No definite features were recognizable. Their hands strained to touch from outstretched arms, and bodies arched as if a force yanked them back. *A romantic catastrophe.* With heavy emotion, she detailed the features into the portions of expressions visible through the half mask and thin veil of hair in motion, accentuating strain and suffering.

Several times, the gallery that featured her work had called, begging her to expand her lovers' series. This would be either the last of the poses or a new series altogether. In representation of the separation, deceit, and violent parting between her and Alex, emotional pain and futility screamed from the mock-up of the sculpture. The real one would be even more powerful.

When she finished the sketch, she faced the driving force to begin another. The personal message would span time. This one represented an unfulfilled promise to her child. With quick strokes, her pencil flew over paper. Two arms rose from a base rippling with churning waves. Cupped in the chalice-like image rested an almost fully formed baby.

The drawing sent a jolt through her, shattering her hesitation in confiding in Liam and bringing into sharp focus the dangers they would soon face. Deep in her bones, she knew something horrible was about to happen.

CHAPTER 20

*E*motionally exhausted, Liv walked through Liam's big house. With a clunk, she dropped her sketchbook and pencils on a table in the living room and roamed the first floor. Which door led to Liam's office? Yesterday's events were foggy. Giving up on remembering, she opened doors and peered inside.

She paused with her hand on the knob of a paneled door at the end of the hallway. Liam's voice carried in tone only. Not wanting to disturb him, she turned and went back to the kitchen. There, she saw the closed door that led below the house. The unexplored space intrigued her. Maybe he stored the wine there. Right now, she could use a glass, or a bottle.

Tapping her fingernail against the thick door that led to what appeared to be a cellar, she made a decision. She flipped on the switch to illuminate the stairs and left the door open as she made her way down. At the bottom, she clicked on another light and gasped. Gold mine. The sight stilled her breath—rows and rows of bottled wine. *Heaven or helluva hangover?*

She skimmed her fingers over the label of one of the many

bottles, and her hand jerked back as if burned. She wondered about the one word she'd managed to see on the sign for the farm, but really, what were the odds? Besides, he mainly spoke of wild blueberries, not grapes. Savage Seas Winery. Tremors shook her hand as she touched the label.

Her favorite wine.

One of Alex's last gifts.

Owned by the man who sheltered her from her husband's family. Was there a connection there or simply a coincidence?

She staggered as images ran through her mind of the innumerable times she'd cuddled against Alex with a glass of Savage wine in her hand and a beer or whiskey in his. He had teased her often about her obsession with the reds this winery produced, which were carried in the finest restaurants, as well as quaint affordable ones she and Alex visited, away from the watchful eye of her parents and their social circle. With single-minded vigilance, Alex had tracked down the manufacturer, bypassed the distributor, and ordered several cases to surprise her.

Never in her wildest dreams had she expected the owner to be the man Alex had spoken to. They had planned a trip someday. *Here.*

What did this cruel twist of fate mean?

A sob wracked her body. The conversation after Alex had given her the crates of wine flooded her mind, and she latched onto it in a moment of weakness, slipping into the memory.

"Hey, Liv."

Setting her book down, she gave Alex her full attention. Excitement and mischief danced in his eyes, and she laughed. "What are you up to?"

"Oh, babe. The question is what will you be up to after you see what I got you." With a tug, he pulled her from the couch and into their study. Two crates sat on the wood floor.

Taking a closer look, she gasped. "How?"

They'd asked at a few of the restaurants they went to together and inquired if they could purchase the wine from the vineyard. Always, the answer had been no. So Liv substituted other wines at home.

Savage Seas made the most decadent wines. Their flavors carried a melody of their own that played across her tongue.

Alex opened the crate closest to them and took out a bottle of cabernet. "Let's open this one and celebrate our anniversary a month early."

"You spoil me." The huskiness of her voice surprised her.

"No." The seriousness of his tone caused her to peer closer. "I treasure every moment I have you in my life. You're a gift I cherish always. Spoiling you is not possible."

On an exhale, she had breathed his name and gone into his arms.

Shaking her head, Liv pulled herself out of the memory, but the aftereffects still plagued her. They had made love, slowly and passionately. He'd told her he never expected to have someone like her to adore, nor did he think he deserved her.

Had he known, even then, the day would come when he would betray their love? Betray her? Their child?

Looking at the unmistakable label she held in her hand, she remembered when Alex told her he'd spoken to the owner, who had said they didn't do tours but had a shop on-site. Alex had mentioned that the store and wine tasting would be moving to the little harbor and had told her they should take a trip there before that happened.

They'd never made it.

Work had gotten in the way, Liv had been featured in another gallery, and the time they'd set aside for a vacation had passed. Instead, they'd gone on another, much later one, which had succeeded in tearing them apart.

The emptiness inside her stretched as long and deep as a canyon. With no one to turn to, she instinctively reached for Liam's friendship, his commanding presence and confident nature. There seemed to be no judgment from him. Not only that, but his strength seeped into her every time she was near him.

The image of Alex's father and brother invaded her mind. So many times, Liv peered into the dark corners, afraid they'd be there...waiting.

To restrain her.

To take her back.

To kill her.

She turned away from the rows of wine in Liam's cellar and fled upstairs into the living room to grab her things. Liam's back was to her, and she swiped the tears from her cheeks before he turned.

The TV was on in the background. Something caught her eye, and she froze.

A red banner ran across the top of the screen, and horrible words flashed within. Their details didn't matter, yet. What did was the beaten man tied to the chair. His head hung, and a clear image of his face remained obscured, deemed temporarily irrelevant. From the shape of his body, the position he held himself in despite being secured, and the men responsible, she knew him. *Alex.*

Of course the world news would show him on TV. Anyone connected to her name and her vast fortune was newsworthy. But this, this wasn't right to air on live TV.

Curt foreign words shouted out a demand, and the network interpreted in English. Words that carried an inevitable threat to her, to Alex, screamed at her from the television. *Unbelievable.* At least to her it was. Their ploy of a ridiculous monetary negotiation in the millions made no sense. Alex was a son to the leader of the Ramirez cartel, being falsely held for ransom. What could it possibly mean?

While the trust fund in Liv's name contained billions of dollars, she and Alex both lived off the inheritance from her deceased parents. She'd granted him access to that. Who did Juan Carlos and Mateo think would pay with her missing?

Did his father and brother not know about all that? Maybe Alex had kept that information tightly guarded. Or maybe Alex's family sought her to gain total control of her fortune.

Wetness coated her cheeks. Absently, she touched her face, only to find tears streaming from her eyes. The possible implications of what she was viewing caused her body to shake uncontrollably.

Her mind screamed with fear and confusion. They had *hurt* him. Was she wrong in suspecting his involvement with them?

Blood dripped down his white, torn, button-down shirt. His arms were restrained behind his back, and a hand reached into view, grabbed the hair on the top of Alex's head, and yanked back. Dull eyes stared right at her. *Oh my God!*

Was this her fault for running?

Wrenching her gaze from Alex's face, she searched for anything that might tell her why. The only discerning thing on the hand that gripped Alex's dark hair was the ring.

A groan tore from her throat, and she fell to her knees. Liam leapt from the couch and helped her up. Her eyes never waivered from the bruised face on the screen that still haunted her dreams and nightmares—her husband.

A distant part of her became aware of Liam as he helped her to the couch. A broken keening filled the room. She sucked in air then realized the wounded sound came from her. *Oh God.* What had really happened?

Liam held her and shut the TV off, but it was too late. The damage from the initial sight was seared into her brain. As

Liam's warmth seeped into her, the newscaster's interpretation played on in her mind.

"Turn it back on," she croaked, realizing there was no point in hiding. She needed all the information available to stay one step ahead of them. She had to see. Was it real? Had they harmed Alex because he worked both sides?

Liam clicked the TV back on, and the images that now filled the screen displayed pictures of her past—images of Alex and her together, splashed in random order, smiling at the camera at various functions, happy. The reporter's words steadied her wavering emotions. The media must have been clamoring for more information.

"We have confirmation that Alex Mudarra, a respected detective at the New York Police Department is being held for a ransom of twenty million dollars. His wife, Olivia Mudarra, heiress of deceased senator John Wrightwood, is missing. No word has been received of her condition or whereabouts. Two weeks ago, the happy couple set out on a delayed honeymoon. Their last known location, Barbados."

The reporter droned on. Liv lost focus as facts played through her mind. Alex sat there, seemingly beaten. The reporter never once mentioned her husband's involvement with his father. The difference in the last names maintained a separation, as if he wasn't connected to the Ramirez family. The fact that his father was not listed on Alex's birth certificate helped too. Born in the United States, he would not come under suspicion, at least not for some time. It would take a zealous investigation to uncover the facts.

Alex had lied. But why?

"Liv."

She startled, forgetting who sat beside her. Leaning back, she yanked her death grip from his arms, slightly horrified she had reached for him and probably cut off his circulation. "I…" She stopped. What could she say?

He held his body rigid, but his eyes softened as she met them. Who was he really? He was too built, too fit, and too observant of his surroundings. The paramilitary and the police in South America were not all to be trusted. Plus, Alex's involvement in his family's organization as well as being an employee of the NYPD left her on shaky footing. The thought of military led her to another question. What was Liam exactly?

"I need you to fill me in on the whole story, Liv." His firm yet gentle words drew her attention.

He deserved the truth. But she deserved to learn who he really was.

She chewed on her lip, wondering if she should ask for information from him first or share her story. Her even being there could cause enormous problems for him—not only from the cartel but also from the government.

Decision made, she met his gaze. "That man on the news… he's my husband." At his silence, she caved. Everything flew out of her mouth, from their life back home to learning who Alex's father really was to her miscarriage and escape. Liam listened without saying a word. Through her sobs and the moments she needed to catch her breath, he sat patiently by her side, letting her tell her story at her own pace. Not once did he appear to judge her. His silence gave her the strength to confess.

Carefully, he enfolded her in his arms. "Is that everything?"

A bitter laugh left her lips, and she pressed herself against the back of the couch. "His father is Juan Carlos Ramirez. So yes, there's more." She tilted her head back to watch his reaction.

He nodded, his eyes turning hard. With everything she had gone through so far, his transformation was the only one that didn't frighten her.

He smoothed her damp hair from her face. "Let's get you some tea or maybe something stronger? Then you can tell me everything."

Wine. Her affection for his label was not something she'd shared yet. It wasn't important. Neither was the fact that he had spoken with Alex about acquiring cases and visiting. "Wine would be perfect."

His arm slipped around her waist, and he led her to the side bar, where he opened a bottle of cabernet sauvignon with his label on it. She pushed all thought of the last time she'd had a glass from her head. Things had been simple then. How could she have not noticed or made the connection when the name Seas was across the sign when they'd turned into the vineyard? When Liam handed her the glass, she took a large gulp.

His lips quirked up at her hearty sip, until his gaze locked on her neck. He hooked a finger under the chain and lifted the butterfly for closer inspection. Because of Alex's insistence and the wide panic swimming through his eyes, she'd left it on even when she escaped.

But she had taken care to keep it hidden from view after boarding Liam's boat. She'd mostly succeeded, except when she'd risked exposure in the pawnshop, where the man had used the information. That had ended badly for him. The fear mixed with envy in the man's expression reaffirmed that parting with the pendant would have been a mistake. The pawnshop man had calmed down when he'd skimmed over her other jewelry. Desire to possess her diamond earrings had burned in his gaze. Those, he had bought.

Another indication the necklace held significant meaning had become clear with the dress shop owner, Marita, her adamant refusal to help, and her demand that Liv leave immediately.

She'd trusted Alex with her life. Now her life lay in another's hands. Her instincts had led her astray once before. Still, she owed Liam an explanation.

"Alex gave it to me." Her whisper broke the silence and drew Liam's gaze to hers.

"I'm familiar with the design…and its meaning."

Panic surged. "What meaning? Wait, are you connected to them?"

He squeezed her shoulder. "No, I'm not. The opposite, Liv." He shook his head when she opened her mouth to question him further. "We have to talk about this more, but I've got a few calls I need to make right away." Standing up, he paused. "Stay inside. I don't want to take any unnecessary risks with you out in the open."

Who does he need to call? Setting her drink down, she worried her hands together. The longer she was alone with her churning thoughts, the more determined she became. Liam would not withhold secrets. She would make sure of it or leave of her own accord.

CHAPTER 21

*D*espite her resolve not to, Liv found herself creeping down the hallway, following Liam's deep voice. A sliver of light shone through the door to his office. Silence filled the air until a chair creaked and his authoritative voice spoke again. He was obviously speaking to someone on the phone.

"No. Be real. No one new started working on the farm. The harvest is done, and only a skeleton crew remained until yesterday evening. We don't have to involve the other part of our team, not yet, anyway." He waited a beat, listening to the other person. "Exactly. With the on-site store downtown, we'll need someone to watch over the employees due to the connection to me. Right. We're close to setting up a base here."

Liv held still, waiting to hear more. So far, his intent to return her to Alex's family had not happened. Even so, she wanted further proof. When Liam spoke again, she leaned closer to catch his words.

"We'll be fine for a day or two, but they won't be far behind. She was recognized in the last port, and you're aware it's only a matter of time before they learn who the boat she was on belongs to." A few seconds passed. "If you can manage to come with Jo and the kids, and Jack too, that would be a huge benefit. Trev can keep an eye on my employees in town."

The pause stretched longer before he responded. "Connor won't be able to be here. He's helping Chris with something. I don't think we'll need our full team. I get he'll be pissed. Too bad, they're still at each other's throats. If Chris is here, Trev would have a coronary. They need a little more time to pass to get over it." He said his goodbyes and hung up.

She turned to make a fast exit but not before he saw her. His gaze caught and held hers through the doorway and he rose from his chair, rounding his desk.

"Liv, there's nothing to worry about while you're in the house. Some friends of mine will arrive and help before the cartel comes."

Her eyes went wide, mainly from Liam verbalizing her fears. "Do you really think there'll be more than a few?"

He nodded slowly. "There's more involved with bringing you back." With a hand on her arm, he guided her into his office. The smell of leather, wood, and Liam invaded her senses.

A huge mahogany desk took up a large portion of the back of the room. Four wing-backed chairs were scattered in corners and in front of his desk. Tall built-in bookcases overflowed along one wall. The inviting room begged her to curl up on the small couch on the left and pluck a book from one of the shelves. As she stepped farther inside the room, she gave Liam her attention.

"The report on TV forecasts your husband's innocence and a lack of involvement with the Ramirez cartel. From what you said, there is a connection. What it sounds like to me is he's been a plant in the NYPD all along. Returning with you by his side will only solidify his identity there. If he fails…"

She took a step back. "I don't understand." How did her

presence change anything for Alex or make her valuable to them? If money was the lure, Alex had access to her net worth, which was a small fortune.

Compassion filled Liam's vibrant eyes, and he rose from the corner of his desk, where he'd perched. "Let's not worry about anything yet. I'm only taking precautions."

She swallowed the lump in her throat. Together, they walked out of his office, and she kept pace as he led her to the back porch and the glider. She was grateful for the fresh air as he lowered himself beside her.

"None of this makes any sense." She turned and faced him. "Alex is part of their family. Hurting him probably had to do with finding out he was a detective. They may think he's building a case against them." With thoughts churning in her head, she didn't allow time for Liam's rebuttal. The thought of what she'd read of the Ramirezes' attacks threw her into denial. "With what happened, I don't mean anything to them. There's no reason to pursue me, or for my existence to affect them."

His arm went around her shoulders, and she leaned into him. If she could just get to Alex, then she could find out why she was important to the cartel. She had to believe some semblance of the man she fell in love with was still inside him.

"We'll figure it out. They have the name of my boat. Eventually, they'll find my name, and in time, my home. They'll be here soon."

"Maybe we should call the police, then."

"I'll handle that now. I'll call my contacts in the CIA and FBI."

"Why would you call them rather than the police?"

He shrugged. "That's who I'm used to working with. They'll notify anyone else if it's needed."

"But we aren't even sure how many they'll send. Obviously, two didn't work. I'd think more would come."

"I do some contractual jobs for the CIA. We'll be ready when the cartel arrives."

Liv's brows furrowed. "I thought you were retired military and you ran this farm and vineyard."

"I do. I was in the service for years. When I came back here to check in on my parents, they told me they wanted to sell and move to Ireland to be close to my sister and her kids. So I stepped up and am running the farm rather than turn it over to a stranger."

"Even though you have another business?"

"That came later. I missed my team in the Navy. We formed the business some time after."

He was not in just any division of the Navy. He was a SEAL. She nodded when he said he would make the calls then be back. When he returned, they moved to the kitchen after Liam's stomach growled, and she realized that she too was hungry. Their conversation continued except for the topic she wanted to learn more about—his training in the military.

"When you were on the phone earlier, you mentioned something about a base?"

He nodded. "My buddies and I expanded a branch to Trev's brother's company. It's special ops but contracted. We'd tossed ideas around for a while about forming one, and it seemed logical to expand Gray Ghost Security Group. We'll have our division up and running soon. I purchased a large plot of land adjacent to the farm. That's where our base will be. There's another plot bordering the east side of my land too. We're thinking of purchasing that just in case it's needed."

Liam rehung the dishtowel on the stove's handle. He picked up the chicken Caesar salads and set them on the table along with tall glasses of iced tea. "Do you sculpt in your home, or do you have a studio somewhere else?"

Liv took a few bites but mainly just moved the food around.

"I have an in-house studio, complete with an offshoot room that houses a kiln."

Liam speared a large helping of chicken and romaine with his fork. "Do you miss sculpting?"

"Desperately." Giving up for the moment on pretending to eat, she picked up the sweet tea and took a sip. "Without it, I feel anxious and almost at a loss for what to do with myself."

Liam leaned back, his salad finished. "Then we'll have to get you some clay when things calm down." He motioned to her food. "Eat."

She smiled. Feeling lighter, she took a bite. Her stomach growled, and she gave in to how hungry she really was.

Liam chuckled. "I'll have you ready to go in a couple of weeks. If there's anything specific you want, just tell me."

She wouldn't be there long enough to acquire all the tools needed and sculpt. What was Liam's objective?

CHAPTER 22

*L*iv slipped outside into the afternoon sunlight and caught sight of a shirtless Liam. She frowned, slightly uncomfortable. Stacked, sinuous muscles gleamed in the sun, so different from Alex's lean, strong body. It gave her a little more confidence in dealing with the fight that lay ahead. Liam talked with another man, whose baseball hat shielded his tan features, and she gripped her hands together. *Who is he?*

When the man he spoke with tilted his head to get a better look at her, Liam turned, and her heart exploded in a staccato beat. She may have made a huge mistake by letting another person see her. If this man lost his life at the hands of the cartel, his blood would be on her conscience.

"I'll catch up with you next week, George. Enjoy the time off." Liam dismissed the other man and walked toward her with silent grace. "I thought we should do something together."

"Who was that man?"

"George, an employee. We're finishing up this last harvest's detail and making sure the farm is good to go. He'll leave, and the crew won't be back until I give George the all clear."

She twisted her hands, anxious about another witness. "Oh."

Liam chuckled. "Don't worry. George will be fine and won't say a word to anyone about you. I need to grab a shirt. I'll be just a minute, but in the meantime, you should head inside."

Liv followed him inside, walked around the living room, and took note of a picture of Liam in uniform. Having a SEAL on her side had to help.

Liam rounded the couch, a tight blue shirt stretching across his chest. His corded arms hung at his sides, and as her eyes traveled their length, she froze at the gun in his hand.

"What's going on?"

"Have you ever shot a gun before, Liv?"

"Ahh, no." She took a step back, wanting as far away from it as she could get.

"Come with me."

Oh God. Should she run? "I'd rather not."

The deep, rich sound of Liam's laughter rolled over her. "I promise, you'll be fine. I'm going to teach you how to shoot at a target. A *paper* one."

With his words, the reality of her situation solidified even more. During his phone conversation to his friend, or business partner, he'd said a few days was the most they had. Soon, she would have to deal with violence and death again. Should she learn to shoot a gun?

Liam had done nothing untrustworthy, and maybe it would be a good idea. At least it wasn't a knife. The involuntary shudder coursed through her at the memory of Alex's brother slicing the man's neck when they'd docked.

Trailing behind Liam, she shoved the gruesome thoughts away. It was time to put on her big-girl panties. Liam pushed open a door she hadn't noticed before. And why would she have? It was between two built-in bookcases. With a shove of his hand, it swung wide to reveal a steel door, complete with an access panel. Liam punched in a code, and it popped open, revealing a stairway that led down.

A chill traveled along her skin. No one would find her down there. If he had any ill intent, he could do whatever he wanted to. Well, he could have done that on the boat when they were far out to sea. No, this was stupid. She had to put her full trust in him, even if it meant handling a gun.

Soft light overhead helped them navigate the stairs. When she reached the bottom of the landing, an enormous space stretched out before them. At the very end of the room hung two targets, like the ones she'd seen on TV shows with shooting ranges.

Liam grinned. "It's soundproof, but you'll want these." He handed her headphones. "Before you put them on, let me go over what to do. We're going to start with your stance. Which is your dominant leg?"

"My right one."

Hands on her shoulders, he turned her to face the target. "Feet shoulder width apart. Now slide your dominant foot slightly back. I want you to try this position, and if it's not comfortable, change to both feet shoulder width apart."

Shuffling her feet, she decided to try the stance with her foot a tad behind.

"With your right hand...I'm assuming that's your dominant one?" At her nod, he continued. "Firm grasp on the grip, and finger extended to the trigger. Your other hand goes lower on the handle, overlapping, for support."

The gun's weight and texture felt alien to her. She did as he instructed, her arms straight out from her body, finger lightly resting on the trigger, gun pointed at the bull's-eye.

"Good. Now line both sights for the center of the target. When you have it sighted correctly, what you're aiming for will appear blurry." He slipped her headphones on for her, stepped behind her, adjusted her aim slightly, and told her to fire.

The recoil was minor, not as bad as she thought it would be. Of course she completely missed the target. She lowered the gun, and Liam took it from her hands and winked. With his own earphones in place, he fired off several rounds.

"Ready to go again?" he asked.

At her nod, he stepped back and handed her the gun, nudging her in front of him. His arms came around her, and she worked to focus on the target and the strange weapon in her hands. He made it appear so easy. Liam helped her to aim, put his finger over her trigger finger, and squeezed off a shot.

When she lowered the gun and squinted at the hanging piece of paper, elation swept through her. "I hit the target!" She turned to smile at him.

"Knew you could do it, love. Now try it yourself." Liam's easy lilt relaxed her, and she lifted the gun again. "Look through the sight, aim, and squeeze."

A rush of power and trepidation filled her. So long as she focused on the target, she didn't have to think about pointing the weapon at an actual person. She could see the draw in going to shooting ranges. That was where she would prefer to keep her newly learned skill.

Liam reached over and adjusted her aim. On an exhale, Liv squeezed the trigger and hit the black space on the target. He took the gun from her hands and switched out the cartridge then continued to show her how to sight as she went through the next batch of bullets. When he assisted her alignment, she hit the target. On her own, she missed horribly.

When the chamber clicked empty, she handed the gun back to him. He pressed a button, and the target zoomed along a track in the ceiling to them. She grinned at his answering smile as she removed the headphones. Liam took the gun from her, reloaded it, and put it in a cabinet on the wall.

The space was enormous, and Liv's curiosity spiked. While one side of the basement must have been used for the cellar that housed the wine, this portion split into three sections. Wrestling mats with a punching bag took up a corner, and another formed a separate room that divided and looked like storage. Glass surrounded the partitioned walls for the lone room, and monitors were set up. The final area contained the shooting range, with bulletproof glass enclosing the entire thing. In a million years, she would not have expected to find this room, accessed via a hidden door.

Liam was way more than he appeared. He'd told her he was special ops and that he and his group were forming a venture. Regardless, she remained shaken from Alex's betrayal, afraid to put her trust in anyone. She shoved that thought aside for later and gave Liam her attention. Even though shooting at targets was fun, firing at live ones would not be. She did not intend to do that. "Why are you teaching me this?" her voice whispered between them. Even though she knew, she wanted to hear his explanation.

Liam leaned against the table and crossed his arms over his wide chest. "You know the answer to that, Liv. You have to be prepared. They're coming." His steady gaze never left her. "Hey, I've got this, and my buddies will be here to help us."

Wringing her hands together, she agreed with what he said. They would be coming, and she did need to be ready.

While Liam watched her silent acceptance, she wondered exactly where his willingness to help her came from. She pursed her lips, ready to ask him what had bothered her for a while now. "Why you? Why did the man who flew me here tell me to go to you?"

A spark of amusement flashed in his eyes, and he grinned

the crooked smile she adored. "You mean why did Trev tell you to find me? He's a part of my team, plus we go way back. He probably thought you could use some help when he saw your bruises." He stood to his full height and ushered her back upstairs.

Then why didn't Trev help? That wasn't an answer, not really.

THE DAY WAS COMING TO A CLOSE, AND THAT MEANT THE arrival of the cartel was even closer. Liv's anxiety about how Alex was doing peaked. Right now, there wasn't a whole hell of a lot she could do. With her brows furrowed, she drew her knees to her chest, just sitting quietly when Liam walked into the kitchen.

He moved to the small wine rack and retrieved a bottle and two glasses. "I promise not to ply you with alcohol. I wanted you to try this, to give me your opinion since you seem so fond of the cab we make." He poured the dark red liquid and handed her a glass. Its spicy, woodsy smell teased her senses.

She took a sip, aware he was distracting her. Even so, she decided she was onboard with his change of subject. The full notes danced across her taste buds and soothed as they went down. It took two more drinks before she lowered her glass. The slight tingling that spread along her body relaxed her as the alcohol took effect on her nearly empty stomach. "What is this one?"

"It's a new sangria cabernet blend we're launching over the holidays."

"Oh. I love it. I have a half a case left of your cabernet at home."

He chuckled. "You do, huh? I'm glad you like it."

"Yes." Her smile turned wistful, and she only let the happy part of the experience come through, not the betrayal. "It's my favorite wine. Alex called here and bought it for me as a surprise."

His mouth pressed into a flat line. "How many cases did he buy?"

"Two. I realize that's not a lot, but we planned on visiting, well, here."

"I remember that conversation."

"With Alex?"

He nodded. "Yes, he was very insistent at the store, something about leading up to an anniversary. Anyway, they transferred him to me."

Air rushed from her parted lips. What he said, and didn't, was like a punch to her gut. It wasn't a shock. She was aware they had spoken, yet hearing it tilted her world all over again. Alex had planned to bring her here as a surprise for their anniversary. When she'd told him she was pregnant with their child, their plans had changed. She'd assumed it was because she couldn't enjoy the wine, but something about Alex's awful response led her to believe the reason wrapped into their altered lives.

She smiled, despite the aftershocks, and took another numbing sip while contemplating how fate worked in mysterious ways. "Did you finish the work you wanted to?"

Liam set his almost-full glass down. Hers, on the other hand, needed a refill, which he complied with. "Enough. There are a few things I want to look into, but my contact isn't available until late tonight."

No… Alex had informants, odd calls, and, she'd come to learn, an even stranger family. What did Liam hide?

He reached over and squeezed her hand. "It's a friend I have that's a detective, one who's met Alex before. There are a few things about his reappearance I wanted to hear about from Fred's perspective. More of an inside advantage."

The knot forming between Liv's shoulder blades lessened marginally. "I don't think you'll learn anything. Alex has worked at the New York precinct for years. He's well respected and connected."

"Maybe, maybe not."

CHAPTER 23

*L*iv woke on the couch under a blanket Liam must have covered her with. Waking to an empty room caused agitation to itch along her skin, another reminder of her separation from her husband. After her shooting practice with Liam and all the worrying she'd done about Alex and the cartel, her exhaustion had caught up with her.

Her heart hurt. There would be no more crying. It was time to do something, even if it was only gathering information. She'd realized she would have to fight when she left the hospital and Alex. With a good start on easing her grief, she was ready to assume control of her life, her future—this time, with her eyes wide open.

She should have tried to find out about Alex, to see if there were any recent developments. Guilt sat heavy in her stomach. Liam had told her not to call home or anyone she and Alex were friends with. He'd said that would lead Alex's family to her faster, and they needed a couple more days to prepare. It was time she woke up and dealt with her situation. She couldn't hide there forever.

Liv picked up the remote from the end table, turned the TV on, and surfed through channels until she found the one that covered the world news. When nothing about Alex came on, she flipped to another, then another.

Until one did.

She froze as the news of Alex's release flashed across the screen. From what the newscaster said, he'd returned home yesterday when an opportunity had opened for him to escape during the confusion of rival cartel warfare. He'd come home with no real harm, miraculously, other than cuts, bruises, and fear over his wife's absence.

I'll bet he's worried.

Perhaps his family wanted to give aid to the image of him undercover in case news of his presence in Colombia had leaked. A proactive exposure of a hostage's situation in which he was tied and beaten could be beneficial. In reality, she knew what the cartel would do to a real hostage. His family would have killed him, not released him.

The reporter droned on until he made an announcement that held her immobile. A statement surrounding the disappearance of Alex's wife and the circumstances that led to her whereabouts would be aired later that night. She pursed her lips at that partial untruth. She wasn't missing because the Ramirez cartel had killed or sold her.

Would Alex confess to everything?

She paced the length of the living room, her burner phone clutched tightly against her palm. Liam had left a note saying he would be in his office for a few hours and to come get him when she woke or if she needed anything. She needed to find out what Alex had planned.

Underneath her worry for him, anger simmered.

He owed her an explanation. In the background, she kept the news on, and every few seconds, her gaze strayed to catch the headlines, hoping for more information about the cartel, about Alex.

The sound of her fingernail tapping against the cell's plastic egged on her ire. She despised secrets, and Alex knew that. The one he'd kept from her about his family had cost them too much. His betrayal soured in her stomach. Unable to stop herself, she pressed in the numbers she knew by heart.

Not even a full ring, and Alex barked out an answer.

"Alex?" Her heart stuttered a beat. Even with anger burning in her, the sound of his voice slew her.

"Where the hell are you?"

At his harsh demand, her hand shook. With a fortifying breath, she held firm. "That's not important. You owe me answers."

"Liv." A desperate note threaded through the deep timbre of his plea. "It's not safe. Tell me where you are so I can come to you."

God, no. She couldn't do that. Her life wasn't the only one on the line there. She would not repay Liam by just telling Alex where she was. "And I was safe where you took me?" She shut her eyes and tried to calm her frayed nerves, resolving to work around her anger and focus on getting answers to her questions. "I called to find out what happened to you, to us. *How* are you involved with your family?"

"I—Liv, if you're not going to tell me then just come home. Fuck, baby. Where the hell are you?"

She sucked in a breath at the fury in his voice, picturing him raking a hand through his hair. He still hadn't answered her question, so she let silence be the answer for her.

"No, just…never mind. It doesn't matter. Get on a plane or train from wherever you are. Things will go back to the way they were, but you *need* to come *now*."

"I heard you're back home after being kidnapped. What was

that about? Money? I don't understand. Who would've paid it with my parents dead, me gone, and you held captive? What was the point?"

"That was my brother's stupid idea, and my dad went for it to try to flush you out from hiding."

"What? Why? Is-is your family there with you?"

"No."

None of this made sense. What was the point of Alex being at his father's house, of his return home, of attempting to bring her back to his family. And now he wanted her home?

No words came. Her gaze was glued to the TV screen, and her mouth fell open. *Rachel.* Her beautiful face, so full of life, had a headline underneath it that made Liv want to throw up.

Murdered.

"Oh my God! Rachel." The reporter said the killer was still at large. Rage and horror filled Liv, and through clenched teeth, she demanded, "What have you done?"

CHAPTER 24

*R*achel's laugh and a million shared conversations burst in Liv's mind as devastation hit her like a ton of bricks. *My God, my best friend is gone.* How could he have done that? Tears flooded her eyes and fell unchecked down her cheeks.

"What had to be done." An audible sigh carried through the line. "You shouldn't have called her, Liv."

She jolted. Alex's voice sliced through her memories and yanked her back. A seed of hatred took root for what he'd done, for what he insinuated, for all of it.

"I didn't, I…" *Oh no.* She'd sent Rachel a few texts about what she'd learned, the last saying she was safe and would fill her friend in on everything when she could.

Tears streamed down her face, and she swiped them away. "She was your friend too, Alex."

"She'd become a liability. You shouldn't have told her anything. I couldn't let her ruin everything I've worked for, Liv. Besides, it was better me than Mateo."

She slammed her finger over the disconnect button and

threw the phone. The cheap device bounced along the sofa, undamaged, as she stood shaking. No matter how she used to feel about Alex, she no longer entertained the idea that there was a shred of decency for her to salvage. He was lost to her.

Unable to listen to any more, she paused the TV, which was frozen on Rachel's picture.

"What happened?" Liam's steady voice calmed her, marginally.

Her bottom lip quivered, and a dam broke inside her. Tears poured from her eyes, and sobs racked her body. She flew at Liam, slammed into him, and clung. *Gone. Everyone she cared about was gone. Her parents. Rachel. Dead.*

Liam's strong arms wrapped around her, and she took the strength, support, and friendship he offered. He'd done nothing but be there for her, and she was eternally grateful for his friendship.

"Shhh, love. Whatever it is, we'll figure it out. I'm here for you."

His big hand rubbed up and down her back as she soaked his T-shirt. Out of all this hell, she was grateful to have someone to lean on and share her burden, all in friendship. If she could focus on one thing, it would be that gift.

Holding her close, Liam let her cry without pressuring her for answers. Sniffling, she let him hold her as they dropped onto the couch. After wiping her face with the Kleenex he handed her, she met his steady gaze, ready to talk. "Alex was—is—home." Her hand fluttered toward the TV, where the paused picture of Rachel was still painted across the screen. "I wish he'd never gone back. Rachel, my closest friend…she's dead. Murdered."

A tic pulsed along Liam's jaw. "Did you call him?"

Tears filled her eyes again, but she refused to let them fall. "Yes. I-I couldn't stop myself." *And Rachel, I contacted her too.* Liam grasped her shoulders as she continued. "I don't understand. On the news, it said he was home and unofficially back to work. There was a picture of him exiting the precinct. How do the police not know?"

"They're not completely in the dark at this point. I have a few friends on the NYPD who are damn good men. We've been in contact."

Rachel must have kept her suspicions from her supervisors. Instead, she probably confronted Alex about them and sealed her fate.

Liv nodded as Liam's words penetrated her racing mind. Still, she needed him to understand why she'd done what she had. "When I saw him on the screen, I had to find out. Why things changed, why he treated me the way he had, why he wasn't searching for me." She grabbed fistfuls of Liam's shirt and growled, "He's not the same. When he answered, he was angry. The voice on the other end wasn't the man I married. It belonged to the stranger I met in Colombia, the one associated with his family's world, not mine."

Liam kissed the top of her head before he rested his chin on her hair. She burrowed closer, chilled to the bone from what she had learned.

"How do you and Rachel know each other?" he asked.

"From college."

"Was she close to both you and Alex?"

"Yes. She was my best friend. She and Alex worked together on the police force." Her voice broke. "God, Liam. He killed her. They said her throat was slashed. It's how Alex's family kills." Bile surged up the back of her throat. "I've seen them use acid too. Thank God not this time. But it wasn't them; it was Alex."

"Are you sure it was him?"

"Yes," she choked out. Bitterness coated her words because

of Alex's actions and her own in bringing her best friend into the situation. "I asked him what he'd done, and he said 'what was necessary.' That she knew too much." Nausea churned in her stomach. "I don't get why it's so important for me to go back home. What does he want from me? I need to figure out what to do, what's best. I could go back to him to stop the killing, at least until I understand the next steps. Maybe that would stop anyone associated with me from suffering." Oh no. If he killed Rachel, did that mean he had a hand in the car accident? *My parents. If not Alex, then one of the others working for his father.*

"Stay here, inside, and let me take care of you."

With her fists, she pushed on his chest. "Why?"

"You're safe here, Liv. Friends of mine will be arriving, and we'll protect you. I'll protect you."

"What *are* you? I mean, I get you're a SEAL. I get that, but why would you take on my problems? They aren't yours." She shook her head. "I don't think that's a good idea. I should go to the FBI or CIA or something."

"Liv, your husband is involved with the Ramirez cartel. He killed your friend, and his family *will* come for you. Haven't you wondered why he behaved differently once you were around them? And now that he's home, there's no mention of a connection on the news? His life is back to normal, aside from the worried husband role he's playing."

She gasped. "Playing?" The word was like a slap to the face. She knew it was true. Hearing someone else say it confirmed Alex's deception from the onset of their life together. It revealed her detrimental judgment in character. She had brought this on herself.

Liam's hands dropped from around her back and raked through his hair. "I'm not insinuating your entire marriage is fake, but the evidence points to his continued involvement. Why hasn't he said you ran? Why is he insisting the cartel sold you?"

Her brows furrowed. "How do you know that's what he said? I haven't even heard that."

"I have a few military and police connections. I've seen his statement. They haven't released it because the paparazzi are like vultures when it comes to your family and the recent tragedies."

No words came out as her mouth opened and closed. Her entire life felt like one big string of inside connections between family and influential friends. Why did Liam's association shock her?

Fierce determination hardened his features, and she shivered for an entirely different reason, one her grief-stricken brain refused to process. The only thing she did pay attention to was her intuition. Around Liam, she didn't fear for her life. That alone was what she focused on. If only she could forget her other life, the people that would surely come for her, and the husband who wanted her back under different pretenses. Alex would have access to her financial accounts. What was she to him now?

With or without Liam's help, she planned to find out.

"What do you propose?" Her former rage sizzled out, leaving her tired from learning of Rachel's death and from the release of grief and acceptance that her marriage wasn't what she'd thought. She looked to Liam and borrowed his strength, temporarily. Depleted, she allowed him to pull her to his side.

"Nothing for tonight. You've processed enough. Just know things are in motion and that this is what I do."

"Thanks, Liam. If you don't mind, I need some time alone."

"I have a friend arriving late this evening and another in the morning. I don't want you to be alarmed if you run in to either of them before I get a chance to introduce you." With a light squeeze to her shoulder, he left the room.

Memories of Rachel bombarded Liv, and she dropped her

head into her hands. Alex peppered into many of those recollections too—her husband, the killer, liar, master of deception, and the person responsible for Rachel's death. He didn't deserve Liv's time. He didn't deserve to linger in her thoughts. Rachel did. If Liv allowed her mind to dwell on how Rachel had died and on her mistake in involving her friend, she would succumb to days of crying and misery. Rachel would hate that.

Tomorrow she would put it all to rest, attack her impending problems, and move on with her life, at least mentally. Divorce would be imminent. She would be free once again, this time in an entirely different manner. She would have no parents dictating the direction of her life, no husband, and she would no longer be a pawn for others.

CHAPTER 25

*W*anting to be alone, Liv sat on the front porch with a cup of coffee. Her hand shook as she raised it to her mouth. The cold water she'd splashed on her face had failed to ease some of the swelling from her grief-induced crying jag over her best friend. *I can't even go to her funeral.* She flinched as memories punched through her foggy brain of all the times she and Rachel had shared over the years. *Why did he do it?*

It didn't make sense to her that, as a member of the forensics team, Rachel would have been a threat. What had she done or said to put herself in Alex's way? Liv wiped a strand of hair from her clammy forehead. Marrying Alex had been her escape, a little over a year ago, from her parents' mapping of her life and their controlling ways. Now her actions led to the unraveling of her world.

Knees to her chest, she rested her chin on them, her coffee growing cold on the side table. Puffy clouds inched across the sky, and she shifted her focus to faint sounds carrying on the gentle breeze. More than one voice carried to her, the clarity of the words lost in the distance they traveled. Whoever it was must have been on the patio.

Sifting through the conversation she'd had with Liam, she remembered he had said friends of his would be there today. Pushing herself to her feet, she picked up her cold mug and went to replace it with fresh coffee before heading to the back.

With a steady grip on her now steaming coffee, she pulled open the glass door and stopped short. She found the owners of the voices she'd heard. Two men turned, and their conversation immediately halted.

Her brows furrowed. They reminded her of Liam. They looked like soldiers without uniforms. They had to be the men Liam talked of last night who were on his team.

"You must be Olivia." The one with lighter-brown hair advanced, hand extended. "Hope we didn't wake you. We got in pretty late last night. I'm Matt, a friend of Liam's."

With a tentative smile, she stepped closer and shook his hand. "Nice to meet you. Liam mentioned he had guests arriving soon."

The one with dark hair, a similar shade to Liam's, laughed. "Guests? Is that what he said?"

She tilted her head, confused, and jumped a little when two large hands landed on her shoulders from behind. Liam's spicy, woodsy scent wrapped around her, and she relaxed amidst the intimidating strangers.

All of them, Liam included, were frightening in their own way—big, built, and tough looking. She curled her hand, nails digging into her palm. She studied their faces, their relaxed stances, and the easy way they spoke to one another. Each positive trait eased her mind further. They were very different from the men tied to Juan Carlos's organization. That alone boosted her confidence that they were in fact there to help, not make matters worse for her.

Liam's deep voice brushed her ear. "They're more like brothers, Liv." He gave her a gentle squeeze then released her. "The beauty queen over there is Matt. He's married with two teenagers and harmless."

Kids. The quick stab of pain caused her to duck her head. She pressed her lips together, annoyed by her behavior. Shoving it down, she straightened her spine and met Matt's gaze. "It's not safe to bring your kids here right now. I'll be leaving soon, and maybe then it will be."

Matt grinned. "My kids can take care of themselves, don't you worry. Leave the worrying for me and Jo to do. They'll be here tomorrow."

"The rude, brooding one over there is Jack. Don't let him get to you." Liam moved away from her and clapped Jack on the back. "Good to see you, man. Appreciate both of you coming."

"That's what we do," Matt chimed in. "Jack and I were about to go over the property unless you wanted to talk strategy?"

"No. Let's wait until Joslyn gets here, then we'll all be on the same page. Liv and I'll probably be in the training room when you get back."

When the guys took off, Liam faced her. "You doing okay?"

Longing she wasn't prepared to experience filled her, as did an equal helping of guilt. Her cheeks heated at the memory of Liam's arms around her and how she'd burrowed into him, an embrace that shouldn't have happened. "Yes. I want to apologize for my behavior last night."

"Stop right there, Liv. I understand you've been hurting. I'm not reading anything into it." He tweaked her nose. "You need some more practice hitting targets, so let's get moving."

Thankful for his understanding, she set her coffee down and followed Liam.

The sidearm felt less foreign in her hands. But she still only wanted to fire it at the targets. If the need arose, she would find the strength, especially if it meant protecting Liam or those who'd sheltered and risked their lives for her.

Liam's arms wrapped around her again, and he adjusted her aim. His finger over hers, he squeezed the trigger and hit the target dead center. The small amount of recoil pushed her back into his chest, something she was becoming achingly aware of. He made her feel safe. It was an illusion, one she was all too familiar with. Ultimately, she would need to be on her own or be in a place where she would be responsible for her survival. With renewed determination, she noted the position and sight so she could hit where he directed her aim instead.

When he dropped his arms, she missed his warmth and the steadiness of his presence. The cold, foreign presence of the gun affected her more than she'd let on.

"You've got this." He adjusted her hand position when she moved it a smidgen. "The goal is to keep you out of harm's way, but I want you to be prepared just in case. No matter what, Liv, don't hesitate. Take the shot."

Five shots later, she was pleased with her accomplishment. One hole sat close to the center, thanks to Liam's help. The rest were at least on the target—the white space, but it was better than she'd done last time.

Needing a distraction from the direness of his direction, she questioned him. Besides, she was determined not to be in the dark again. "Matt and Jack look an awful lot like you."

"Really? I don't think we look alike." A grin teased the corners of his mouth. "I'm bigger."

She rolled her eyes. "You were all joking around, but there's this, I'm not sure, presence about you all. Maybe a take-charge attitude, but different than what I'm used to being around."

He laughed. "I'm sure it's just because we're a unit, a team."

"Right, the SEALS. I get that, it's just, there's more there."
Her brows furrowed as she mulled over what he'd told her. "Are
you all still active or reserves? I'm sort of confused by that since
you said you work with the government sometimes."

"We served our last term several years ago. On occasion, we
contract out, but not on a regular basis. Most of us would like to
more, but there are some things we're getting in order for our
base of operation."

"Just the three of you?"

"No. There are five from our original team. Five in the one
we partner with as well. We have other contacts that join in if
we need them, and Jo, of course, but that's all that's needed to
get the job done."

"Since you have government contracts and connections, you
must have access to all sorts of information." Her gaze met and
held Liam's. "Were you aware of who I was when I asked for a
ride out of Rhode Island?"

He shook his head. "Not right away. I got Trev's text, and
he'd run a light background check on you. I had that too.
Nothing flagged us there, at least not at first. I don't want you to
be alarmed, but I bugged your phone, so don't beat yourself up
over calling Alex."

She walked over to the table and set the 9-millimeter down,
processing what he'd told her. He always seemed so accepting of
anything she told him. He probably knew a lot of it before she
confided in him. No wonder he never seemed alarmed. For
some reason, the invasion of privacy didn't bother her. "Why
help me? I'm still having a hard time understanding that. I'm
not the job. You didn't get a contract to keep me alive, to fight a
war for me."

"You looked wounded and lost. When we got back here, I
did some further digging."

She nodded, processing. "Then you know all about the cartel and Alex?"

"Yes. No one within the precinct made the connection, not officially. He's still free to move around." He shrugged. "They're watching him. Sometimes that's better to draw out more of the players and keep them semicontained."

What did that mean for her? She locked gazes with him. "You think I'm in enough trouble to call in your Special Forces team?"

CHAPTER 26

*S*eated in a sitting room with large floor-to-ceiling
windows facing the bluff, Liv wished she were in her
studio back home. The gritty feel of clay between her fingers
would have gone a long way in easing some of her anxiety. For
the time being, she could draw her ideas.

Picking up her graphite pencil and sketchbook, she flipped
to the drawing she would sculpt someday. Her back to the door,
she added intricate details, and her heart bled out further. Two
arms, forearms flush and hands opening from the palms, formed
a chalice, which rose from rippling water. What they held was
where she focused her attention. A tiny baby, curled up as if it
were still in her stomach.

In careful charcoal strokes, she made adjustments to the little
eyelid and paused to look at the completed sketch. A tribute,
really, to the baby she'd lost. Hers had been a peanut, not really
as formed as this child. In the curve of the hands, the gentle
cradling promised safety, and she poured her love and released a
majority of her pain into it.

Even without being there, Rachel was a part of her letting

go, in healing, with what she crafted as well. Her best friend had been ecstatically happy for her, unlike her husband and his family's odd reactions.

Someday, her child's soul would have another chance at life. If not to her, then to a mother whose life offered the world she could no longer provide. Never would she think it was best this way, but in essence, drawing and sculpting her infant was starting to set her free.

Mentally exhausted, she sat back against the couch. The world around her trickled back into her awareness and, with it, the peel of laughter. *Children?* Her heart pounded at the thought of Matt's kids there. She would never forgive herself if something happened.

Leaving the sketchbook, she whipped around in panic, intent on pleading with them to go. She couldn't endure the death of innocence again, especially not because of her.

A small woman stood in the doorway, her platinum-blond hair brushing just past her shoulders. Her beauty shone bright in her fey-like face. Fighting the impulse to rub her tired eyes, Liv fast-blinked. Was the woman real, or had she finally lost it?

The woman shook her head, breaking contact from scrutinizing the sketch. When their gazes met, Liv sucked in a breath. Compassion and understanding swam in the lady's azure eyes. "I'm sorry for your loss."

The quiet voice grabbed her by the throat. Swaying, she nodded, unable to do much else. She'd already bled out, putting everything she had into her art. She needed to recover, a few moments to reenergize, and with the stranger talking to her, she wasn't sure if it would be possible.

The woman offered a small smile as she stepped into the room. "I'm Jo. Joslyn actually, but please don't call me that. Jo is good. And Liam told me your name. He didn't tell me you're an artist."

Liv returned the smile, somewhat halfheartedly. "Yes. Your husband mentioned you and your kids would be here today." She paused, thinking of the best way to say what she needed to. There was no reason she couldn't. From what Liam had said, this woman would be just as informed as the men. "I'm concerned about your kids being here. It's not safe as long as I'm here."

Jo laughed. "Oh, you don't have to worry about them. They've been through more than you could even imagine." She swept away her words. "You'll be shocked once you see them in action."

"Aren't you worried about their lives, their safety, with what'll be coming for me? Liam said it's only a matter of time."

Jo winked. "Come meet them. And to set your mind at ease, Matt told them they would be guarding you. I will too, just not in the same secured room." She rolled her eyes. "That man is way too protective and thinks he's going to shut me out of the action."

Liv followed Jo to the door that opened onto the patio. Beyond the glass sliders, two teenagers laughed. Unable to help herself, she scanned their features—the shape of their faces, their tall, lean builds, the placement and color of their eyes— and compared them to Matt and Jo. As a sculptor, that's what she did. She studied people. The kids looked nothing like either of their parents.

Liv halted, and so did Jo beside her. "They're mine in every sense of the word, except biologically. Same with Matt." Jo's sure voice answered Liv's unspoken question. She must have seen the confusion on Liv's flushed face when she looked between the kids and her.

Jo grasped her elbow and led her to the couch rather than outside. "You're going through an awful time. I can't begin to understand what you're feeling. Liam did fill me in on everything, but that doesn't explain where you're at in terms of your heart."

A tear rolled down her cheek before she could catch it. Dammit, she swore she wouldn't cry anymore. "I just don't know. I love Alex, but everything changed."

Jo pursed her lips. "Back home or in Colombia?"

Liv leaned against the pillows, needing the support. "He'd been acting a little off at home. Honestly, we didn't discuss his work. He preferred to keep it separate, not wanting to involve me, which made me happy for some stupid reason." *Because of my parents' relationship and influence in my life.* "It wasn't until we were face to face with his father and brother that his personality completely shifted."

Jo squeezed her hand.

Not wanting to talk about it anymore but grateful to have a woman to commiserate with, Liv switched topics. "Were you in the Navy too?"

Jo grinned. "With these bozos? Nope. FBI."

Unease skirted along her skin. "Are you still?"

"Don't worry. I'm one of the good guys, promise. And no, I'm not actively with the FBI any longer. I'm a stay-at-home mom for the most part. How strange is that?" She laughed. "I knew nothing about kids when Dylan and Jilly landed in my lap." Love blazed in her eyes before she turned to catch a peek of her kids through the windows. "When needed, I work with Matt and the others. I'd prefer to do more, but the kids come first."

"Why would they be here? It's so dangerous."

Sadness swamped Jo's eyes. "This isn't something they haven't seen before. Before they came to live with me, their lives were filled with abuse and intense poverty. They watched their father murder their mother. Their world was hell. So this…it's good for them. Gives them a semblance of control back, discipline, and doing something good rather than fall into the destructive trap of their former upbringing. Being included in our team teaches them they can make a difference, be part of a family who protects each other instead of harming."

Liv shivered. "I'm so sorry."

"For their past, yes. Their future is bright." Jo grinned. "They're amazing kids, and I'm so lucky to have them in my life. Come meet them."

Liv followed her outside. Two teenagers laughed and joked with Matt, Liam, and Jack. Their attention immediately turned to her and Jo as they stepped out, their smiles still intact.

Her gaze collided with two pairs of eyes way older than their years, and she shivered from the knowledge of why they didn't seem their age. Jo was right; these two were no ordinary teenagers. Jo introduced her to Dylan and Jilly, and Liv interjected, telling the kids to call her by her first name. There was no point in being formal. This was an unusual situation, and from the looks of these teens, the dangerous and strange events they would learn about would not be a shock.

Liv accepted the water Matt offered and took a small sip. Liam stepped close, his strength lending her the support she needed but would not ask for. His pinkie linked with hers for a fraction of a second before he let her go.

Everyone seemed to look to Liam as if he was their leader. She could see it. He had a commanding air about him—fair but firm.

"It's settled, then. The perimeter is secure, so tonight, we relax and have some fun. Tomorrow, we plan," Liam announced.

CHAPTER 27

*W*ith coffee in hand, Liv crowded into Liam's office. Matt, Jo, and their kids were already seated. Jack leaned against the windows, and Trevor turned and offered her a wink when the door clicked closed behind her. She gave him a small smile, surprised to see him there. Taking the empty seat in between Jo and Trev, she braced herself for what would be discussed this morning.

A sense of unease, of pending danger, permeated the air. She sank back into the chair and listened as Liam's deep baritone filled the room.

"There's been no movement yet from Alex. So far, approximately twenty men are en route from the Ramirez cartel. I've been in touch with Stevens and Jamison."

Her lips pursed at the unfamiliar names, and Liam caught her confusion. "Rich Stevens is our contact at the CIA, and Drew Jamison is a senior detective at the NYPD."

"Drew said he's been suspicious of Alex for some time now. They haven't had anything to pin on him to indicate he's on the take, until now. Things aren't adding up with his release from the Ramirez cartel. That wouldn't have happened since they rule with a brutal presence."

Nails digging into her palms, Liv waited for condemning looks from the others. None came. Trev reached over and tugged on her hair, and his lopsided grin provoked an answering smile from her. Jo gave her hand a squeeze. No shoulders stiffened, and no shocked or appalled glances were cast her way. She got the impression from their easy acceptance that the uncertainty and danger they would be facing were nothing new to any of them. With that, she relaxed a tiny bit more.

Liam recounted everything she'd told him about Alex. Rich was tracking Alex's and key cartel members' whereabouts. For some reason, it was important for Alex and the cartel to get Liv back. They didn't have a definite answer as to why.

"We know Alex planned on changing his career." Liam nodded in her direction.

I guess that means I'm supposed to talk. Liv took a deep breath and shared what would've come next for them. "My father basically told Alex he would be a shoo-in for senator. We believed it too, especially after Senator Radcliff told him Davidson would be retiring soon and all three of them would pave his way to fill the spot."

"So the reason could be political? Liv's connections?" Jack offered.

"Maybe. I mean, Alex has the financial means from money my parents put into a campaign fund for him, and then there's my trust. Money isn't the issue. He has the support and backing, even though my parents are dead."

"Let's assume he plans to go into politics for power," Matt reasoned. "From what Drew said over at the NYPD, Alex basically single-handedly took down more than one cartel. Now he wants into politics. What are his motivations, and why is Liv a necessity to get back?"

"Because I know too much. I've been inside his family's home, seen what they do, and they're not sure what I learned while I was there. Alex may want to protect me or to kill me before his brother can find me. I've witnessed what he does, and it's horrifying."

Now she understood Alex's unique skills for dismantling the organizations in the manner and speed in which he did. He had firsthand experience with the inner workings of a cartel and must've had insider information from his family.

"There's another angle we haven't talked about," Jack said. "When I spoke to Drew, he said there was evidence of foul play in your parents' accident. The brake line was corroded by acid. Could this be about money? You're an heiress. Your parents probably left everything to you." At her nod, he continued. "If you decide to divorce him, especially since you learned what you did about his family, he wouldn't get anything. If he gets you back, he can either control you or kill you."

It might not have been an accident. Alex had never told her that, just that her parents had been in a terrible crash. The details, other than instant death, had been kept from her. While she dove headfirst into grief when she'd learned about her parents, any news surrounding the cause would have escaped her notice. He could have told her. But he hadn't. Anyone she came into contact with would have assumed she knew the details and would not have wanted to cause her further pain. Had Rachel found out and confronted him?

"That's an angle that has definite possibilities." Liam stopped talking, and his penetrating gaze locked on her. "Liv, you okay?"

She nodded that she was okay, not wanting to get into her tremulous emotions in front of everyone. What could she have said? Not really? It was a very real possibility Alex was involved in her parents' death. After learning about Rachel, she would have been foolish not to think so.

Liam kept an eye on her as he asked if there were questions.

"The NYPD is still mostly unaware of Alex's involvement with the Ramirez cartel?" Matt asked.

"From all the digging I've done, yes, the precinct is in the dark to his connection to Juan Carlos. The FBI has looked further into his disappearance and seemingly miraculous return. Liv, our contact at the CIA wants us to be in on this, to keep you safe. Even if they hadn't requested we get involved, we would've helped you. It's something I thought you should be aware of." Liam turned to Jack after Liv's acknowledging attempt at a smile. "Are all the cameras and trip wires installed?"

Jack nodded. "Every inch is covered, and the drone is in the air. Motion lights are set up, and the ones surrounding the house have the higher-watt bulbs, also on. I can take the first shift for surveillance."

Liam agreed before his focus turned to Liv. "You have to stay in the house."

"For how long?" The thought of being forced to remain inside made her feel caged, albeit a very large and luxurious one, but a cage nonetheless. She had already felt that way at Alex's father's house and again in the hospital.

Jack's chilly gaze swung her way. "As long as it takes."

Jo rolled her eyes. "Stop being so dramatic." Facing Liv, she smiled. "Don't mind him. He's had something up his ass lately." The teens snickered, and Matt grinned at them. "Dylan and Jilly, get all the stuff from the garage and spread it out over the lawn. Everything—basketballs, set up the badminton and volley-ball nets, whatever you can find to make it difficult to navigate. And Liv? It won't be too long, and Jilly and Dylan will be restricted to the inside of the house too."

The older boy groaned.

Jo shot him a look. "Maybe you could get a video game going after and challenge Jilly or Matt. It would pass the time until we have a sighting."

Dylan's attitude did a one-eighty as he leaned back in his chair and eyed Matt and his sister. "You're going down."

Liam spoke up, the matter apparently settled. "Jack will be on surveillance for the next four hours, Matt and Jo will prep the weapons, and I'm going to need to ensure none of the workers come here for the next week. We'll do a normal rotation for monitoring. I'll take the roof lookout with Jo when I get back."

"Why are you doing this?" Liv's voice whispered through the room, snagging all attention. "I mean, why would you all risk your lives to help me?"

"It's what we do, despite the CIA's involvement in your situation," Jo answered. "If Matt, the kids, or I needed something, the rest of us would come in a heartbeat and lend a hand. It's the same with each member of the team. We're a unit. Don't take on unnecessary guilt, Liv."

Too late.

CHAPTER 28

ALEX

*a*lex's shoes crunched over broken glass. Another wave of helpless fury detonated. He swept his arm over the dry bar in the dining room, sending several small figures, a half-full decanter, and two empty glasses crashing around his feet.

It didn't help.

Nothing helped.

If only she would come home, then things could be salvaged.

He stepped over more debris and picked up a framed picture of Liv and him. His arms circled around her, happy grins on both of them. He clutched the frame with one hand and ran the other through his thick hair, tugging at the strands.

From the time he was young, he'd had a goal, a job to accomplish, and within the parameters of that, he'd found Liv —his mark. In a matter of days, she had become more, so very much more. She was his life, at least the one worth living. Now he needed her like the air he breathed.

Still holding the picture, he sank onto the couch and pulled his phone from his pocket. He dialed her number, and it rang a few times before her sweet voice reached his ear.

"Liv." Voice hoarse, he cleared the frantic emotion from his constricted throat and tried again. "I *need* you to come home, where it's safe. Things will go back to the way they were."

Silence ticked, and he held his breath, waiting. Desperate anger clawed at him, but he refused to expose her to the frustration that rumbled within him. She would only want more answers. Those, he couldn't give, not if he wanted her home.

"I can't, Alex. I don't think it would be a good idea."

Every muscle tightened in his body, and his fingers whitened against the black picture frame. "I'll hire a plane to take you back. This is the best thing to do, babe. Where are you?"

"No." Her voice reverberated with conviction. "I'm not ready to come home. You didn't answer any of my questions the last time we talked. And there's Rachel. How—God, Alex—how could you?"

"Everything will be clear when you come home. Liv, trust me. Think of the life we share. Think of who we are together. In your heart, you know I'd never hurt you."

"You have, and that's not what I asked, Alex. I need you to tell me why. Why you've changed. Why you kept secrets from me, the one thing I told you I hated and couldn't live with. Why you're involved with your family. You are, aren't you? I don't understand. Your job—"

"Liv, I can't talk to you about details, or the why of things, on an unsecured line. Please, tell me where you are so I can keep you safe."

"That ship sailed, Alex. As soon as you learned about the pregnancy, and we made plans to visit your family, everything changed. You brought me to them, if not physically at first, within reach. I don't feel safe around you right now."

"Babe, I love you. It'll all make sense once we talk face to face. I promise."

"God, Alex. Too much has happened, so much changed between us, all so fast." She sob-hiccupped. "You shattered my heart, *killed my best friend.* I just, I can't. I won't *ever* be with you again." The line went dead.

"God dammit!" Alex kicked the coffee table in front of him, sending it careening into an armchair. The burst of violence did little to soothe his agitation or his racing heart.

When the phone rang, he answered it on the first ring. "Liv?"

Familiar, aggravating laughter immobilized him, injecting ice through his veins. "What do you want, Mateo?"

"The same things you do. Can't keep your wifey on a leash, hmm?"

"Mind your own damn business. I'm going to get her today." Twice now, he and Liv had talked on the phone, both times long enough for him to trace. And he had. He knew exactly where she was. He'd suspected it after Rodrigo had dropped the name of who owned the speedboat. He only wished she had told him.

"Not if I get to her first." For the second time, the line went dead.

Panic held him momentarily still. *Fuck!* If Mateo got to her first…he didn't want to even think about the possibility. Alex raced to the bedroom, threw a suitcase on the bed, and shoved clothes inside. The steel case contained a secret compartment, one impenetrable by airport security cameras. No need to check and make sure his guns, extra cartridges, and knives were all in order. He had not taken anything out since he'd returned home.

Alone.

Without her.

Desperate.

He double-checked his tracking equipment, noting she hadn't moved from the Maine location. Calling in to the precinct wasn't an option, nor was it required, as Alex hadn't officially started back to work. If he could keep his trip to retrieve Liv as secretive as possible, he would.

Whiskey stained his clothes from when he'd thrown his glass and the decanter. Sparing a few minutes, he changed into a clean pair of slacks and an oxford. The blazer and tie didn't matter. Where he was going didn't require he worry about his appearance.

What did concern him was the head start Mateo had on him.

CHAPTER 29

*L*iv rocked back and forth, her arms around her stomach, tears running like rivers down her cheeks. The phone lay on the couch beside her, still warm from her tight grip. She hadn't thought it was possible to hurt any more than she did. *Wrong.* Her heart had broken into a million pieces all over again. The sound of Alex's voice, pleading, had shattered her.

It was over—completely and irreversibly finished.

Two loose ends remained: the cartel confrontation and officially leaving Alex.

She'd told Alex no. Stood up to him like she had rarely ever done with her parents. They'd all used her, and she was done. When things calmed down, after the pending attack, she would make it official by divorcing him. Once more, she realized it was time she took her life into her own hands…after Liam and his friends helped her with the cartel. By then she would take ownership of her actions, reactions, and plans for her future.

She was done with the political scene, with keeping up

appearances, with fake people and being used. All she'd ever wanted to do was sculpt, wear what she wanted, be with whom she wanted, and go where she wanted without her parents' circle of friends watching, always watching. *No more.*

The couch dipped, and strong arms wrapped around her. She collapsed against Liam's hard chest, accepting the support he offered. *Again.*

This time, her tears fell in acceptance that her old life had ended, and she fully embraced a new existence. Her tears were not many, nor did she feel crushed, defeated, or helpless. Strength seeped into her being.

Liam's hand stroked her back, offering comfort. Stopping for a minute, he handed her a Kleenex then resumed the hypnotic motion on her back. "Is this about the call from Alex?"

"Oh, right. I forgot you were monitoring the phone." He was trying to protect her. She got it, really. And it didn't even bother her in the least. From the very start, since he'd found her on his boat, he'd done nothing but keep her safe.

She sucked in a breath, so confused. *Not with my decisions to leave or to trust Liam.* Just the charade of their marriage.

"Do you want to talk about it?"

A bitter laugh ripped from her chest, escaped her lips, and sliced through the air. The surrealism of the situation wasn't lost on her. "He wants me to tell him where I am so he can send a plane and bring me home. I didn't tell him anything about where I am. I stood firm and told him I'm not coming back." She needed to get it out, to talk to someone, even if Liam probably knew what she and Alex had discussed verbatim.

"It doesn't matter if you did, Liv. By now, he knows where you are if he didn't before. We're ready for him; we want him to come."

Her body was strung tight, every muscle straining, leaving

her unsure if she should jump up and run. Making the decision to move on with her life without Alex was one thing. But being forced to confront him in a situation not of her choice, most likely with a full cartel regiment, didn't appeal to her.

Liam tilted her head back. "You don't need to worry. We're expecting him and are ready. Did he say anything you found to be unusual?"

Air whooshed from her mouth. "No. I don't think so. Only that he could keep me safe if I went home, that things would go back to the way they were. That's the thing, though. They wouldn't. Too much has happened. Not only that, I don't know why his family did that fake kidnapping or the exact reasoning behind their interest in me, or how he could have killed Rach. She was his friend too." She pressed her hands flat on Liam's chest.

"I understand it's confusing, Liv." He brushed a strand of her hair from her cheek and tucked it behind her ear. "He's still in the States, in New York. At least for now. We'll keep you safe, and things will get better."

Shrugging, she let another piece of her life go. Nothing tied her to her old life, not really.

"Is there anything I can do to help?"

"No." She wiped her eyes with fingers that shook. "I think I need to be alone for a little while." A wobbly smile touched her lips for a brief moment.

She retreated to the room that faced the bluff and stood there, letting the emotions swirl and bounce inside her. The nearly completed sketch of her shattered intentions cast invisible threads, grabbed her by her broken heart, and pulled her near. If she had her clay, she would bury her fingers in it. She was desperate for the only thing in her life that gave her any semblance of peace, of release.

Sitting on the couch, she skimmed over the form she'd drawn while gauging if anything else was needed. Longing shot through her for what could have been, should have been, but what would not due to the shove down the stairs.

Who had done that to her? She was almost positive it wasn't Alex.

The stress of the phone call still coursed through her and tried to weaken her resolve to stay away from him. A very small part of her thought that if she went home, she would spare someone else's life. As she played through the exchange with Alex, the sketchbook slipped from her grasp. The sound of it hitting the wood floor, of the pages crinkling, never came.

Liam held it. Mere inches from her, he placed it on the table and sat down next to her. His presence was a simple offering of support, letting her know she wasn't alone.

That confrontation with Alex over the phone was the last one she intended on having. Liam's steady heartbeat under her ear soothed her racing thoughts.

"I hate that you went through so much. I realize we haven't known each other long, but I want you to realize I'd have done anything to prevent what you've been through."

Liv wished she could forget for a while in Liam's arms. It was wrong, though. Even with the evil she'd experienced at the hands of Alex's family, he remained her husband, and she would not break her marriage vow. The question was, how long until her marriage was legally severed.

Liam squeezed her shoulder. "I promise I'll keep you safe, Liv."

"Thank you." This time, she would keep herself safe.

"What can I do for you? What do you need?"

What did she need? *This nightmare to end.* She wished she hadn't met Alex's family. No, nothing Liam could do would restore her old life, but maybe he and his friends could help her attain a new one.

Despite her thoughts of starting anew, one question still burned inside her. *Who pushed me down the flight of stairs?*

CHAPTER 30

ALEX

*A*lex lifted his hastily packed bag onto the conveyer belt and passed through the security checkpoint. He'd shaken the paparazzi and hoped they wouldn't pick up his trail there. With a flash of his badge, security would ignore anything that looked a little suspicious. He'd left his standard-issue gun for them to see in the middle of his shirts.

A minor repair to their private plane meant he would have to wait to leave. When he'd called earlier, they had said it would be completed late in the day. That wasn't an option. So commercial it would have to be.

Clothing rustled from fellow passengers as they too went through the scanners. Heels clicked, and conversation buzzed as people rushed to their gates in the busy airport. No beep sounded as he stepped around the metal detector and x-ray point. And there would not be any alerts, thanks to his badge paving the way for him to carry a weapon on the plane.

With a nod to the guard, he slid the bin that held his passport and ticket closer. Bending, he retrieved his carry-on suitcase, which had passed through the cameras without fail, probably without more than a cursory glance. *Stupid.* If he'd wanted to, he could have fixed all their homeland inadequacies. But that wasn't his focus. He had bigger plans, orders, which were almost within his grasp. If only Liv would come home.

A young boy ran from his mother, giggling as she chased him through the busy terminal. Her long, dark hair and bright smile reminded him of his own mother before everything had changed, before he'd learned his lot in life and the orchestrated path laid out before him.

Excitement shone in the young mother's eyes as she bent to her child and told him it was time to greet his father at the gate. When Alex was five years old, the concept of meeting his father had elated him. He had no recollection of laying eyes on the elusive man before then.

There were times during those early years when his mother had tried to take him to see Juan Carlos. For some reason, his grandmother had been set against the idea. She'd stopped his mother's attempt every single time, finding a loophole in his mother's plans to thwart her. He hadn't understood why. Now he did.

What she could not stop was the accidental meeting that had occurred when his father happened to be in town. Alex's small hand securely in his mother's, he walked out of a clothing store, packages in tow. His mother's fingers spasmed on his, and he jerked to a halt. A man and his son strolled toward them, the man's gaze locked onto his mother. There was something familiar about the man, and Alex's curiosity got the better of him.

"Who's that, Mama?"

She drew him closer to her body for a brief squeeze. "Your father, Alexander."

The man before him quirked his eyebrows, a small smile playing around his mouth. "Rita."

Pulled forward by his mom as she went to the man and kissed him, Alex tugged until she let go. He stood before a boy about his age, maybe a year older. Hatred shone in the boy's eyes, and Alex's spine stiffened.

His parents separated, their attention now on him and the other boy. With a quick turn of his head, Alex caught the shock on his mom's face before she hid it. Did she not know about the other boy?

"Hello, Alejandro," the man greeted. "This is your brother, Mateo."

Alex clutched his mother's leg, studying the boy opposite him. A brother? Squaring his shoulders, but not moving away from his mom, he mumbled a quiet hello. Identical brown eyes stared at him, and a slow sneer spread across the boy's face. After that, the boy ignored him. That had only been the beginning.

The jostling behind Alex brought his thoughts back to the present, and he moved along the narrow aisle on the plane to take his seat in first class. After stowing his case above, he belted in, and waited for the seats to fill before they taxied down the runway. With time to kill, he mused over the things his family had put him through over the years.

His grandmother had been the only one who'd wanted the best for him. Even his mother thought of him as a pawn, her ticket to a better life. In time, he'd learned what his father really was. All through his early years, his mother had sung Juan Carlos's praises. She gushed that Alex was the reason his father's interest remained and why he blessed them with so much, including buying them a beautiful home to live in. She didn't have to instruct or dance any longer at the Latin club, except for pleasure, and she had everything she ever wanted. Almost.

When his mother went on and on about his father, his grandmother usually left the room. She was getting up there in years, her body frail and not moving as fast as it used to. But she took care of him whenever his mother spent a long weekend away—with him, his father. Agitated questions swam like piranhas in his thoughts, but he held them back. His grandmother cautioned him, but in time, he would learn the answers.

Why didn't they live with his father? Why didn't he go to his father's house, ever? Why did the other boy, his *brother*, live there?

When he did find out, he wished he had not. The other boy was the legitimate son of Juan Carlos and lived in the same house. Everything his father had—his business, his home, expensive cars, money, gold-plated and diamond weapons, the control of the town, and so much more—would be left to his successor, not him. The unfairness burned inside him.

Unless… A chance remained to take it all, one that his mother drilled into him with every opportunity she got. The main idea came from his father, but his mother altered it in subtle ways to benefit him…them. And he had followed her carefully laid plans in exact detail, except one.

The baby.

The baby's conception had happened sooner than his mother, his father, and apparently, his brother, had agreed upon. To his father, a baby meant opportunity. His brother no doubt viewed anything related to Alex as a distraction from their father's attention. A risk. Even his wife seemed to pose a threat to Mateo. Sharing wasn't something his brother welcomed.

A memory jabbed his brain like a viper's deadly bite of a time when he'd visited his father at age sixteen. Alex had stood behind his father's house, his back to the bushes, while he faced Mateo.

"Why do you bother to come here?" Mateo sneered, his latest birthday present—a gold-plated handgun—dangling from his right hand. "You're nothing. No one would even miss you."

"Fuck off." The parted curtains closed again. Mateo's mother. She hated him too. "My father wanted me here; that's why I came."

Mateo lifted his gun and fired. The bullet had whizzed by Alex, narrowly missing his ear.

Alex ground the heels of his palms against his closed eyes, dispelling the memory. Mateo resented Alex's existence because it got in the way of his inheritance of an empire.

A part of Alex wished his grandmother still lived. Before she had passed, she gave him the brooch and told him of the secret compartment housed within the family heirloom. She'd said there may be a time he would need to use it and to pass it along to his future wife. It was something she hadn't trusted to her daughter. But she had told him there was goodness in him, not the greed that festered inside her daughter.

That's where she was wrong.

He thirsted.

He wanted.

And he took.

All the carefully laid plans to go to America, finish college, work his way up in his career, marry the right girl with the right connections, then reach his ultimate career goal just like his wife's father. A senator.

He shut his eyes to the flight attendant demonstrating preflight instructions and leaned back as the plane taxied to the runway, almost ready to take off. As they bumped along, he continued to ponder his future and the mistakes of his recent past.

His importance would exceed his brother's with the dual connections, the influence, and the ability to do what was needed. If only his brother's snitches hadn't gotten wind of Liv, of the baby, of their marriage. They had been watching.

They may have learned a few things, but thanks to Alex's grandmother, they didn't know about the bracelet Liv wore.

The last private conversation he'd had with Mateo had not gone well. Over ten years later, his brother's stinging words still rang in his ears. "You'll never have his love, respect, or business. You are nothing but a bastard-born pawn. It's my legacy."

Now he had to get to Liv before his brother did.

CHAPTER 31

*L*iv cupped her jewelry in her hand as she entered Liam's office. The ting of metal and gems against his wood desk rang with finality. Why she'd kept the necklace on after leaving Colombia was still a mystery to her. Well, it was probably because she hadn't been ready to let Alex go completely. She was now. With a tug, she broke the delicate chain. The bracelet that held Alex's grandmother's brooch was the only piece of jewelry that remained on her body. That she needed help getting off later. It was enough to unburden herself by parting with the rest of her jewelry.

Liam disconnected his call, set down his cell, and looked at her, waiting.

The knot in her throat made it impossible to speak. After clearing her throat, she confided to him what had taken her days to admit to herself. "I can't keep pretending to myself that Alex is undercover." She wrung her hands. "I mean, I get now he's not. I have for a while, but I wasn't ready to fully move on until now. The things that happened with his family were too real."

Liam didn't say anything, merely waited for her to continue. He was right. There was more she needed to get out, so much more. If only Alex was here for her to say it to. However, Liam would do.

"I know I told you Alex kept his business separate. I liked our happy little bubble, so I didn't push to change anything. Expect when my parents intervened. But I don't think they really wanted me to be a part of the intricate workings, the gory details, and the emotional downfalls Alex waded through in his job on a daily basis. The life of a detective is not always an easy one. What they wanted me to involve myself in was his rise to the Senate. To a degree, I did. He was close. So very close." She swept her hand as if waving the words away. "That's not important here. What matters is how he never treated me differently while we were dating or the first year of our marriage. Not until I told him I was pregnant with our child."

Liam stood, went around his desk, eliminating the space between them, and leaned against it in front of her.

"Everything changed in that moment." The memory of Alex's anger and the sound of the bottle smashing against their backsplash erupted in her mind. "He was in a panic, mumbling something about it not being time. When he got himself under control, he talked to me about a vacation and also finally meeting his mom. So we went. That was the first time I learned about his father. That he was known, alive."

Liam's gaze turned wary. "Juan Carlos isn't listed on his birth certificate."

"Yes, that's right."

"There would have been a reason for that. If he had a plan, and I firmly believe he did, that gave him the anonymity to accomplish what his family desired. I looked over Alex's career in great detail. It was impressive. Liv, he dismantled his father's competition in the States. It looks as if he was making way for the Ramirez cartel. My best guess, due to the groundwork he'd laid, when their infiltration was slotted to happen would be by the time Alex rose to the Senate and no longer pursued drug trafficking and detective work."

She gritted her teeth with the full knowledge of being used. Lies, so many of them, by people who'd supposedly loved her. All her life. Her parents and Alex had lied to her. Would her future also be false?

"I'm sorry to tell you that, Liv. I understand——"

"No, you don't. Not really. I knew the issues with my parents, what my worth to them was, but Alex? He was supposed to be mine. Instead, he used me for what he could gain a hundred times worse than anything my parents ever did." She squared her shoulders and put on a brave face. That was the thing with pretending—soon, it would not be a farce anymore. And she was close to being okay. Once she and Alex finalized the divorce and she took further steps to move on with her life the way *she* wanted to live it, she would be. That, she felt ready to do.

Liam reached behind him and scooped up the butterfly necklace and her wedding rings. "What would you like me to do with these?"

"Get rid of them." She extended her arm with the difficult-to-remove bracelet. "And I need help with this one." The words were said in raw sincerity, even though she couldn't look at him. Did she want it off right now?

When she did, the frown that pulled Liam's mouth down echoed the one in her heart. "I'll put them in the safe for you. There will be a time when you're ready to fully let go of them. I don't think this is it." He lifted a hand to stop her words. "I know you're hurt, done with the lies, and want to move on. Don't rush yourself. We'll deal with one thing at a time, Liv. The first is to make sure you're safe and that Alex lets go."

She dropped her arm and offered him a small smile, not ready to admit he was right. Accepting his hand, she laced her fingers with his and followed him out of the office. His hand enveloped hers. She liked it. Same with the rough callouses and sureness of his grip. The land and his home were beautiful, and the change was welcome—change she would make permanent. If not there, then somewhere else like it. There was no way she would return to her life in New York. She had plenty of money with the trust from her parents and their full fortune that she'd received after their death. Even though she did not need to work, she would. Sculpting was a part of her.

Maybe Maine would be a nice change of scenery. She could buy a house somewhere and enjoy a quieter existence. The galleries that displayed her artwork would continue to do so. All she needed to do was ship her pieces to them. The life she was expected to live in New York and the people she had to associate with were never her thing. Rachel was more her type, and Liv missed her sorely.

"Let's go find Jo and go over the drills. I don't think we have long until we have company."

CHAPTER 32

ALEX

*T*he door slammed behind Alex. The chair closest to him received a solid kick. *Fuck the others on the hotel floor.* He couldn't care less if he disturbed them. The quaint Victorian inn overlooking Maine's coast wasn't booked for the breathtaking view, charm, or ratings. It was a necessity, a stop along the way to getting his wife back whole and alive.

The beauty of the area was not completely lost on him. He scrubbed his hand over his scruffy face. Liv would love Maine. The inn boasted a grand deck that wrapped around most of the old home. He envisioned how the lights would blaze from the many windows in the dark, the single dormered one at the top acting like a beacon. The place was beautiful, and she would have instantly fallen in love. His heart sank as he remembered he'd planned to surprise her with a trip here for their anniversary, before she'd told him about the baby and turned his world upside down, and not in a good way.

Alex tossed the heavy case on the bed with a thud. It bounced once before lying still. He reached into the pocket of his black Armani pants and pulled out both phones. One he turned off and removed the battery. There was no way he would risk the microphone or the camera being used against him. With his work phone securely disabled, he thumbed through the coded contacts on his other phone.

Bristling with tension and the need to act, he forced himself to find out where the pieces had fallen while he'd chased his missing wife to their home in New York, only to find she'd never returned. He'd lost valuable time, sort of. The news painted a picture of a grieving and desperate husband. *True.* And it focused on the lie centered on his time and treatment in the hands of the Ramirez organization. He'd claimed he escaped. *Not even close.*

His real escape, planned to unfold in the future, was now compromised.

He pushed the number he wanted and lifted the phone to his ear. His father's direct line rang, and his impatience bristled as he itched to be on his way to get Liv. *Come on, answer.* Grinding his teeth, he rubbed the back of his neck raw with his free hand. When Juan Carlos answered, a mixture of relief, fear, and anger surged in a dangerous cocktail.

"I took care of loose ends in the States and am on my way to retrieve Liv. She'll return home with me, where we'll proceed as we did before our visit. Everything will go as planned."

"That's no longer an option. Spin her death however it will benefit the career laid out for you. This little hiccup may even help gain sympathy and escalate your political rise. Go home and stick to the original timeline."

Fuck!

He waited a beat, mentally counting to slow his volcanic

rage. "There's no need. I'm here to collect Liv. I'll keep the schedule *with* her. It's less messy."

"No. Mateo is there to handle your loose end."

She is not expendable. Veins in his neck and temple throbbed. "Liv is mine to deal with!" Not Mateo's to toy with...*and slowly kill.*

Before he could damage the progress he'd made with his father over the years, he hung up and threw the phone on the bed. It bounced several times only to land, undamaged, on the floor. *Shit!* His scalp stung from thrusting his hands through his hair and yanking on the strands.

Mateo would *not* interfere with his life. His destiny. *His wife.*

Alex's mind raced. Mateo was either on his way or already there. *What can I do?* He paced back and forth in front of the hotel bed. As Alex made one last pivot to resume his tread in the opposite direction, the cell phone that had bounced off the bed and landed on the floor caught his attention.

He smacked himself in the forehead. *I can't believe I didn't think of that.* He retrieved the thankfully intact phone and thumbed through the coded contacts until he found his informant, David, within Mateo's men. He shot off a quick text and dropped on the bed to wait. Not even a minute later, a reply came through about Mateo and his team's pending ETA.

An hour.

Mother fucking shit! He tore open his suitcase, dumped his clothes out, and popped the hidden compartment open, where his guns, ammo, and knives hid. Checking the cartridges in his gun, he shoved the extra ones in pockets and strapped the two knives on either side of his calves. His father and brother's vision for the future could go to hell. It was time for him to take charge and teach his brother a lesson.

And to save Liv.

~

THE SUV ALEX RENTED BUMPED OVER THE WINDING COASTAL road that would take him near the winery. As he drove, his mind wandered to one of the first times he'd visited his father's home. Mateo had been there. No matter how much he tried to push the memory away, it came of its own volition.

Alex swatted an insect buzzing around his face. The heat from the sun blazed down on their heads as Alex walked behind his brother, Mateo.

He hadn't wanted to come, not really. His dad, whom he didn't really know, had requested he come for a visit. At eight years old, he didn't have a say in leaving his home when his mom said it was time to go.

Taking a step to the side, he continued to follow Mateo through the fields—coca fields. Mines littered the outskirts to keep unwanted trespassers away. He tried his best to step in the same spots Mateo did. If he didn't, he ran the risk of an explosion, one where he could lose his legs, if not his life.

Voices carried from ahead, and he squinted to see what they were doing under the lean-to. A man used a long stick to stir something in a metal drum. Others stomped around a squared-off area, trampling on the leaves underfoot.

Mateo stopped, and Alex clipped the back of his shoulder. Smirking, Mateo broke off a long, green leaf and offered it to him. Alex took it from his hand, unsure what he was supposed to do.

"Eat it. Take a bite."

He didn't trust his half brother but couldn't figure out how taking a bite of a leaf would be bad. Lifting it to his mouth, he tore a piece of it off with his teeth and chewed on the bitter, fibrous plant. Scrunching up his face, he spit it on the ground and dropped the leaf. Brows furrowed, he balled his fists and glared at Mateo's laughing face. One punch. If he didn't get that his older brother would beat him into a pulp, he would do it.

"You're just like them." Mateo indicated the workers in the field. "Necessary, but replaceable. You'll never be like me. This, everything my father owns, will be mine. You're nothing." He had spat on the ground by Alex's feet, shoved him out of the way, and walked in the opposite direction to Juan Carlos's home.

With a growl, Alex tore himself out of the childhood memory. Mateo was right. Alex never should have allowed them to manipulate him. This time, he would turn the tables on his brother.

CHAPTER 33

"**M**orning, Liv." Joslyn smiled, ushering her further into the kitchen. "Have a seat and some coffee with me."

Just the thought of sitting at the kitchen table with Joslyn made her miss Rachel that much more, but she needed some girl time. Liam had sensed it too, or maybe he was afraid of another female meltdown, and had suggested she seek Joslyn out. So she had.

She and Joslyn were such opposites in looks. Jo embodied the essence of a spring day, with her platinum hair and dainty features, while Liv contrasted with darker tones. Despite Jo's diminutive five feet two, her mere presence filled the room and made it clear that she could go toe to toe with anyone. Liv liked that about her. According to Liam, Jo's role was to ensure that everyone had an extra set of eyes on the approaching enemy. She did that by staying on the roof and monitoring the drone.

Liv's heart skipped a beat at the thought of Alex being included in that group of enemies. The realistic part of her understood the way it had to be. Even though she longed to hide behind the assumption that he played both sides and worked undercover, she knew deep down that wasn't the case.

Then when Liam had pieced together the puzzle for her of where and why Alex grew up apart from his father, the lack of legal connection to Juan Carlos's empire, his strategic marriage to her, and access to her father and their friends, her final hope that he was working undercover had disintegrated.

Joslyn's smile eased Liv's bubbling anxiety one step further, and she flashed a smile of her own. The sounds of video games and good-natured teasing from the teens trickled into the kitchen, where their mom sat, coffee cup in hand.

Liv fixed herself a cup and joined Jo. "Your kids get along so well. That seems a little unusual from my experience, especially an older boy with his younger sister."

"Yeah, there are moments they don't. With two highly trained teens, that leads to a recipe for disaster now and then, but you're right. They are really close. Makes sense with every-thing they went through." She waved her hand. "That's a topic for another day. How are you doing?"

Liv lifted a shoulder and let it fall. "I'm all right." A myriad of emotions played through her mind. "Alex will be coming soon, and I'm conflicted. I've talked to Liam about my feelings so much that I'm surprised the man doesn't lock himself in his office or flat out leave the house."

Joslyn chuckled. "Deeper conversation can make the toughest man run for the hills, and Liam's pretty alpha." She snickered. "Ya know, I see the way he looks at you." She held up her hand. "Don't misunderstand me. You're going through a difficult and confusing time. Just understand Liam can handle way more than you think, despite the instant flash of panic at the thought of tears or emotions. Matt's a big softie when it comes to me and the kids too."

With another sip, Liv asked one of the questions that burned inside her. "There's so many variables with Alex and his involvement in the Ramirez cartel." She met Joslyn's gaze with a tortured whisper. "I know what I have to do, and I'm letting Alex go. It's not an overnight thing, to be able to shut my emotions off when I'm still married to the man. I mean, it's easier since he's done terrible things. God, he killed my best friend. How could I love someone like that? Then there's Liam. I've come to see him as a friend. It's nice. And while I'm grateful for his support, when this is all sorted, I want to stand on my own two feet."

Leaning back in the chair, Joslyn nodded. "It's incredibly difficult sifting through all that."

Air rushed from Liv's lungs. "It is, and it doesn't change the fact that I love Alex in some twisted way. Not the person he's revealed himself to be but the man I used to know. We built a great life together. Well, apparently it's pretty unhealthy, just like my parents' marriage was, based on secrets. In a way, the cycle repeated itself. Still, my parents would never wish Alex's ambitions, his secrets, on me." She grimaced. "Well, that's not entirely true. Alex's goals were in line with their expectations. But he let me lead the life I wanted and mostly kept that part separate. Now I get it. His family had plans of their own for him, and I'm coming to understand he must share them."

Joslyn took another sip of coffee, her attention never wavering as Liv gathered her thoughts. "I'm letting him go, piece by piece. With my…accident at his family's home, a large portion is just numb."

"You'll heal. The key is finding something to help you cope and leaning on those who care about you. I can tell you that Liam does. I've known him for a while now, and he's stronger than you think. Lean on him." Her eyes narrowed, and her gaze pierced Liv. "You said accident?"

"Oh." The sharp pain she'd lived with since then had dulled

enough over the past few days that she could answer without breaking down. "I tumbled down a flight of stairs and lost..." She waved the last of the sentence away when understanding flashed across Joslyn's face. There was no reason elaborating on *how* she fell; it wasn't relevant to their discussion. When Joslyn reached across the table and squeezed her hand, Liv let go of even more discomfort. Still, she preferred to change the subject, and Joslyn let her.

"Tell me about the kids. You said they're fully yours, but I sense there's more to the story." She fought the yearning inside her that the mere mention of children evoked. Someday, she would have another chance.

"They had a rough beginning. Their parents..." Joslyn shook her head and frowned. "At the time, I was an agent for the FBI, and their parents were my targets. The things those two witnessed, experienced... But life's weird like that. Sometimes something you never thought you'd want, that you didn't think you could do, falls in your lap. That's sort of what happened, and honestly, my life is better for it. They're pretty amazing. Before, I didn't want anything to do with having a family. I worked well on my own. They changed that. So did Matt."

Joslyn's face lit up as she spoke of her family, and Liv shoved aside her envy. "You all seem so perfect together."

"We're happy but far from perfect." Joslyn chuckled. "They have gone through so much in their young lives, and it's only made them stronger. That's part of why they're so close. I'm fortunate that Matt came into my life when he did. Dylan needed a male role model, and we couldn't have found a better one than Matt."

"I'm glad it worked out so well for you all."

"Liv, my point is that sometimes things happen for a reason. Even terrible ones. There's always another door, and it's usually the one you're meant to go through."

She nodded, having similar beliefs.

"Go ahead and rely on Liam. After the next twenty-four hours, you'll see all of him. There'll be no secrets, no worries."

Fear settled in her gut. "Because Alex will be here." *Any hour. Same with the cartel—any minute or any hour.*

"Yes, and he won't be alone."

"No, he won't, but I'm not scared of him. It's his brother that worries me. Mateo commands a small army of his own. For some reason, I'm caught in the middle of Alex and Mateo's battle for power. I'm the pawn."

CHAPTER 34

"J've got movement," Jack broadcasted through their earpieces from on the roof. Not too long ago, they'd received word from Trev, who took the harbor stakeout. Men were headed their way. Now, with Jack's sighting, the reality of the situation hit her like a truck. Liv's breath sawed in and out, and her grip tightened on the banister, her gaze darting around for anyone—Joslyn, the kids, Liam.

Jack's voice commanded they take action. "Liv, Jilly, and Dylan, head down to the secured room now." *Where's Liam?* "Jo, take my position. I'm going to ground."

Liv couldn't move. The only thought playing like a loop in her head was that Alex might be there. Things needed to be said between them, face to face. Lost in thought, Liv paused until she caught a glimpse of Jilly's dark-blond hair as she sped to the kitchen from the living room. The touch at Liv's elbow made her jump and whirl around. Dylan stood slightly behind her, his lips pressed together in a grim line.

"We need to go."

She reacted to his quiet command. Still so young, but his

tone and demeanor belied his youth. Jilly clutched the secret doorway at the opening to the lower level, waiting for them. Dylan's frown deepened, and he scolded his sister. "Why are you waiting? You should have headed down as soon as Jack gave the order."

Jilly rolled her eyes before she led the way downstairs. Locks slid into place, and she dropped a steel barricade rod across the door. Liv looked behind her. Was that there before?

Dylan winked. "Just a precaution. It's doubtful they'll get into the house."

Liv took a stuttered step into the cavernous space. Jilly and Dylan walked with purpose to the cabinet that housed weapons. Dylan took out guns, ammo, and knives and distributed them between him and his sister. He took another gun and extra clip from the cabinet and handed it to Liv. It was the 9-millimeter Liam had shown her how to use. He must have told Dylan which one to give her.

"The safety is on, but I loaded it for you. Keep this on you, okay?"

She nodded, stunned at the change that came over the teens. They were too young, in her opinion, to handle the situation she'd brought them into with calm acceptance. How was it possible that they handled weapons with such ease and took charge in a way that would rival almost all the adults she knew?

Jilly jogged across the open area to a room filled with computer equipment and a wall of monitors. She clicked on the light and turned on all the screens. Without realizing it, Liv found herself in the doorway, glued to the pictures on the wall. The images were of the vineyard, all angles of the outside and inside of the house, both levels, and even an aerial view.

Jilly pressed the button on her earpiece. "Screens are up."

Dylan did the same, their words connected to the earpieces they all wore. "Armed." Dylan's hands settled on her shoulders, and he maneuvered her into one of the chairs. "You can sit here and monitor the house. If you see anything, report it in, okay?"

Liv nodded, but she struggled to tear her gaze from the monitor in front of Dylan, specifically, the three SUVs parked outside the gate. Each held eight—a total of twenty-four—dangerous men against Liam and two other men, not counting Joslyn, the teens, and herself.

She watched in horror as Ramirez cartel members streamed through the vineyard with guns raised.

"How?" She swallowed the lump in her throat. "How will we…" Terror gripped her and froze her words before they formed. It would be a slaughter.

Jilly reached over and squeezed her shaking hand. "This is a piece of cake. Don't worry."

Liv turned to Jilly. "There's too many of them."

"Nah. They can handle this. If they need us, we'll go up."

"Not you, though," Dylan chimed in. "You'll be our eyes down here. Jack isn't watching the monitors any longer, and we need someone on them. That would be your job."

"But this isn't your fight. If anything happened to you… I don't think I can do this." Liv stood and started for the door.

"No, no, no," Jilly chanted as she grabbed Liv's arm and Dylan blocked the way. "We're a team, which is pretty freaking cool. The others have been doing this for as long as we've known them. They've totally got this. Promise."

"Where is Jo? Your mom?"

Dylan brushed off the question without a care. "She's on the roof with an M2010."

Jilly looked back at Liv and rolled her eyes. "Dylan is such a boy." At his glare, she laughed. "Why would she know what that means?" She redirected her attention back to Liv. "It's a sharpshooter. Mom's a great shot. Well, if we had Hawk here, she'd be on the ground, in the action, in a heartbeat."

"Who's Hawk?"

"Oh, he's an amazing sharpshooter. Dad says he's the best he's ever seen. But he's mainly on the other team." Jilly's eyes sparkled before she turned back to the monitors.

Again, Dylan ushered Liv to her seat while her head spun.

"They go out on missions sometimes. This is nothing. Trust us. Turning yourself in will only cause more problems." Dylan pointed to one of the outside monitors. "Look at the way the cartel members move, their guns. Do you really think those men will leave anyone who lives here alone, even if you tried to turn yourself in to them?"

No, he was right. They were ruthless. She'd seen it firsthand when she had docked with Alex's brother and father. His family would kill them all for aiding her. "I made a mistake. I never should have come here." Her body trembled with the weight of the lives of the people she had come to care about. "Now you're all marked. They won't stop."

"Not going to happen," Dylan answered, his attention back on the monitors. He pressed the button again and spoke to their team. "They split into six groups, all entering through the vineyard from the front and sides of the house. Three men downed by trip wires. Arrival approximately ten minutes. New lone wolf from the rear."

What? Squinting, she scrutinized the monitors to see what Dylan was talking about but only saw a group of men, not one. A burst of speed snagged her focus, and she watched in awe as Jack jumped up from a hiding space, virtually undetectable, to take down three men. The fourth, he disarmed and fought. It didn't take long.

Liam executed a similar tactic, eliminating three, then two more, in fast succession. On another monitor, Liv watched as men fell, clean shots to the head and chest taking them down. When a few of their buddies noticed the direction they took fire from, they gave up stealth and aimed their machine guns at the roof, spitting bullets in a deadly spray. Matt sprinted behind them, threw a knife at one, fired a shot at another, then engaged in hand to hand with the remaining thug. Fast and efficient, Liam's team advanced. She understood what Jilly and Dylan meant, but it still didn't ease her guilt for putting them in danger or her worry for Alex.

Her racing heart never got a chance to settle because she shifted to the rear monitor, where a man was making his way through the trees. There was no mistaking who it was. *Alex.*

She mimicked what the teens did when they spoke to their group. "The rear is Alex." She took a breath and scanned the other monitors. "I think his brother's leading the group from the front, by the blueberries."

"Thanks for the identifiers." Liam's voice braced her.

Liv rose from her seat and paced. Dylan and Jilly tapped keys and made one of the other screens pan closer. When she saw Mateo, her heart skipped a beat. He split from his group and dashed to the side of the house, toward Alex. What did that mean? Were they working together?

After meeting Mateo, her worst nightmare had been learning Alex was related to him and could potentially have some similar characteristics she had not yet seen.

Her attention split between the monitors, and she watched in horror as Matt neared the center group at a full sprint. He stopped maybe twenty feet from them, crouched down, and took aim. He fired no shots but held still, his whispered words telecasting to the team. "In position."

Alex stopped and faced the direction Mateo approached.

Jack looped behind another cluster of cartel members coming in fast from the left, the group Mateo had abandoned. Mateo changed direction, but the men following him did not. Liv flipped her attention back to Alex, who stood still. Was he waiting to rendezvous with Mateo? She alternated from watching Alex to Mateo. Would Alex agree to this ambush?

With Jo on the roof and Matt and Jack out front, engaging three groups of armed men, Liv looked for Liam. *There!* Slipping around the house on the opposite side of Mateo, he focused on Alex, who was obstructed from Liam's line of sight by the trees.

CHAPTER 35

$\mathcal{N}$ ot able to watch anymore, she backed away. Jilly and Dylan didn't notice. They assumed she sat, mute, behind them. As soon as she was clear of their sight, she made her way up the flight of stairs, unlocked the steel bolt, and slipped through. Her breath came in quick pants as she raced through the house to the back. With her hand on the slider, she pressed the button on her earpiece. "Dylan and Jilly, lock the door at the top of the stairs." Then she walked outside to the cursing of the boy who now tracked her escape on the monitors.

Curses rang in her ears as the team realized what she'd done. It didn't matter. Her focus remained on Alex. If she could get to him before Mateo, she would make him explain. The need for answers burned within her. With so many of the cartel there, Alex's prior unwillingness to let her leave Colombia, and his urgent pleas for her to come home, she needed to find out what her importance to him was in terms of the organization. When they'd spoken the last two times, she had thought he only wanted things to return to how they were. Now, with the show of force spreading across the farm and Liam's words ringing in her ears, her suspicions ran wild.

In the back of her mind, she wondered if Alex knew who'd pushed her. Had he approved? He hadn't wanted children, not for a long time, if at all, and his reaction when she'd told him about her pregnancy had been far from positive.

Wind tugged at her hair, and with one hand, she tucked it behind an ear while she scanned the backyard. As fast as she could, she ran through the garden and across the sprawling lawn, until she neared the thick trees on the back of the property. She had time. The gun weighed heavily in her hand, and so did her resolve. Alex had killed her best friend and probably her parents too. He would answer her.

With a glance over her shoulder, she noticed Liam sprinting toward her, a good fifty feet away. She didn't dare look in the other direction, where Mateo would come from.

Several feet from her, Alex emerged from a cluster of trees, gun in hand. His eyes widened when he caught sight of her. With his free hand, he urgently gestured for her to move aside as he raised his gun. Oh God, Liam!

In that moment, realization slammed into her. She cared about Liam more than she'd thought. He made her laugh, feel safe.

Tears welled; the wind tugged at them and whipped them from the corner of her eyes. "No, Alex!" She shifted in front of the path of his gun, blocking his line of sight to Liam. With a steady hand, she raised her weapon and aimed it at his chest.

"Shit, Olivia!" Alex angled his weapon to the left, away from Liam. His words growled through the dwindling distance separating them. His fierce glare only boosted her conviction to reach him. He owed her answers.

Heart in her throat, she picked up her speed, sparing a quick glance over her shoulder to where Alex aimed his weapon.

Mateo. He was still too far away. She and Alex would have a few moments until they were in shooting range. Then things would escalate even more.

Not bothering to check how far away Liam was, she met Alex at the line of trees. She held the gun between them in a steady grip.

"Put that away," Alex snapped, his sight trained over her shoulder and to the left. He'd deemed Mateo the bigger threat over Liam, and her. That told her so much.

With a roar, he grabbed her shoulders and flipped their positions. Off balance, she jerked forward, like a ragdoll. Alex's back now faced Liam, while hers slammed into the tree. Close, he was too close. Alex pressed his body to hers. With her view blocked, she clenched her jaw at how his grip dug into her. She struggled to shift the gun wedged between their bodies, pointing up.

"Liv." The tortured sound of his voice almost gutted her. He crushed her to his chest, buried his face against the top of her head, and inhaled. "So worried. Why didn't you come home?"

Nausea punched her in the stomach. "I couldn't." *You're a killer.* Straightening her wrist, she shoved the barrel at his chest. "You owe me, Alex. Tell me why. The baby. Your father and brother. A cartel! And, oh my God, Alex, Rachel."

With a quick twist of his hand, he yanked her weapon free of his chest, forcing the angle down. "Babe, you have a million reasons to hate me." His mouth pressed into a stubborn line. "Just hear me out for a minute." He took her face in his hands, the flat of his gun pressing on one side, and brushed a kiss on her forehead. "I would have answered them, or as many as I could, if you'd only come home."

Anger simmered, and her body trembled. His touch was a reminder of what else he'd killed. Time dwindled. Soon Liam and Mateo would be on them. The stiffening in Alex's body told her he was aware too.

The whirlwind of her thoughts rushed her. None of them were good. She and Alex had a past, a history. No matter how much she despised him, a part of her still loved him. She deserved a moment or two to hear him out, to learn why he'd shattered their lives. That was all they had left.

"Let's go, Liv. There's a small window for us to escape. If we take it now, we can leave and go back to what we had. You liked our life, didn't you?"

Her pulse quickened. "That was never the issue. You know what was. From the moment I told you about our baby, you changed. Everything did."

The breath seemed to burst out of him, and a small tremor in his hands ran against her cheeks before they stilled. "Babe, you were it for me. My life, my salvation. I tried to, wanted to, give you everything."

"I know." She allowed the veil of her fury to part for that one response. "There are too many questions, and I need answers. There's no way I can risk the possibility of interaction with your family. They're murderers, Alex. And you…" She choked on what he did to Rachel, to her parents.

Smells and sounds came and went with the awareness of her surroundings. The urgency of the situation pushed her to make him talk. The pungent scent of pines gave the illusion of safety, of time. But they weren't safe, and they didn't have time. Liam rushed to save her from her husband. More terrifying than anything else, Mateo neared.

Wind rustled through the trees, once more making her aware of both men pursuing them.

Dizziness swept over her from the sadness swimming in Alex's eyes. "I'm sorry, Liv. For not shielding you better, for bringing you into this life, for risking your safety and happiness." He dropped his forehead to hers.

The crunch of pine needles echoed like drums in her ears. Shots rang from both directions. Her heart pounded against her ribs.

"I can't answer your questions, babe. It's too late." His fingers toyed with the bracelet on her wrist, the only thing she wore from him. "Look inside. I've given you the answers you need." When he drew back, his face lost the desperation and longing that pulled his features taut. Only sadness, acceptance, and a chilling resolve remained. "You were supposed to be my salvation."

She shook her head no. He'd told her what she meant to him in his words, his touch, but she couldn't do it, not anymore. "I thought you were mine, but I was wrong, Alex. I'm my own."

Bullets rained all around them, and Alex pressed her tightly against the tree, exposing his body instead. The rough bark scraped her skin. His arm extended, the gun held steady. Loud pops and whizzing noises from Alex's gun and return fire filled the air. When Liv registered the searing thud of flesh being hit so closely to her, she released the scream she'd held. Alex's body jerked into hers repeatedly with each bullet, the grunt of pain the only sound he emitted.

"Doesn't matter anymore, Alex," Mateo shouted. "She's not needed, just as the baby wasn't." He raised his gun again. "Neither are you."

"Mother fucking shit, you did it. You pushed her." Furious, Alex took a step away from her, dropped his empty cartridge, slammed another one home, and started shooting again with renewed fervor.

To her horror, blood seeped from Alex's back and shoulder. He stood strong, seemingly impervious to the damage he endured.

More bullets whizzed by them. Not aiming at them but at Mateo. *Liam.* She peeked around Alex, who'd stepped away from her enough to get a better shot, but he remained a human shield between her and Mateo.

Liv pointed her gun around Alex and squeezed the trigger. She missed. In between her and Alex's shots, more rang out. *Liam.* His aim was true, and Mateo jerked back as bullets riddled his chest. Still, he kept coming.

Alex wavered on his feet. His whispered words of love for Liv rang in her ears as he crumpled to the ground, ripping out her heart all over again. The finality of his death stained her soul. She dropped to her knees, an anguished scream filling the air around them.

Gunshots continued to fill the air. She no longer cared. Mateo neared, and it didn't matter, not anymore. The thump of a body, Mateo's, hitting the ground a few feet away, didn't draw her gaze, nor did the rustling sounds of him getting back up, determined to reach her. Only the sight of Alex, lying in a pool of his blood, held her attention.

With shaking hands, she turned him over. *So much blood.* Sobs shook her, and she fell over his still body. Regret, anger, and sadness collided. Warm stickiness coated her, the iron smell filling her nose with each breath. Nothing mattered. Not now.

Let Mateo come for her.

If he reached her, she would make him pay. Her grip on her gun tightened with resolve.

Strong hands gripped her shoulders and lifted her to her feet. The gun left her hand as Liam crushed her in a hug. Words were spoken, to her, to the others. They made no sense. The only thing that did was his embrace. In a movement that had her world spinning all over again, he lifted her to his chest, and she found herself cradled against him. Wind whipped her hair as he ran back to the house. "Cover us" were the only words that registered.

Later, she understood he'd requested cover as they ran. Most of the team rushed to their aid, as the threat had been neutralized everywhere else on the property. Now all she could do was sob in Liam's arms. With each step, she worried about the burden she'd placed on him. Popping her eyes open, she ignored the streaming tears and did her best to be another lookout for him.

"Dylan, take the roof," Liam said. "I've got her, going to home. Jilly, keep watch where you are."

Her body shifted as Liam pulled back the slider, brought them inside, and slammed it shut behind them. Their pace slowed as he carried her upstairs and into a large bathroom.

"Are you hurt?"

She felt dead inside, and his comment made no sense. *So much death.* Even though she'd let go of Alex, she'd lost everyone that had been a part of her life, her past. "Everywhere," she whispered.

Liam swore, turned on the water, and put her under it, fully clothed.

Slowly, her eyelids shut, unable to watch the sight of Alex's blood turning the water pink and trickling down the drain. She just needed a little time to deal with the shock of Alex dying, of all she'd lost. Right now, she was so very tired.

"I don't see any bullet holes, Liv. Are you hurt anywhere?"

Her head lulled forward, thumping into his solid chest. The softness of his T-shirt separated her forehead from his skin. She was so grateful for Liam's friendship, his kindness. He lifted and held her in the shower before she fell. The warm water rushed over her, slowing the shivers that chattered her teeth.

Blinking, she looked around, her gaze again following the direction of the water. Liam ran the showerhead over her, and the pink-tinged water acted like a punch to her stomach. Nausea hit hard, and she threw up, all over both of them.

Liam didn't say one word. He just continued to hold her, even when she was coated in blood and puke while she cried. Minutes passed as he stroked her back, and slowly, she relaxed enough for him to wash both of them off. The water shut off, and he covered her body with a towel. He squeezed her hair out and wrapped another around her head. He helped her to sit before he left for a moment. When he came back, he pushed a shirt and a pair of sweats into her hands then tilted her head up so she would look at him.

"Can you change? Get out of those wet clothes and put these on?" When she nodded, he left, closing the door behind him.

She struggled with her wet clothes, finally getting them off and tossing them into the shower. After she pulled on the sweats, she cinched the drawstring to accommodate her smaller waist and rolled the pants legs over and over until her feet peeked through the openings.

At Liam's soft knock on the door, she told him she was dressed. When he came in, he was no longer dripping wet. He'd changed into dry clothes in the other room. He lifted her once more, ignoring her protests that she could walk, and carried her to the large bed, where he settled her under the covers. The bed dipped, and he lay down next to her, taking her in his arms. No words were spoken. He simply held her.

Exhausted, she fell asleep in his arms.

CHAPTER 36

*B*irds chirped outside the window, their sound pulling Liv from sleep, and she blinked her unfocused eyes in the soft rays of sunlight. How long had she been out? Extending her hand, she reached to the indented spot next to her. It was cool to her touch, and she realized Liam had left some time ago.

Yesterday remained a dull ache in her thoughts as she rose and showered. She wanted to make sure everyone was okay and thank them for helping her.

Pulling the towel from her damp hair, she turned her head, curious about the room she'd rested in. There was no mistaking the masculine touch in the various shades of gray and white. The bed she'd spent the night in was king size. On the opposite wall hung a picture taken at dusk. She stepped closer to look at the print of rippling, inky water and a worn stretch of dock. At the end was a tethered boat. Bending, she peered at a silhouette shot of five men and one woman on a hill. A small smile pulled at Liv's mouth as she recognized a few of them from their stance and outline alone.

Without anything else to distract her, the impact of everything that had happened yesterday rolled through her like a slow-moving freight train, and she dropped onto the bed. It made sense now. Well, most of it. There were a few things about her life with Alex she didn't understand.

She choked back a sob. She'd loved him, the man he had been, not the one she'd come to learn of. And he'd loved her in his way, as much as he'd been capable of with the borrowed existence he'd had. Her time with him and his family had challenged her conviction and given her a glimpse into a warped world.

In the end, he'd been a puppet to his father's whims. It had cost her dearly. For that, she had come to accept his death. However, she wasn't heartless. All the loss, especially Rachel and her parents, left her scarred.

You're my salvation. Alex's whispered words played like a record in her mind. She believed he'd meant that. But his family ties were so much stronger. If he'd made it to the Senate without her pregnancy, would their outcome have turned out differently? Would he have been a better person rather than a murderer?

Somehow, she believed he would have kept her and their child safe, free from his brother and father. He would have if he hadn't fallen into the same pattern he had been thrust into. His mother had traded in the life of her son to ensure one of luxury for herself. And his father had used Alex to pave the way in the States for his organization to move in and take over.

The competition between him and his brother for a father's love and respect had eaten at him like a cancer. As a child, Alex hadn't stood a chance. As a young man, he'd learned to spread his wings. Finally, as a man, he had pledged most of himself to his family, except for the life he'd carved out with her. The small things he had done told her she'd meant more to him than the plan his family had concocted. If she hadn't truly mattered, he too would have pushed her for constant connections as her parents had. He would have involved her in the darker side of his world. And he would have killed her. But he didn't.

In the end, they'd both been used as pawns. If she'd learned the truth under different circumstances, she never would have allowed it. That was, if she could have gone against his family.

In her heart, she liked to think Alex would have saved them, kept them from the evil waiting in Colombia, possibly cut ties. She had to believe it.

God, she'd loved Alex—the version of the man she'd married, not the one tangled in his family's web. She shivered with the realization that she was a widow. Life would be different, reinvented. That part, she longed for.

The sound of the door opening drew her from her thoughts, and she swiped the few tears from her cheeks that escaped. Liam walked in, holding a steaming mug of coffee and a bowl. His lips pulled up in a crooked grin. "I brought you breakfast. Coffee and some blueberries over yogurt, sort of our specialty around here."

The bed dipped as he sat next to her. Shifting to a sitting position, she accepted the drink. He put the yogurt on the bedside table.

Guilt and pain flared bright. "Is… " She couldn't finish her thought. The image of blood and dead bodies littering the ground wasn't a pleasant one. By the void in Liam's expression, he understood.

"Yes. The FBI was called right away. They sent a cleanup crew."

With a nod, she accepted that it was over, she hoped.

Twisting the bracelet that held the brooch around her wrist, she told Liam what gnawed inside her. "The last words he heard from me weren't kind. I rejected him. And he…he told me he loved me." She swayed, and he took the coffee from her hand.

Strong arms surrounded her, and she pressed her cheek against his chest. He held her until she calmed. Time moved slowly, and she stayed in his embrace, a temporary numbness seeping into her veins. This man had come to mean a great deal to her.

"Did you—were you able to find anything out?" she asked.

"Yes."

When Liam's deep voice rumbled, her fingers tightened their hold on him, and she listened, waiting for the remaining puzzle pieces of her time with Alex to click into place.

"There were a few men we interrogated before we found someone apprised of the details we were looking for. What Alex didn't realize, or didn't count on, was Juan Carlos would never have relinquished the power of his organization to him. It was always meant to go to Mateo."

"It doesn't even make sense that he'd want it. I know we talked about why he would have cleaned up drug trafficking in New York, but if he wanted to make way for the Ramirez cartel to gain a foothold, how would that benefit him if he wasn't going to get something in return? I mean, if they would be in the States, wouldn't it make sense for him to come back to his family then?"

Liam's chin brushed the top of her head. "I think there was more to the story, to his plans. The only other thing we learned was about the rivalry between the brothers."

Liv nibbled on her bottom lip and twisted the bracelet once more as she remembered Alex's urgent plea. "He told me to open this." Her nail tapped against the stone.

Lifting her wrist, Liam turned it to get a better view. "There's a tiny hole by the clasp."

"Can you open it?"

"Should be able to. Let's go into my office. We can try the end of a paperclip."

Intent on learning what Alex had meant in the last moments they'd had together, she followed Liam to his study.

Her wrist in his hand, he bent over her and inserted the piece of metal. With a pop, the bracelet opened, and she slid it off her wrist. Leaning over it, they both looked for an inscription. When none was found, Liam turned the bracelet to look along the edges of the brooch's setting. His hands stilled as he brought the same paperclip end up to a small hole imbedded beneath one of the intricate swirls in the antique design. A soft pop sounded, and the stone released to reveal a tiny plastic object.

"What's that?"

Liam's gaze swung to hers. "A micro SD flash drive."

Liv followed him behind his desk, watching as he woke up the sleeping screen on his laptop and inserted the flash drive. "There're a few files, one with your name on it." He moved aside so she could sit. Leaning a hip against his desk, he gave her space to find out what Alex had meant for her alone.

With shaky fingers, she clicked the file and opened it.

A letter addressed to her filled the screen, and her breath hitched.

Liv,

If you're reading this, then something terrible has happened to me. I pray you're safe and unharmed.

There's so much I've wanted to tell you, to confide to you, but I didn't want the ugliness of my world to touch the bright one you shared with me. Those days must be over now, at least for me.

You'll have questions, and I want you to hear the answers from me. No matter what, know that I loved you. Our feelings were real, ours alone, and no one can tarnish them.

I'm going to share some things from my background to try to shed some light on why things may have unraveled the way they did. There was a plan in place even before I was born. That's when it all started. It was between my mom and Juan Carlos. He decided my birth would be the key to get him inside the States to grow his organization. He wanted to expand his territory exponentially.

My mom agreed with him. Until we ran into my father and half brother. I was young, maybe about five years old, the day I met him for the first time, and she my brother. That's when her rose-colored glasses developed a fracture and her obsession with power truly began.

I didn't know. She kept her thoughts from me until I was ready to go to college in the States. My grandmother despised my father, and if she were alive, she would have agreed with the second half of my mom's plan only.

Juan Carlos wanted me to infiltrate the NYPD, to wipe out his competition, and for me to remain on the force as his eyes and ears. My mom wanted me to find a wife with political connections and money. To do as much of my father's requirements as possible, then get out of there and into politics, where I would no longer have a direct line to what he wanted. She planned to move by us, and to establish a stronger relation-ship with my father far away from his wife, possibly even be the only one for him, as he'd surely frequent his expanded enterprise. I have no idea why my mom had that delusion, but it was a driving force for her to surpass whatever his wife and first-born son had. To be the only one for him.

Then, and only then, did she think I'd be able to start a family, or our child would be my father's leverage, his puppet. She cautioned if I had a child before then, my father would expect that I meet with him and discuss what role my son or daughter would play in the family business. One he never intended to pass on to anyone other than Mateo.

A child represented a tool to him, just as I've been. I didn't want that.

What I didn't count on was falling for you, babe. My infatuation for you began that very first night in the bar. I couldn't take my eyes off you. When you agreed to be my wife, a whole new world opened up to me, one I knew I didn't deserve. You brought light, happiness, and hope to my every day. I wish I were able to do the same for you.

You were my freedom, my true escape from a world I was born into, one

I never expected to crawl my way out of, until our eyes met for the very first time.

Babe, the only part of my life that ever meant anything was when I was with you. I wish they weren't watching us; wish I didn't give into the malignant part of myself that was connected to them. It was too late for me; they'd learned the truth of your pregnancy. The only way I could try to keep you safe, us intact, was by going to them first. It was my last Hail Mary. If you're reading this, it didn't work.

I love you, Liv.

There were terrible things I had to do. If I hadn't, their fate would have been much worse at the hands of my brother. I will always regret what I've done. Pressure from Mateo, from my father, was unbearable. They wanted to move faster than we had been. Their demands escalated. It was them or you. I didn't have much choice at the time. Mateo was closing in, and I feared he would hurt you. It was a contention, and I had no other option but to prove to them my loyalty. I tried to find a way to stash your parents somewhere, keep them safe, but I couldn't. Mateo knew more than I'd thought and sent one of his spies to the restaurant where we celebrated our anniversary. I'm truly sorry I didn't have the foresight to stop him.

My atonement to you, for what little it's worth, is everything I've gathered over my lifetime on the Ramirez cartel. There's more. I don't want to strand you with this information and not help you deliver it into the right hands, as well as find a way to ensure your safety. Because they'll come for you. I won't be there to protect you, and I can't have that.

When I purchased your favorite wine from Savage Seas, I did a little research. Liam Savage owns it, and I've learned all I need to about him now. I hope he can protect you, as I could not. I have to tell you, babe. It kills me to tell you this because I've failed you. The owner, Liam Savage, is someone I'd trust with your life. From everything I've learned and contacts I've spoken to, I'm confident in sending you to him. I've left his information in the right-hand drawer of my desk. Go to him, tell him everything, and share these documents on the cartel with him. He'll understand what to do.

It's breaking my heart while I'm writing this to know you'll be at his home, at the orchard I planned to take you to. But I also wouldn't have it any other way. It can't be a coincidence that led me to finding out about him. I have to believe that.

I love you more than words, more than life. You were my chance at redemption, my heart, my everything.

Your husband,
Alex

CHOKED UP AND WITH TEARS STREAMING DOWN HER FACE, SHE ushered Liam over. Part of her wanted to laugh at how there were no coincidences. Through her crazy escape, she'd found her way to Liam. She hadn't needed to open Alex's desk to find Liam's address; fate had taken care of that for her.

Wiping the last of her tears from her face, she gave Liam a small, reassuring smile. She'd gotten what she needed—closure. He could do whatever he wanted with the files.

Skirting around the desk, she noticed Liam take her place behind the laptop, a concerned look crossing his features as she walked out the door. She had to go. The rest of the information didn't matter to her. The letter had given her what she'd needed.

Quietly, she slipped through the house until she reached the front door. The sun traveled higher in the sky since she and Liam had talked. It was closer to noon now. A light breeze rustled the leaves on the trees by the wraparound porch as she sat on a wooden swing.

She drew up her knees, loosely wrapped her arms around them, and pressed her back against the wood. To some degree, Alex's explanation made sense. She would never understand parts of what he'd written about, but the tragic revelation was that Alex had been used for what he could bring his family, just on a different level than she'd been for her parents.

Soon, she would have to figure out what to do with her life.

Going home to live was out of the question. It was time for a fresh start, one where the decisions were hers alone.

For the first time, perhaps in her entire life, she took a full breath, devoid of responsibility to others. This time, she would start over again and do what she wanted.

EPILOGUE

SIX MONTHS LATER

*W*ind whipped Liv's long hair into a tangled mess as she stood near the edge of the bluff. Undulating waves hurtled toward the coast. A storm was coming. Angry clouds rolled overhead in the darkening sky. Liam had finished his swim in the heavy undertow an hour ago. It wasn't until he'd set foot on land again that she'd drawn a full breath.

With a last look over the craggy shoreline, she turned and headed toward her studio and the breathtaking views the floor-to-ceiling windows provided of the tremulous ocean on one side and the wealth of greenery on the other. The inspirational scenery and serenity the area offered had made her decision to stay tempting. Liam had cinched the deal.

When land adjacent to Liam's had gone up for sale, Liv snatched it up. A small house was located on the vast property, and she'd enjoyed putting her own touches on it. Living close by, Liam would come over, see how she was doing, and lend a hand with the minor remodel. They'd fallen into a pleasant routine with long walks and occasional evenings of dinner and wine out on his patio. Until he'd flipped her world on its axis again with a toe-curling kiss.

A little over six months had passed since Alex and Mateo died near the opening to the forest in Liam's backyard. In that time, she'd found her footing once more. The few attacks after Alex's death helped her process her grief faster than she'd ever thought possible. The CIA had offered all and any support they needed to continue to deter Juan Carlos's vengeance. She was safe. Thanks to Liam, his team, and the CIA.

The CIA was ecstatic, as Liam had copied the files from Alex, detailing the Ramirez cartel operations and key players, and handed it over to their contact, Rich Stevens.

Liv had let it go, officially closing the door on that part of her life. She kept the good memories she'd shared with Alex, but the rest were not worth her time. Instead, she'd learned from them, determined not to let history repeat.

The blinders she'd worn when dealing with unpleasant reality had been discarded, and she faced the world as an active participant, an informed one.

Hand on the doorknob to her studio, she gave the knob a turn and push. Arms wrapped around her and pulled her back against a solid chest. Her lips twitched as she fought a smile, knowing exactly who held her. *Liam.*

"Mail came for you," he said. "Think it's from the gallery owner from Nantucket."

"Oh, good. That'll be the contract we discussed." So far, shipping to her other galleries had proved to be a simple matter, one she planned to continue. She could always catch a flight if the gallery owners requested her presence, if she was available.

Liv tilted her head back to look up at Liam. A dusty shadow of hair covered his square jaw, amplifying his sexiness. She threaded her fingers through his, across her abdomen. "Is that the only reason you're here?"

He dropped a kiss on her forehead before the slow, seductive grin she loved spread across his face, making her heart flutter. "Guilty. Just can't stay away."

Turning in his arms, she looped hers around his neck and rose on her toes to brush a kiss along his scratchy jawline. "You were gone this morning when I woke up." Her gaze locked on his lips.

It had been two months since they'd started living under the same roof. After the cartel incidents, he had made a deal with her. At the time, she had refused to live in the same house together. She needed to stand on her own two feet. Liam had seen things differently. Her safety was a priority. Even so, she'd stayed firm in her convictions. They'd compromised. If danger headed their way again, and he'd assured her it would, she would move in with him. Temporarily.

That had happened a few times. Even so, she had enough space while she was in her own home to process, to heal, to move on. It's what she'd needed and he respected that, when things were quiet.

Maine was beautiful. She had wanted to stay, and so she'd purchased her own place. Since she'd bought a house right next to Liam's property, he'd been marginally appeased. Honestly, she liked being near him.

The choice had been an easy one. There wasn't anything back in New York for her. The circle of people she'd grown up around didn't interest her in the slightest, nor did the paparazzi that would regularly snap pictures when she left the apartment or house. Liam had offered her time to figure out what she wanted next, and she'd taken it.

One thing she did compromise on over time was his offer to

build her a studio. She just hadn't realized it would be on his property. Secretly, she was glad.

Liam attempted to tuck a strand of hair behind her ear that, with the tug of the wind, defied his efforts. They stood half in and half out of her studio entrance. He'd had it built in less than a month and a half. Rather than taking full charge, he'd asked her to do the design. It had given her a much-needed project and grounded her decision to stay in Maine even more. The area was beautiful and constantly fed her creativity. And…there was Liam.

Their friendship had developed into more. It hadn't taken too long for him to kiss her and elicit a chemical explosion within her. Dropping her arms, she stayed close, but with the thoughts swirling in her head, she needed a little space. Absently, her finger rubbed over the fading indent where her wedding rings had sat.

"Thinking about the past?" Liam raised her hand to nip along her finger.

"Only a little. It led me to you." Desire flared in the depths of his eyes. He'd hinted at putting a ring on her finger again. She wanted nothing more than to share her life with him. That was what it would be—a shared life, not one with secrets between each other. He was giving her time. She didn't need it. She hoped he would ask soon.

Hungry lips parted hers, and his tongue swooped in, taking immediate possession. The wind picked up, and a *thump thump thump* beat inside her head. With excruciating slowness, Liam broke their kiss, and the noise she thought had been her blood pounding made itself known. A helicopter circled overhead.

Hands flat against Liam's chest, she pushed back so she could get a better view of the bird that flew above them. Long blades sliced through the air as the helicopter lowered to the landing pad in the distance. She smiled.

Liam's thumb brushed across her bottom lip. "What's got you smiling, love?"

She shrugged. "Just happy you came for me." With a head tilt, she indicated the area where the helicopter had landed.

"Yep. It's Stevens. There's been a development. Jack's already here. Do you want to sit in on the meeting?"

"Of course. I need to reschedule the meeting I had in town with Martin. We have a lot of marketing to discuss with the new line of blueberry soap and lotion going into the store. Have you heard what's going on, why Richy is here?" The CIA agent had earned a warm spot in her heart when she'd met him. He'd handled everything Liam had thrown at him and made sure to include her in the debriefing after Liam shared how she had been in the dark regarding her husband's motives. After that, she'd started calling him Richy, a name she swore the gruff, cigar-smoking man secretly loved.

After all, she and Joslyn were the only women who were a part of the Gray Ghost team. They offered a softer side to the rough and tough alpha SEALs he was used to dealing with.

The sculpture she'd finished flashed in her mind. It was in their private collection, one she wouldn't ship to the galleries that represented her in New York, London, and Chicago. Rachel had said a long time ago that some of her sculptures seemed prophetic. She'd come to believe her friend. So the mystery woman standing over a prone man, who looked remarkably like Trevor's brother, would remain in her and Liam's private study, the one only they used.

Liam closed the door behind them with a click and tugged her by the hand to the garage. They climbed into their SUV, and she pulled her phone from her pocket. The meeting with Martin was the only thing on her agenda for the day. Taking over for Liam as the liaison between their wine representatives and their local store had entrenched her into his life further, gave her the purpose she needed, and kept her close by his side. He'd confessed that was where he'd wanted her since their time on the boat over a year ago.

More and more, he shared his world with her—from the farm and winery to Gray Ghost Security, LLC, which took up a large portion of his time when they were on missions. She enjoyed the behind-the-scenes part of the winery and had taken over many of his former responsibilities with the vineyard and farm, which made both of them happy.

After rearranging her calendar, she turned in her seat to face Liam. There were only a handful of minutes left before they arrived at the large steel building that housed a meeting room, or war room as the men liked to call it. "Do you know what this meeting is about?"

He gave a curt nod. "A little. It's a rescue mission. A member of Stevens's department went missing when their plane crashed."

"From the CIA?"

"At least one. There were others on the plane. We'll find out when we talk with him."

She worried her bottom lip. While she demanded to be in the loop of all operations, fear ruled her with the thought of something happening to Liam—to all of them, really, but mostly to him. "Will you go?"

He pulled into a space next to the door of the secure steel building and flashed a cocky grin. "Yep. There's nothing to worry about. I've done these types of missions more times than I can count."

The huge helicopter sat on the landing pad, empty. The men were inside. Liam's hand rested on the small of her back as he opened the heavy door to the building, which was lined with cameras and floodlights. Inside, masculine voices led them to the large room a few feet away.

Liam pressed a kiss on the top of Liv's head as they walked through the doorway. Richy sat at the table with several photos fanned out in front of him and a thick file spread open. As they settled into chairs around the large oval table, Jack stopped pacing and dropped into a seat opposite them.

Richy's shaggy eyebrows climbed his wide forehead. "Are we all here?"

"Yes." Jack gave a clipped response.

Liam expanded for Stevens. "Trevor is on his way. We'll fill everyone else in when they get here."

Richy took off his glasses and pinched the bridge of his nose before settling them back on his face. "We're combining the teams. Chris, Bret, and Mike will be going, and we want the two of you. If you need more after you hear the mission, that's up to you to decide."

Liv placed her hand on Liam's thigh under the table. It wasn't unusual to request certain members of both teams, but the hairs on the back of her neck were standing up. Something didn't sit right with her. She leaned forward and glanced over the scattered pictures of headshots and surveillance photos. None of the people looked familiar, but the sense that she should pay close attention still prickled along her skin. "Won't Trev be needed to fly them in?"

With his mouth pressed in a thin line, Richy turned to her. "No. When Chris is on an air mission, Trevor seems to play it overly safe. This one won't allow for that. The area we plotted where Military Chief of Staff Johnson's plane went down is in rough, hostile terrain, surrounded by the sea, trees, and has poor visibility from the rainy season. It's far from the rebellion camp, in the midst of sympathizers or relatives, and way too close to the stronghold."

"How many were on board?" Liam asked.

"Besides the pilot and co-pilot, four others—the Secretary

of Defense, Henry Williker, his executive secretary, and two of our assigned security agents. From the surveillance photos, we recognize a few. Johnson, one CIA member, Henry, and the secretary were taken hostage. Our other security guard is presumed DOA."

They went over the mission, from entry point to extraction, and all foreseeable obstacles. Liv paid attention and mentally shifted her schedule around so she would be in close proximity to either Trev or another member of their team that would be monitoring and communicating back and forth with the guys. About an hour after Rich Stevens arrived, he departed the same way, hoping to miss the worst of the incoming storm, both literally and figuratively.

Liv rode back in heavy silence with Liam. When he parked in the garage and they got out, he nudged her toward the back of the house, taking her hand.

"Where are we going?" She laughed as he tugged her toward the bluff behind their house. That was another new development. She no longer thought of it as his house. The sprawling Victorian was her home too.

Not for the first time, she marveled at how much Liam's powerful persona and form fit the rough and wild backdrop of the sea. Huge, white, crested waves rolled to crash against boulders and rush along the sand, carving out an ever-changing shoreline.

His hand dropped to the small of her back as he led her close to the edge. "I can't wait any longer." He stopped and turned to face her. "There's something I want to do."

The urgency melted from Liam's features, and a calm determination settled over him instead. Her heart pounded against her ribs as he dropped to a knee before her. "You came into my life when I least expected to find you. Fractured, but with an inner strength and will blazing deep within you. I offered you my protection. You gave me so much more—friendship, under-standing, peace, love, and passion. You're the last thing I want to touch at night and the first beautiful sight I want in the morning. You're imbedded in my heart. Without you, I'm no longer complete. Marry me, Liv. Share forever with me."

Happy tears overflowed and spilled down her cheeks from the sheer joy this man brought her. "Yes. I'll share forever with you, Liam."

Once, she'd thought she had her heart's desire. Now she knew the truth. She snuggled into Liam's embrace. A future to rival her wildest dreams spread out before her.

AFTERWORD

If you enjoyed reading BROKEN CIRCLE as much as I did
writing it, I hope you'll consider leaving a review.

Follow Amy McKinley here:

www.facebook.com/amymckinleyauthor/
Newsletter | http://eepurl.com/b_Dc91
www.twitter.com/AmyMcKinley7
https://goodreads.com/author/show/14257449.Amy_McKinley
www.instagram.com/amymckinleyauthor/
https://pinterest.com/amymckinley7/

You can also find her at www. AmyMcKinley.com

ACKNOWLEDGMENTS

I'd like to express my sincere gratitude for the invaluable support of all those along this journey.

With heartfelt thanks to my critique partners, fellow authors, and friends for all they do. To Victoria Van Tiem, for her zeal in bouncing ideas and brilliance with structure. To Emily Albright, for her steadfast encouragement and phenomenal suggestions and catches. To Kris Kisska, for her lovely character insight and in-depth knowledge that made the story richer. These three incredible ladies are rock stars in their own right. Each one of them has been there from first draft to final edits, providing insight, candor, humor, guidance, and camaraderie.

A special thanks to Taylor Anhalt for helping to make this novel shine with her grammar skills, editing, and willingness to jump in despite her hectic schedule. Not to mention all those texts and emails she's graciously answered.

To Neila Y. and Kim H., two wonderful editors at Red Adept Editing, who did a fantastic job and made this story so much better. To T.E. Black for chatting at all hours and creating so many wonderful things for me, from Facebook banners, to formatting, and of course, this gorgeous cover.

To my amazing beta readers Maryellen, and Maria Vickers, for providing incredible feedback. As an award-winning sculptor, Maryellen Newton, provided tremendous insight on Liv's artistic creations. And for and to her unwavering friendship—basically for keeping me sane.

To all the readers, bloggers, and reviewers who went out of their way to help and support this release—you're all so very generous and kind. Your support and encouragement continues to inspire me. A special thanks to my PA, Jackie V. Booknerd, for her ongoing support, unwavering enthusiasm, and friendship.

And last, but in no way least, to my husband, two daughters, and two sons, for supporting and believing in me while I follow my dreams. For their patience and understanding when the house is messy and general chaos reigns. I can't imagine life without them.

ABOUT THE AUTHOR

Amy McKinley is the author of the Five Fates Series and Gray Ghost Novels. Her romance books have strong heroines, sexy alphas, and just the right amount of heat, danger, and always an HEA. She lives in Illinois with her husband, two daughters, two sons, and three mischievous cats.

You can find her at www.amymckinley.com

ALSO BY AMY MCKINLEY

Gray Ghost Novels

Broken Circle

Eye of the Storm

Beneath the Surface

The Five Fates Series

Hidden

Taken